MIDNIGHT HOUR

MIDNIGHT HOUR

An Anthology

Abby L. Vandiver

CROOKED
LANE

NEW YORK

Published in the United States by Crooked Lane Books, an imprint of The Quick Brown Fox & Company LLC.

Crooked Lane Books and its logo are trademarks of The Quick Brown Fox & Company LLC.

Library of Congress Catalog-in-Publication data available upon request.

ISBN (hardcover): 978-1-64385-752-7
ISBN (ebook): 978-1-64385-753-4

Cover design by Nicole Lecht

Printed in the United States.

www.crookedlanebooks.com

Crooked Lane Books
34 West 27th St., 10th Floor
New York, NY 10001

First Edition: September 2021

10 9 8 7 6 5 4 3 2 1

To our fellow crime writers of color—keep pushing.

FOREWORD

My Dear Reader,

I'm usually not one who enjoys reading the foreword to most books, fiction or non-fiction; frankly, I find most forewords boorish wastes of time. An unnecessary delay in gratification. "Let me tell you *why* what you are about to read is *important*." Dear God. Just let me get into the meat of the thing and decide on its importance or lack thereof myself. Forewards to books are, at least for me, much akin to a droll, self-satisfied waiter unctuously describing the mesmerizingly delicious taste of a medium rare, bloody-centered steak paired with a superior pinot noir. All the while said waiter is taking perverse pleasure in listening to the carnivorous hunger-rumblings of my stomach.

Ditch the preamble.

Just give me the damned steak.

With that in mind, let's not think of these few words as a "foreword."

Think of this as the only fair and true warning you will receive: put this book down right now and move on to a read that is less—alive. Something with less than a quickened pulse. Fewer shadows twitching in midnight's periphery.

Midnight Hour, a crime fiction anthology composed completely from writers of color, will draw you in—seduce you—with its brilliant, luminescent storytelling. Storytelling that revels in the often-quiet, dark carnivore lurking at the back of your mind and in the suppressed primeval corners of your soul. You will see through the eyes of "the other" different perspectives. And you will dance through these pages under a starless canopy of deliciously harrowing experiences and breath-taking moments of criminal terror. But again, be forewarned: seduction is not—nor was it ever—without its costs. You may well be at risk of having your dreams infected with nakedly revealed fears and an unusual assortment of criminal perversions, sicknesses of the soul and grotesqueries of the mind that make our shared humanity sometimes considerably less than human. Therefore, I would suggest you *not* wait until the midnight hour to begin reading this anthology, should you decide—against your better judgement, of course—to invite the deformed lives of many of these characters home with you.

Writers of color have long produced a litany of extraordinary fiction including the genre of crime fiction. Writing that, without preaching or proselytizing, uncovers and reveals the distortions and delusions, fallacies and myths of an American society that has often pushed such voices to the back of the literary bus. Writing that exudes the multifaceted poetry of underappreciated or unrecognized cultures and ethnic histories.

The voices that speak in this volume are without question or hesitation some of today's most uniquely original fiction writers. Full stop. Period. They include (but are hardly exclusive to) Tracy Clark, David Heska Wanbli Weiden, Abby L. Vandiver, Jennifer Chow, H-C Chan, V.M. Burns and Christopher Chambers. They are voices that will linger long in your mind. Take up residency in your soul. Add a new, extradimensional degree of sight to your peripheral vision and continue to walk just beneath the surface of your skin for an indeterminate amount of time.

All of which may very well be quite pleasant.

Then again . . .

Stephen Mack Jones

LUCKY THIRTEEN
By Tracy Clark

Henry Pearse made his way up the quiet street, a bag of groceries light but cumbersome in his arms. He walked slowly, mindful of the icy sidewalk and the slush beneath his feet. He was of a certain age now, not as surefooted. Caution was the ticket. He wasn't feeble, by any means. He got around just fine for a man of sixty-two. Still to himself, as the old folks liked to say. But sixty-two was not twenty-two, and ice was ice.

He stopped a few feet from his cracked front stoop and glowered up at the old frame house, then turned to scan the raggedy block, his eyes narrowing, his look accusatory. He would have to say, if asked, that he could just about smell its despair, its cowardly resignation. It had died years ago but hadn't the good sense to lie down and toss the dirt.

The town had had a thriving factory once and jobs that paid decent wages, but the factory folded and snatched the jobs away. Now the town was as close to nothing as nothing could get. The left-behinds, the ones caught sleeping by change and innovation, now stumbled like zombies after an outbreak. Aimless. Henry hated them. They hated him right back.

He made his way up the cracked walk, wanting to get inside and settled before the fools came out. They always did on New Year's Eve, as though clowning it up at the appointed hour would make their lives any less of a waste, any less insignificant. Shooting off cheap pistols and even cheaper firecrackers like it was the Fourth of July was nothing more than meaningless noise, Henry thought. Childish.

If they knew anything, they'd know how important New Year's Eve was, especially midnight. The stroke of twelve was a gift, a sparkling moment of transformation from old to new—a new day, a new year. It was a renaissance.

Henry looked up at his mother's house and scoffed. Robin's-egg blue. It had been that color for as long as he'd known the place. As though the lightness of the paint could cancel out the darkness inside.

"Gone now, you old cow. And good riddance."

The woman had never understood him. Tried to remake him, hadn't she? Turn him away from his passion. Stuff him in a box like everyone else. What kind of mother did that?

He'd known early what he was meant to become, and he had considered that certainty heaven sent. Henry had had a calling, a talent, drive. All behind him now, though he missed the thrill of it, the sense of accomplishment. But a man had to know when to hang up his cleats, when to take his bow and leave the field.

Henry climbed the front steps, opened the door, and pushed inside, damp mustiness smacking him in the face as violently as the snap of a wet towel. He drew in a sharp breath, held it, until he could ease into the stench of his mother's rotting belongings and the ghostly remnants of her disapproval.

The stink seemed to seep up through the floor cracks, slither out of the heating vents, bleed out of the walls.

Straighten up and fly right, Henry boy, she'd say. *You got to learn to get along in this world.* And later when she saw she couldn't change him, *You're the devil, Henry Pearse. The devil come straight from hell.*

Henry smiled, remembering. She hadn't known anything. But it was always the ones who knew the least that never shut up about a damn thing, wasn't it?

Whistling his favorite tune, Henry walked the bag back to the kitchen, past the worn couch and end chairs with those infernal doilies on the arms. His mother had made them one after the other like it was an obsession. *Crazy bat.* He trailed a finger along the length of the dining room table as he passed it, making sure not to disturb the single neat place setting at the table.

He'd left a simmering pot of mulligan stew on the greasy stove, and he checked it now to make sure it wasn't sticking to the bottom. He loved stew. All kinds. Stew was efficient, offering several things all at once, no need for a second pot. He'd learned to make it a while back. Another useful skill he'd acquired along the way. He'd had such a productive life, really. He had few regrets.

The kitchen was small, outdated, painted white, but the paint had long since yellowed with grease and gunk singed into the many coats. The old woman hadn't even noticed, he bet. Just kept cooking her tasteless gruel in this grimy, dark witch's kitchen, never caring how it might look to the outside world. To him. And on the yellowed walls more of those damned doilies, like sooty butterflies spread wide and matted for display. God, he hated this house.

He hadn't planned on coming back here, ever, but there'd been unfinished business, and Henry hated leaving anything undone. Maybe he'd sell it, move on. There was nothing tying him here, really.

The doorbell rang. Henry turned, stared down the long hall, then took a deep breath. He peeled off his jacket on his way to answer it, stopping at a chair to fold the coat neatly and place it over the back. When he got to the door, he stood for a time, his hand on the knob, watching the obscured figure of a man through the glass.

He looked back over his shoulder, scanning the front room, past the threadbare couch, the scarred coffee table, his eyes landing on the mantel over the neglected fireplace where he'd lined up his treasures. Clocks. All the same.

They were no more than a few inches tall, small, the kind folks used to travel with back in the day, before cell phones made that unnecessary. Each clock had little silver hands, the second hands no wider than a hair. He'd placed them side by side like a stilled phalanx of minutemen waiting for a call to battle. Twelve of them. Henry counted them again now, taking great pride. The bell rang again. He opened the door.

The man on the doorstep was in his twenties, average in every way, Henry thought. A man most people would walk right by without noticing. Not dark or light, short or tall, thin or not thin, just unremarkable, like a mailbox or a light pole. The man held a clipboard and wore a bomber jacket with the left pocket ripped. Henry's keen eyes took him in, unimpressed. He kept his face blank. "Help you?"

The man consulted the clipboard, a little nervous, Henry would have to say, unsure. "Yeah, this is forty-three thirty-nine, right?"

He had beady eyes, Henry noted, and if he had to describe the man's hair, he'd have to say it was darkish, not blond, not quite black, ashy maybe? Whatever it was, it came to a point in a prominent widow's peak. The eyes made him look rat-like. They were shifty too, making him appear no-account, his mother would have said. "Not interested in whatever you're selling, son."

The clipboard came swinging toward Henry's face fast as anything and clocked him on the chin, tumbling him back. The blow was followed by a violent shove that sent him crashing to the gappy, ratty carpet, all of it, the hit, the shove, happening so quick Henry barely had time to register surprise.

On the floor, Henry squeezed his eyes shut to quiet the ringing in his ears as the man slammed the door closed and locked it behind him. Henry lay there, the wind knocked out of him, dazed. He raised a trembling hand to his chin and drew back bloody fingers, the sight of his own blood a fascination. He looked up at his assailant. "*I'm* bleeding."

Bomber Jacket grinned, revealing yellow, crooked teeth, then reached down and dragged Henry by the back of his shirt into the living room, depositing him next to his mother's whiskey-stained lounger. It smelled of hooch and of her. Henry held his breath, not wanting to take it in.

"If you don't do what I tell you, old man, you'll get a lot worse."

Henry struggled to get up but faltered on the cheap carpet, worn thin by years of his mother's hateful pacing. "You've made a mistake. You need to leave."

Bomber laughed. It was a deep, sour, soulless sound, full of menace. "Shut up. I'll leave when I'm ready. First, you're going to tell me where you keep it." He pulled a .22 from his pocket, aimed it at Henry's head. "Or I'll end you right here."

"What are you talking about?"

He kicked Henry hard in the side, grinning as though he enjoyed the pain he caused. But Henry denied the young man even a groan, which earned him a second kick. Still he made no sound.

"So you're tough, huh, old man?" Bomber leaned down, pressed the gun to Henry's stomach. "Well, I'm tougher. Now you're going to get your old ass up off that floor, and you're going to give me everything you got in here that's worth anything." He pulled Henry up by his shirtfront and pushed him onto the couch. He sneered, glancing around the place, taking it in, finding it wanting. "What a shithole."

Henry massaged his wrists, rotated them to make sure he hadn't broken or sprained them. He'd fallen hard. His eyes held the man's. "Ask yourself, then. If I'm living here, what could I possibly have that you'd want?"

"You think this is some random hit? I been watching you. Coming and going. An old lady used to live here. I don't see her anymore, so I'm guessing she kicked off." He pointed the gun at Henry's head. "I'm betting she left a little something behind when she did."

Henry shook his head. "All I've got is what you see."

Bomber scanned the living room with its mantel full of clocks. An even dozen. All frozen at the same time. Midnight. He chuckled. "You're so far gone, man, you don't even know what time it is." He shook his head, watched Henry sitting there helpless. "But what does it matter, right? You with practically one foot in the grave." He sniffed, his eyes following his nose toward the kitchen. "What's cooking?"

"My dinner."

Bomber tucked the gun in his waistband, hovered over Henry. His breath rancid, foul. "*My* dinner now. Get it dished up." He pulled Henry up, took hold of his collar, and thrust him toward the pot. "I got time enough to eat, then deal with you." He leaned over, whispered in Henry's ear. "Because you're just a lonely old fool, aren't you? Nobody ever visits. Nobody comes. Not even the mailman."

He watched closely as Henry scooped the stew out of the pot, making sure the old man came nowhere near the knives in the drawer. Then he made Henry dish up a bowl for himself. At the table, Bomber sat with the gun in his lap, Henry across from him eating slowly as the thief ate like a man who hadn't touched a meal in days. He noticed Henry.

"Don't like your own cooking?"

Henry stared back at him. He could feel the blood drying on his chin. "I like it fine."

The thief put his spoon down, his eyes hardened. "Then fucking eat it."

Henry dipped the spoon into the bowl and slid stew into his mouth.

"More like it." Bomber ate half the bowl before he spoke again. "Don't you ever use salt?"

"It's bad for you." Henry slid in another mouthful. He figured it was going to be a long night. Best to be fortified.

The thief chuckled. "Just like an old grandpa. No salt. Nothing crunchy because you don't have teeth. What good are any of you?"

"You don't like the stew, don't eat it."

The man's eyes fired. He raised the gun from his lap and showed it to Henry, in case he'd forgotten who was in charge.

"You're going to want to cut that crap out right now, you get me?"

Henry flicked a look at the salt shaker between them. "There's the salt. Add it yourself."

Bomber put the gun back in his lap, grabbed for the shaker, and sprinkled salt generously over the stew before digging in again. After one taste, he smiled, finding the improvement satisfactory. "More like it." He sprinkled a little more, then winked at Henry playfully. "When I'm done, we'll do business."

Henry let his stew go and sat with his hands clasped on the table. His side ached from the kicks, but he'd get over that in due time. He'd always been a patient man. He'd had to be in his line of work. The breaks didn't always go his way. Sometimes when he went out, he didn't get anything, and he'd have to wait for another try. Like fishing. Fishermen weren't guaranteed a catch, were they? Sometimes they had a good haul, sometimes the nets came up empty. Henry had learned to deal with disappointment, to delay gratification.

Henry moved the shaker back to its original spot, next to the pepper shaker, touching, perfectly aligned. "Three days this week. Two the week before," he said, his voice placid as a summer lake.

The spoon stopped halfway to Bomber's mouth. "What?"

"That's how long you've been watching. You stood across the street, down two houses, behind that big elm." Henry smiled. "Nothing wrong with my sight or my hearing."

Bomber registered a slight confusion but not worry. He was a man with a gun in an old man's house. He smirked and went back to the stew. "Good for you, then. When I finish this, you'll do what I need you to do, and then I'll be out of here."

Henry pushed his bowl toward the center of the table, checked his watch. "Okay." He ran a hand along the table-top. Not a scratch on the dark, polished wood. It had been his mother's pride and joy, a big, heavy table, a lace runner down the middle. Handed down by some dead relative, it was the only thing of real value she'd had to her name, other than the house.

Bomber looked up, frowned. "What the hell are you doing?"

"Admiring the table. It's worth something. You want it?"

"What the hell am I going to do with some old table?"

"Sell it."

Bomber leaned back, taking the old man in, slightly amused. "Listen up. I'm here for money, and that's all. You got that?"

Henry's eyes met his. "Sure."

Bomber looked around the room, his eyes landing in the corner where a chair sat covered in a paint-splotched drop cloth. "What the hell's all that?"

"It's a chair."

"I see that. Why's it covered up?"

Henry sighed. "You cover furniture if you're not going to use it for a while."

Bomber blinked, dullness in his eyes. "And, what? You don't use *that* chair?"

"Haven't in a while."

Bomber shook his head. "That's dumb as hell. You even have plastic under it, like it makes a difference if this jacked-up carpet gets any dirtier."

Henry let a few moments pass. "How old are you, son?"

"Not your son, gramps."

"I need to call you something. What's your name?"

Bomber pushed the bowl away, clattering the spoon. He leaned back again in the high-back chair, his stomach full, certain of how this was all going to go. "You can call me the man who's going to break you, right here, right now."

"On New Year's Eve, no less," Henry said. "A special day. Will you wait for midnight or no?"

"Midnight? Man, I'm going to be gone way before then. I got plans with my lady tonight—and I'll be using your scratch to show her a real good time." He shoved up from the table. "Now get up and go get my money. I want all of it."

Henry stood, smoothed down his shirt, straightened his belt. "It's upstairs. In my bedroom. I have a safe."

"That's more like it. Let's go, then." Bomber took a step, blinked, a stunned look on his face, like he'd seen a ghost or been put into a trance. "Hey."

Henry said nothing, just watched.

Bomber shook his head as though trying to clear it, then began to sway, his eyes glassy. Sweat formed on his forehead right below the widow's peak. He began to cough. "Get me . . . some . . . water. That stew's sticking . . . in my throat."

Henry didn't move. He didn't have to.

"You hear? . . . Old . . . man?"

Bomber's face paled, then his eyes fluttered. Henry calmly reached over and took the gun from him and waited for the man to fall unconscious to the floor. He grinned then. "Night-night, *son.*"

The gun was nothing special. You could buy one just like it in any dark alley for fifty bucks. He set it on the table, then swept the bowls and spoons up and walked them to the kitchen sink, where he set them in soapy water to soak. Henry hummed as he opened the refrigerator and pulled out a pitcher of ice water, then poured himself a glass. Again he checked his watch. An hour to midnight.

"All the time in the world."

* * *

Bomber's eyes flew open to find the room dark except for a single lamp shining in the corner. The drapes had been drawn. The place cold. He couldn't move his arms and looked down to find they'd been strapped to armrests by nylon zip ties. He was sitting in a high-back chair, his legs bound to the legs. He flicked a look into the corner. The chair under the cloth was gone, the plastic too. Realization dawned. He was sitting in the chair, the plastic now under his feet.

"Hey. What the hell?"

Henry walked calmly out of the shadows, leaned in, a leather apron covering his clothes, plastic goggles hanging from a strap around his neck, exam gloves on his hands. "Wakey, wakey, *Albert*. That is your name, isn't it? I checked your wallet. According to your driver's license, you're Albert Grant. Twenty-six." Henry offered a playful pout. "But not an organ donor. You selfish bastard."

Albert fought the restraints. "Let me out of this chair, you crazy fool!"

Henry turned his back to the chair, walked over to the corner. "I will. Eventually I'll have to." He shot Albert a sly look. "You had forty dollars in your wallet. What say I take that off your hands? Funny, isn't it, how tables turn? You came here to rob me, but I end up robbing you instead."

11

Albert struggled to free himself but made not a single bit of progress. The ties weren't budging. "I said let me go, you son of a bitch."

Henry laughed. "You've got that right. It's too bad you never met my mother. She was quite something."

Albert bucked in the chair, desperate to free himself. "Call the police, then. Let them take me in, but when I get out, I swear, I'm going to mess you up. Count on it."

Henry pulled a rolling cart from the corner and moved it close to the chair. He looked over at Albert, who had no idea what kind of trouble he was in. "No police. It'll just be you and me tonight." His eyes held Albert's. "And you won't be coming back."

Sweat trickled down Albert's face, his eyes wild with rage, frustration, fear. He was prey caught in a trap, and he was just now getting it. "I'll kill you! I'm going to gut you like a fish." He issued his threats through clenched teeth, each one as toothless, as impotent, as the one before it. "I'll make you *bleed*."

Henry nodded, adjusted his gloves. "Funny we should have such similar plans for the evening, isn't it?" He drew the covering off the cart to reveal rows of silver scalpels, drills, saws, knives, needles—all polished to a brilliant gleam.

Albert's breath caught. "What's all that? What're you going to do?"

Henry stood captivated by the display. He'd taken good care of his tools since he'd used them last. He'd put them away, he'd thought for the last time. Who knew he'd get another chance? "I used to be the best." He picked up a scalpel, felt the point. "Funny how I was watching you as you were watching me, isn't it? Your mistake was assuming I was too old to notice. How could I not? You wore the same clothes every time. Rookie mistake."

"Hey, c'mon. I apologize for busting in on you, okay? Just let me go. I didn't take anything. We call it even, how's that?"

"Apology accepted, Albert." Henry drew a small clock out of his apron pocket, showed it to Albert, and set it on the cart next to a small hand drill. Albert stared at the clock, then turned to look at the ones over the fireplace. It was the same.

"What's that?" His voice shook, fear having stolen whatever bravado he'd come in with. "What's it for?"

Henry winked. "That's you, Albert. Lucky thirteen."

"*What?*"

"I had a long career. I earned a bit of a reputation. Newspapers always like to give you a catchy name. It sells copies, I guess, but it doesn't really mean much otherwise."

"What the hell are you talking about!"

Henry swept his hand over his tools, reverently, as though he were almost afraid to touch them. "Doesn't matter. I knew you'd pick tonight." There was a twinkle in his eyes. "It's the perfect night to get up to mischief. The perfect time to steal what isn't yours . . . money . . . other things."

Albert's lips were dry; he licked them. "Please, Henry, *sir.* You don't want to do this. You can't be serious. Just untie me."

Henry readied his tools, the small saw just perfect for fingers and toes. The hand drill for the eyes and ears. His blood raced through his veins in anticipation. How many people got a chance to relive their glory days? To pick up again what they'd loved and been forced to put down? He breathed in, his eyes closed, lost for a moment in remembrance. Henry twanged the saw. It was music to his ears.

Albert screamed. "Help! Somebody!"

Henry placed the saw back on the cart, picked up the drill and revved it. "No one's listening, Albert. New Year's Eve, remember? They're all either out for the evening or shit-faced drunk." He scanned the room. "And everything here is locked up tight." A quick glance at his watch. Just minutes till midnight now. He winked at Albert. "Soon."

He eyed Albert's wrists. The man had worn them raw by struggling. He came closer, holding the drill, plotting his first strike. It was always the most important one, Henry felt. How it went determined how everything after it would go.

"Don't come near me with that!"

Henry chuckled. They always did that. Forbid him, as though *they* had the power. "I will come near you, Albert. I'll come very near." He leaned over, whispered in the young man's ear. "Remember when you knocked me down, dragged me around, then kicked me?" He pointed to his bruised side. "Right here. Twice."

The sound that came out of Albert's mouth was a pathetic whimper. "I'm sorry. Sorry-sorry-sorry. *Please.*"

Henry straightened. "You were quite the big man with that gun."

"I got dizzy. You took it. I blacked out. The stew." Albert glared up at Henry, tears in his eyes. "But you ate it too. I made you."

Henry moved around the chair, still plotting. "I did. I like stew. I learned to make that particular variety in a prison kitchen. But I didn't touch the salt."

"The salt?" Albert's brow furrowed. "You roofied the *salt*? You . . ."

Henry laughed. "I'm having such a good time. Aren't you, Albert?"

"You're crazy. You're sick! Psycho freak!"

Henry turned his back to the chair again. "Well, now you sound just like Mother." He picked up the clock from the cart. Its hands frozen straight up at twelve.

"What *is* that?"

Henry smiled, happy to talk about it. "A clock. One for each of my special projects. There are twelve on the mantel now. This one's for you. I had thought I'd have to leave my job undone, but then you chose *me*, Albert. I couldn't believe my luck. Lucky thirteen."

"Help!" Albert screamed, fighting the chair, the ties. "Help. *Help*."

Henry padded back over to the cart and grabbed a roll of duct tape from a drawer. It was almost time. He peeled off a stretch of it and slapped it across Albert's mouth. "A man is lucky to find his true calling, Albert. To do what he must do." Albert's muffled screams went nowhere. " 'The Midnight Killer.' " Henry shrugged. "That's what they called me. Not the name I would have chosen, but what're you going to do, right?" He looked the room over. "Maybe I'll stay put. Wait for someone else to wander by." He grinned at Albert. "A venus flytrap waiting patiently for . . . someone." Henry exhaled deeply, mindful of the time. "I'm waiting for the countdown to start the drill. You will go out with the old year. It's quite an honor, young man."

Albert's body was drenched in sweat; fatigue and terror had weakened him. How could he have known? Henry was an old man. Just an old man. Now he was going to die.

He slumped in the chair, little fight left in him. *Just an old man.*

Henry's smile was so serene, so content. He revved the drill, having decided gleefully where he'd strike first. The fates had delivered him the world's best belated Christmas gift.

"Old man, you said. Shithole. You ate my stew as though I'd made it just for you—which, I guess you could say, I did. You, Albert Grant, were expected."

Henry checked his cart. He checked his tools. All present and accounted for. Thirteen. A baker's dozen. "Almost time," Henry announced. "Just one more thing."

He walked over to the turntable against the wall. It was ancient by today's standards, but it still worked. His mother had rarely used it; didn't know how, Henry suspected. He dug into the pile of old LPs and found the one he needed, the one that had always spoken to him and spurred him on to greatness. Unconventional choice, maybe, but okay by him.

The album cover was near pristine, the plastic film over it just a little ragged. He slid the record out and put it on the turntable. Before the music even started, Henry began to hum the tune, then sing it with great feeling.

"I'm gonna wait till the midnight hour . . ." He turned, smiling devilishly at Albert, who'd come to steal and got stolen instead. *"When there's no one else around . . ."*

Henry whistled along to the song, happy. "Wilson Pickett," he told Albert, who appeared to give less than a shit. Right at the moment, he had other concerns. "Before your time, of course. I like it because I also wait until midnight. It's just how I'm wired, I guess. And, of course, there's no one around but you and me, Albert. See how it all fits?"

He stood by his tools, checked for time. Less than two minutes now. Albert's struggling had ceased. He was too exhausted to go on. Still, even in his weakened state, Henry could see in his eyes he wasn't keen on dying.

"I get it, Albert. It's human nature. We fight to the last, even if it's futile. Self-preservation. It's instinctual." He palmed the drill, caressed it. Albert's eyes pleaded for mercy but found none. "Eyes first?" Albert wailed behind the tape, then wept. "Maybe you're right. One minute." The song replayed on the player. Henry sang his favorite part.

Henry walked over to the window and cracked it, though it was winter and cold. He could hear the revelry from his neighbor's house next door as the countdown approached. He knew for a fact everyone over there was likely too drunk to hear a bomb go off. He inhaled deeply, let the breath out slow. The old year was dying, a new one coming. A cleansing, Henry thought, a blank page.

Ten, nine, eight . . .

Henry revved the drill. "I had thought eyes, but now . . . temple?"

Six, five, four . . .

"I'll only have a few seconds, though; then I'll move on to the rest."

Three, two, one . . . HAPPY NEW YEAR!

The drill punched a hole in Albert's skull and burrowed its way through his brain. There wasn't much blood, and what noise Albert had managed to make never made it above the roar next door. Henry savored the moment Albert's life drained away, then calmly padded over to the window and closed it. He turned off the player.

He stood for a moment watching what he'd done, anticipating his next steps. He moved back, breathed easy, plucked the clock off the cart, and walked it over to the mantel. He placed it next to the others, then stepped back to admire its placement, making sure it lined up just so.

"Right next to Mother, Albert. How's that?"

He began to hum. He was happy. He had all night to play.

"Not bad for an old man, is it, Lucky Thirteen?"

SKIN

By David Heska Wanbli Weiden

"**Y**ou want the usual, Virgil?"

    I nodded and put three dollars on the counter. The barista set the cup down in front of me. Pejuta sapa. *Black medicine* in Lakota. The coffee was good, strong but not bitter. The place had opened a few years ago, the first coffee shop on the Rosebud reservation. Now we had four restaurants, not counting the food truck that served burritos and tacos out by the grocery store—Rapper's Delight Tacos, all their items named after hip-hop artists: Snoop Dogg Nachos, 2Pac Carnitas, the Biggie Burrito. I liked their stuff, but nine bucks for three greasy tacos was a little steep for the rez.

    I took a seat out on the patio and settled in. A few cars passed by, no one I knew. I thought about heading out and joining my friend Tommy at the fast-pitch game. His team, the Rez Sox, were playing a crew from the Pine Ridge reservation, the Wild Oglalas. The games were usually pretty laid-back, but I knew there might be some tension tonight, given the traditional rivalry between the Sicangu and Oglala tribes, so I had promised Tommy I'd stop by. I was wondering if I had time to order a brownie when my cell phone buzzed.

"Virgil, it's Charley. You got a minute to talk?"

Charley Leader Charge. The attorney who'd represented my nephew—for free—when he was falsely arrested for possession of narcotics.

"Hey, Charley. How's it going?"

"Not too bad. Trying to keep up with the paperwork, keep my clients happy. How's Nathan?"

"He's all right. Goes to a different high school now, seems to like it. Even got himself a girlfriend."

"Good to hear. That whole thing—what a mess. Nathan didn't deserve any of that."

No, he didn't. My nephew had gotten caught between warring heroin and pill dealers, and he'd barely escaped with his life. Charley had stuck by us the entire time, and I hadn't forgotten. Even though he was based in Rapid City, he was known for helping out folks on the rez, where he'd grown up.

"Thanks again," I said. "Appreciate what you did."

"My pleasure. Just glad it worked out." He cleared his throat. "So, I'm calling about something else. A favor."

"Yeah?" I waited for him to say more.

"It's a little complicated. Deal is, I've got a longtime client—can't say who it is, but he's an important person here in Rapid. I've worked with him for years. Anyway, he's been in this long-running battle with the Hampton School. You know about them?"

"No." I took another drink of my coffee.

"The Hampton Theological Seminary. Or just Hampton. The oldest seminary west of the Mississippi. Very wealthy, very connected. The mayor sits on their board, along with state senators and reps. You get the picture."

I didn't, actually. When I'd heard the word *favor*, I'd assumed that Charley wanted me to beat up somebody here on the rez. That was my job—or used to be, anyway. I was the person you called when you wanted some rough justice, usually after the federal government or the tribal police released some child molester or rapist without any punishment. A hired vigilante, although some liked to call me a thug or worse. But that didn't matter, because I'd stopped giving beatings after the problems with Nathan. I'd had plenty of offers but turned them all down. I didn't understand what some school in Rapid City had to do with me.

"Okay," I said, "it's some fancy place. What's the favor?"

I heard papers rustling over the phone. "I'll get to that. But first, I need to explain; this is somewhat, ah, delicate. As I said, my client has been in a legal battle with Hampton, and it's gotten personal for him. The favor, you see, is something that's not entirely within the boundaries of the legal system. I need some assurance as to your discretion."

This I understood. "Yeah, sure. I'll keep my mouth shut. Always have."

"Good. I knew that, of course. I'm in a difficult position, because as an officer of the court I can't advise or recommend any action that's . . . extrajudicial. I'm just acting as a middleman here."

"I get it. What's the deal?"

"Well, the Hampton School has a collection of very rare books. And their prized volume—printed back in 1779—is *The History of Christianity*. They've had it for almost a hundred years, and it's the jewel of their collection. It's displayed in a trophy case in their lobby."

I finished the last of my coffee, now lukewarm. "All right, what's that got to do with me?"

A pause. "My client would be most appreciative if you might be able to . . . appropriate the book from the school. And he'd be happy to pay you for your time and effort. Two thousand dollars. Cash."

Now I understood. This dude was some sort of collector and wanted this old book for himself. But I was no thief. I didn't mind putting the hurt on someone who deserved it, but stealing shit was not my thing.

"Look, Charley, you know I ain't no burglar. I mean, I get that your guy wants this book for himself, but—"

"No, he doesn't want the book. To the contrary, he wants you to dispose of it. The book should be destroyed."

"Destroyed? I don't get it. Why steal a book just to trash it? Makes no sense."

He cleared his throat. It sounded like an old car trying to turn over. "You see, my client despises this book and has tried to persuade Hampton to divest themselves of it. As they have declined to do so, he's decided that he has no other option than to seek alternative methods of acquiring the volume. And that's where you come in."

"Okay, sure. I understand that part. But why does he hate the book so much? He against religion or something?"

"No, nothing like that. It's got nothing to do with the content of the book," he said.

"But I don't—"

"It's the cover of the book." He paused. "The story is that, back in the late 1700s, a white man, Daniel Morgan, was attacked by an Indian but was supposedly able to fight him off and kill him. He claimed self-defense. Who knows what really happened? But we know what Morgan did next. He took the body of the Native he'd just killed, flayed and tanned the flesh from the corpse, and used it for the book's binding." He paused again. "The book is made out of human skin. Indian skin."

* * *

My mind reeled as I started to drive back to my house. A book bound in human skin? I knew Indians had been slaughtered back in the day, but this was beyond anything I'd ever heard. It was one thing to kill someone in battle—and there'd been a lot of battles back then—but it was truly evil to strip the flesh from a body and process it into a book cover. And to display it in a religious school? The whole thing was sickening.

Once I'd gotten past my shock, I'd agreed to steal the book for Charley's client. What choice did I have? I owed Charley, big-time. Not to mention I wanted to take that goddamn book and burn it. But that wasn't allowed. Charley told me to save the binding—the skin—and give it to a medicine man who could follow the proper spiritual procedures and give it a decent burial. I didn't have any objection to that. Besides, Charley said he'd leave the two thousand dollars in an envelope tonight in the lockbox outside his office in Rapid City. That money would come in handy, as I'd been without any income for quite a while.

My only concern was getting into the school without being caught. That and the fact that the book was apparently in some trophy case, which was probably locked up tight. I'd have to go in at night, when everyone was gone. I guessed security would be minimal at a religious school, but there was no way to be sure without seeing for myself.

I tried to focus on the road, but grotesque images of a dead Native being skinned kept drifting into my head. My phone buzzed, and I saw it was my friend Tommy calling. Grateful for the distraction, I answered.

"Yo Virgil! Thought you was gonna come by the fast-pitch! Them Oglalas thought they were hot shit, but our pitcher was fire, man. Dang, he was throwing curve balls, rise-ups, fast-balls, everything. Beat 'em seven to two. Now it's time to par-tay! Where you at?"

"Heading home, I guess. Sorry I missed your game."

"Well, shee-it, meet me down at the Depot! Buy me a cel-ebration beer—I deserve it. What you say?"

"Sure, why not?" I needed some time after the call with Charley, so I turned the car around and headed toward the bar.

Twenty minutes later I found myself at the reservation tavern. It was quiet inside, but that wouldn't last long. Later in the evening the place would fill up, but I had no plans to stay for that. I didn't drink, and nothing good happened at the Depot once the liquor started flowing.

"There he is!" Tommy motioned for me to join him in a table at the back, near the pinball machine. His beer was half-empty. "You want a Shasta?" Without waiting for me to answer, he waved to the bartender, Charlotte, and pointed at me. She knew I didn't drink and came by with a can of Shasta and a glass of ice.

"Toast!" Tommy raised his Bud. "To the Rez Sox! First victory this year. Hecetu yelo! Uh-huh."

I tapped my glass to his. "Good going. Melvin pitch today?"

"Yeah, his arm was movin' so fast, I couldn't even see it!"

I noticed Tommy had chalk on his face and grass in his hair. "Any problems after the game?" I asked.

"Naw, the Oglalas was bitchin' a little, but it was cool. You decide not to come?"

I took a sip of my Shasta and wondered how much to tell Tommy. He was my oldest friend, but maybe he didn't need to hear about this stuff.

"Well, I was just at the Buffalo Brew, you know . . ." I said, and trailed off.

"Something up with Nathan?"

"No, got a call from Charley Leader Charge. My lawyer? He needs me to do something for him. A favor."

Tommy downed the last of his beer. "Yeah, what kind of favor? He need you to put someone down? Thought you wasn't doin' that no more."

"Nothing like that. Different type of job." I scanned the bar to see who was there. No one I needed to worry about. "You know anything about some Bible school out in Rapid called Hampton?"

He squinted and looked up at the ceiling. "Hampton? The old boarding school? North of Rapid?"

"No, it's a Bible college or something like that."

He motioned to the bartender for another beer. "Yeah, it was a boarding school first. Pretty sure. Maybe my grandma went there? Sica, man. Evil. I heard them Rapid City skins won't go near that place."

Boarding school? Charley hadn't said anything about that. Every Native knew about the boarding schools that existed back in the old days. Little kids would get taken from their parents and shipped off to the East Coast or, if they were lucky, one of the nearby schools where they'd at least be closer to their families. But whether on the reservation or off, the boarding schools were tough places for Indian kids, because they'd be punished—beaten—if they spoke their language or tried to hang on to traditional ways. Many never made it back and were buried in the sad little school cemeteries.

"Who runs it now? Got any idea?" I asked.

Tommy was watching some guy play the old Black Knight pinball machine. One of the flippers didn't work, so you always lost when the ball drained to the right.

"No clue, homes. So, what up with that? You gonna tell me?"

What the hell. "All right, but keep this quiet, okay?" I moved in closer and lowered my voice. "I have to get in there, whatever the place is. I guess they got an old book displayed in their front lobby. Long story, but I need to grab it."

Tommy stared at me. "The book? What for?"

I paused. "Uh, this book—it's pretty fucked up. It's a really old book, maybe two hundred years old, and Charley needs me to get it. Some client of his wants it."

"The book is, like, an antique?"

"I guess so. Whole thing is pretty messed up."

"Messed up how?"

I paused again. "Well, the book—it's, uh, made with skin. The cover. It's bound with human skin. From an Indian. I guess some wasicu killed a Native long time ago, then cut his flesh off and turned it into a book cover." I took a drink of my soda. "Told you it was fucked up."

Tommy's face turned three shades paler. He was utterly quiet, which was rare for him. I waited for him to say something.

"This is for real?" he asked.

I nodded.

"Let's go get that goddamn thing," he whispered. "Tonight."

* * *

I'd never seen Tommy so angry. He was generally a happy and fun-loving guy, but he cared deeply about Native issues and indigenous peoples, and this thing had really set him off. I'd tried to talk him out of helping me, but he'd insisted on coming along. Although I usually worked solo, there was no question I could use some help on this job. I didn't know what to expect up there, and I trusted Tommy. He was riled up and wanted to head out there right away. I didn't have any objection. We needed to leave as soon as possible, as it was a three-hour drive to Rapid City from the reservation.

I called Nathan and told him to fix his own dinner and that I'd be home very late. Nathan was fine with that—he'd play his new video game with his friend while he cranked his music as loud as it would go. We drove to Tommy's house first so he could drop off his softball stuff and grab some things.

"You want to come in?" Tommy asked.

"No, I'm good. Just hurry. Got a long drive."

While Tommy was inside, I looked up the Hampton school on my fancy new cell phone. I clicked on the button that said *Our History* and read a little about the place. I saw that they acknowledged being a former Native boarding school, but their website didn't say much beyond that. I skipped the *Prospective Students* button and clicked on *Current Students*. I wanted to find out if the main building was open at night. I hit the *Library* tab and discovered that it closed at nine PM. That was good for us, because it meant we'd arrive long after closing and the place should be empty.

After a few minutes, Tommy came back out carrying a gym bag, which he tossed on the floor of my truck. I saw he'd washed his face and changed clothes. He wore jeans with a hole in the knee and a T-shirt that said SAGE AGAINST THE MACHINE.

"What's in there?" I said, pointing at the bag.

"Couple of flashlights, hammer, crowbar, and some grub. You hungry? Got an Indian taco, but it might be a little moldy. Some chips too—flamin'-hot-nacho flavor."

I shook my head. "I'm good." He opened the bag as I pulled away.

"So, what's the plan?" Tommy asked, between handfuls of chips. "The place open at night? We do a little smash and grab?"

"It's a Bible school, so I'm guessing it'll be closed up by the time we get there. Library closes at nine, so we should be cool." I rolled down the window halfway to rid the car of the nacho-chip stench.

"Aight, how we get in?" he said, sending miniature nacho-chip asteroids flying from his mouth as he ate.

"I don't know. Check the back door, I guess. Go in through a window if we have to."

"You think they got an alarm system? Don't need that boo-shit."

"Maybe. Let's just get in, find the book, and get out. Charley said it was in the main lobby in some trophy case. Shouldn't be too hard."

"What's this book called again? You know, the title or whatever?"

"*The History of Christianity.*"

He snorted. "Like to drop a little Indian history on the mofos who made that thing and kept it. Get some Custer action going, you know what I'm saying?"

"Hope it won't come to that."

I stared at the road, my headlights shining in the darkness.

* * *

After about an hour of driving, Tommy passed out, dead asleep. I listened to KILI, the radio station for the Pine Ridge reservation, until it faded out. I switched off the radio and focused on the highway. As I drove, images crowded my mind: the wasicu settler, having killed the Native man, stripping the flesh from his back and tanning it, turning it into a horrible leather. I wasn't exactly fluent in the Lakota language, but I remembered that the word for skin was *wichaha* or *há*. *Taha* or *tahalo* for animals. How could the killer view the Indian's flesh as that of an animal? I thought about my own mother's skin, how soft it was on her arms, how warm it was when she embraced me, the joy I felt when she picked me up and laughed. When did the Native person become an animal in the wasicu's eyes?

One of the proverbs that was always approvingly trotted out for Natives was that, back in the old days, we used every part of the buffalo after a hunt. The meat, the hooves, the animal's skin. It was all put to use and nothing was wasted. This was thought to be a part of the Indian way of life—a demonstration of wise management of the environment. But the larger point was always overlooked: that it was important for every person to use all of their abilities and talents for the good of the community. A person's gifts should be encouraged and not wasted or ignored. But in modern America, it seemed like any skill that didn't result in greater wealth was devalued and diminished, if not mocked and ridiculed. I wondered if the killer had felt this way so long ago—that the Native person he'd murdered was without value because of his refusal to accept American ways. Or was it just simple racism—the notion that anyone with a slightly different skin tone was not deserving of human dignity? No matter what had happened, the book was a disgrace. It was time to do the right thing, even if it came two centuries late.

* * *

A few hours later, we hit Rapid City. I stopped by Charley's office first and checked his late-night lockbox. Just as he'd said, there was an envelope inside with my name on it. Twenty crisp hundred-dollar bills. I stuck the envelope in the inside pocket of my jean jacket.

Thirty minutes later we arrived at the Hampton school. I looked at the clock on the dashboard of my truck: exactly midnight. The large parking lot was pretty much deserted. Only a few sedans and an SUV were parked on the outskirts. The parking lot had a few dim lights but the building itself was dark, no lights on at all. I drove around to the back and parked a block away on the street.

"Tommy, wake up. We're here."

He opened his eyes and blinked. "What time is it?"

"It's late. Just past midnight."

He yawned. "Oh, man, I was beat after that game today. Good to grab a little shut-eye. That the place?"

"Up ahead. Thought we'd park back here; stay out of sight."

He took a drink from a bottle of water stowed in his bag. "What you want to do?"

"Let's try the front first. Grab your flashlights, the crowbar and hammer too—stick 'em in your gym bag. We run into anybody, just say we're looking for the hospital."

"Hospital! That's a good one. Hoka!"

We walked in the darkness to the school. It was quiet here, only the noise of the wind and faint murmurs of traffic off in the distance. The building was huge, constructed of reddish bricks, arched windows, and a spire towering over the roof. It looked old, and I could imagine Native kids being marched inside long ago and the anguish they must have felt at being separated from their families and their culture.

I raised my finger to my lips to indicate that Tommy should stay quiet and motioned for him to join me. We slowly walked up the stairs to the front entrance. There were no lights on, and I didn't see any security cameras in the corners. I peered into a large window but couldn't make out anything inside. I went over to the old-fashioned wooden door, grabbed the metal handle, and pulled. It was locked. No surprise there. I motioned for him to follow me, and we walked around to the back of the school. There was a little parking lot there, and I didn't see any security vehicles, just an old bicycle attached to a rack with a U-lock.

I spotted a small door off to the side, next to a large dumpster. I motioned to Tommy and we crept over to it. I turned the handle and pulled, only to discover that it was also locked. It was a metal door with a dead bolt, so there was no way we could kick it open. I looked around for another entrance but didn't see one.

We walked around to the eastern side of the building, which was secluded by a stand of trees. It was dark on that side, so I whispered to Tommy to get the flashlights. He handed one to me, and we scanned the area.

"You see that?" Tommy said.

"Yup." A large window was slightly ajar, no more than an inch or so. But that might be enough. The window was about five feet high—just low enough that we might be able to pry it open. I whispered to Tommy to hand me the crowbar and gave my flashlight back to him.

I wedged the tapered end of the crowbar in the side of the window, which had a metal frame. I used all my strength and was able to get it open a little. I motioned for Tommy to hook the claw end of the hammer underneath the front edge of the frame, and I inserted the crowbar on the other end. We struggled for about thirty seconds until the frame finally came loose with a loud cracking sound. I looked around to see if anyone had heard but didn't see any motion nearby.

I was able to swing the window up, and I saw that it opened into someone's office. There was a computer monitor and cords on a desk, which I pushed aside. I grabbed the frame and pulled myself up and inside, stepping on the desk. Then I indicated to Tommy that he should put the tools back in the bag and hand it to me. He climbed up and stepped in.

"Flashlights," I whispered. He nodded and handed one to me. We turned them on and looked around the office. Bookshelves, computer equipment, a large desk chair. A door on the opposite wall, which presumably led to the hallway. We just had to figure out how to get to the main lobby. I wondered if there was some teacher in the building working late, grading tests or papers.

"All right, let's check it out," I said quietly, and pointed to the office door. "Keep the flashlights off until we know there's nobody here."

I slowly opened the office door and stuck my head out into the hallway. It was dark, but there was a lighted exit sign at the end of the corridor, so I could see that there were about ten office doors and an old-fashioned water fountain. I motioned to Tommy to follow me. He closed the door quietly, and we started down the hallway toward the exit sign. It was absolutely silent, and I didn't see any lights coming from the bottoms of closed doors, so I began to think we were alone.

We came to the end of the hallway and turned right. There were more office doors and a couple of restrooms with two lighted signs above them.

"Yo man, I need to pee," Tommy whispered to me.

"You got to be kidding."

He shook his head. "Homes, I'm on Pisscon One. Got to go."

I sighed. "Stay quiet and hurry! We need to get moving."

He slowly opened the door to the men's room and went inside. The door squeaked when it closed, and I held my breath until it was quiet again. After a minute he came out, and I motioned for him to follow me. We walked to the end of the hallway and took another right.

We gazed out into a large open space, and I recognized the front entrance. Although it was dark, the huge windows by the door allowed in enough light from the parking lot that I could look around. Over to the side were two ornate wooden doors and a sign that said CHAPEL. There was a sizable reception desk in the middle of the room and several rectangular yellow couches. I scanned the space and located some large display cases on the other end of the room.

These had to be what we were looking for.

We walked over to them, and I pointed my flashlight inside the first display. Framed certificates, a trophy, framed old newspaper articles and photos. No books. The next case had a sign that said FACULTY PUBLICATIONS, and about twenty books were propped up inside. My heart started to beat faster, and I focused the flashlight on the volumes. *Theory and Countertheory of Homiletics*; *Posthuman Systems and the Divine*; *Ruthless Compassion*. I kept looking, but all of these books seemed fairly new and not hundreds of years old. I checked them again to see if I'd made a mistake, but it wasn't there.

"No book," I said. "Maybe we're in the wrong room?"

"Look," Tommy said. He pointed toward the chapel entrance and shined his flashlight near the wooden doors. He moved his beam up and down, and then I saw it. A freestanding triangular cabinet with a glass front. An old one, with fancy wood trim and a few shelves inside. It looked like something you'd see in a castle in England.

We moved closer to it and peered inside with our flashlights. There was a wooden easel on the middle shelf supporting a large book, dark brown, with faint gold lettering on the front and side. The spine of the book was torn, and the edges were frayed. The book was so old, it was difficult to make out what was embossed on the front cover. It took me a few seconds to read the old-fashioned font, but then it came into focus.

The History of Christianity.

This was it. The object that had haunted this school. The sickening volume that was apparently the pride of Hampton, given its prominent location in the main lobby.

That would end tonight.

"Son of a bitch," Tommy said, "we found it. Let's open this thing and get out of here."

All of a sudden the room exploded with light. I stumbled and shut my eyes instinctively.

"Who the hell are you!" I heard someone shouting at us, but I couldn't see where he was.

"I'm, uh, we're—"

"Get your hands up!" he shouted. I could tell he was behind us. The police?

I squinted and looked around. "Hey, we're just—"

"I said hands up!"

I turned and saw a man wearing black pants, a black shirt, and a ball cap that said SECURITY. He was pointing a small handgun directly at me. I raised my hands, still holding the flashlight. Tommy did the same. Now that my eyes had adjusted to the fluorescent overhead lights, I got a better look at the guy. He was about twenty-five years old, with short black hair and medium-brown skin. I could tell he was Native. Then I took a look at the gun, which was still pointed at my chest. It looked like a little Ruger LC9 semiautomatic, but I couldn't tell for sure. At this range, any handgun was dangerous. I kept my eyes on his face to see what he was going to do.

"Yo man, take it easy," Tommy said. "Why don't you—"

"How'd you get in here?" the man said.

I quickly ran through some possible cover stories in my head. I didn't think the hospital story would wash, given that we had flashlights and a bag of tools. I decided to go with a utility story.

"We're with Black Hills Energy," I said. "Got a report of, ah, an outage. Just checking on it."

The security guard looked at Tommy and me, top to bottom. Tommy was wearing his standard uniform of ragged jeans and a T-shirt, and I had on an old jean jacket and flannel shirt. Not to mention Tommy reeked of sweat and nacho-cheese chips.

"Bullshit," the guard said. "I'm calling the cops."

"No, it's true, man!" Tommy said. "We heard there was some, you know, natural gas here. Just doin' our job!"

The gun moved from my chest to Tommy's. "Uh-huh. Tell it to the police." He shifted the gun to his left hand, pulled a cell phone out of his pocket, and started to press a button with his thumb.

"*Don't do that!*" Tommy yelled.

The security guard stopped, surprised.

"Man, please don't call no cops!" Tommy dropped his flashlight. It banged as it hit the floor. "Look, dude, I gotta be honest with you—I got one strike against me. You call the cops, I go back to the joint for a long time."

This was true. Tommy had spent two years at the state max for assault, and I knew he'd do anything to avoid going back.

The security guard looked at Tommy. "Not my problem. What the fuck are you guys doing here?" The gun stayed pointed at Tommy, but he put the cell phone down.

"Yo man," Tommy said, "are you Indian? You Oglala?"

The guard paused for a second. "Yeah, so what?"

"We are too, homes! Sicangu! From Rosebud."

I didn't know what Tommy was doing, but maybe his rap could delay the security guard while we figured out our next move.

"Look, bro, I'm gonna level with you," Tommy said. "We ain't actually from the power company."

The guard smirked. "No shit."

"How long you been working here?" Tommy asked.

"None of your business."

Tommy held his hands up as if in surrender. "All right, cool! Ain't no thing. I just wanna know if they told you what's in this cabinet here."

"What?"

"This thing right here. The book inside. You know about that?"

He shook his head. "What are you talking about—book? You guys are trying to steal—"

"This motherfucking book! It's made from the skin of an Indian! Just like you and me!"

The guard's eyes widened. "What—"

"It's true, man! We ain't here to steal nothin'! Just want to get rid of that thing. It's some old book—a wasicu killed an Indian back in the day, then took the skin off his body, made it into a book cover. It's right there, bro."

The guard was quiet for a moment but kept the gun pointed at us. "Somebody told me that when I first started working here. I didn't believe it. I mean, what the hell? That's messed up." Now he aimed the gun at Tommy's head. "But that's on them. The president of the school or whoever. You assholes can't be breaking in here, book or no book. I got to do my job."

He raised the phone again.

"Hold up!" I said. "Please. Just stop for a second, okay? Look, man, we get it. You got to work, right? We don't want to cause you no trouble. You seem like a good guy. But can you do us a solid? Just let us grab this book and we'll get out of here. What do you say?"

He shook his head, the gun now pointed at me. "No! I'll get fired if they find out someone broke in here. Now keep your hands up! I mean it."

I saw that he was trembling, shaky. He'd almost certainly never confronted anyone with a gun before, and that made him unpredictable. Dangerous. I needed to calm him down. I noticed he was wearing a name badge that said *Lonnie*.

"Lonnie—that's your name, right?" I said. "How about if we just take off, leave the book? That cool?" I lowered my arms.

"Put your hands up! Now! You guys busted in here—tell it to the cops."

"Dude, why don't you put the gun down?" I said, and took a step toward him.

He moved back about two feet. "Stay right there or I'll fucking shoot! I'm calling right now." He tried to push a button on his phone, but his hand was shaking too badly and he couldn't do it. He kept shifting his eyes from the phone to me.

"Lonnie, just give me that phone, okay?" I said. "And the gun."

"Fuck you." He stuck the phone in his pocket and grasped the handgun with both hands, aimed straight at me.

"You gonna shoot me, Lonnie?" He didn't say anything, but his eyes were blazing. "You really want to kill another Indian?"

"I warned you!" He took a step forward. The gun was just inches from my head.

I stood stock-still, waiting to see what he would do. I tried not to breathe.

After an eternity, he stepped back and lowered the gun. I took a deep breath and looked over at Tommy. His eyes were wide and his head was cocked at a strange angle, like he'd seen something startling and unexpected.

"That book really made of Indian skin?" Lonnie said.

I nodded.

"Shit, go ahead and take it." He stared down at the floor, unable to look at me. "I'm probably gonna get fired." Lonnie moved behind the display cabinet and unlatched the back panel.

I gave Tommy the signal and pointed at the book with my lips. He reached inside and grabbed the book from the easel.

"What are you gonna do with it?" Lonnie asked.

"Get rid of it," I said. "We'll take the skin off first—give it to our medicine man."

He nodded. "I might as well go home; don't need the shitstorm that'll come from my boss." He turned away and started walking toward the main door.

"Wait," I said. He turned to me.

"Take this." I went over to him and handed him the envelope with the two thousand dollars. He opened it, then stared at me with a look of confusion.

I raised my right hand. "Just take it."

He gave a half smile and walked out.

Once the door closed, Tommy turned to me. "What the hell, man? He was gonna shoot you! Goddamn lot of money."

"Yeah, it was," I said.

THE BRIDGE

By Abby L. Vandiver

"He'll be dead by midnight, and I'll meet you at the bridge."
That had been the plan. Probably not a good one. But it was what we'd come up with.

The bridge was old like me, the area dark, and while it was abandoned, it was near a main thoroughfare. A truss, faded black painted steel, the top and bottom cords rusted and dismantled, the floorboards uneven, some ripped out, and the vertical and diagonal poles dangling and scattered about along with the rivets that used to hold it all in place. The waterway underneath had long been dried up and beyond it, nothing. Littered, debris-filled grounds. Abandoned buildings. No place to hide. No place to escape into. Nowhere else to go from there. If we were seen or chased, we'd be trapped.

Well, I would. Me. I would be the one trapped. Chased. Because I was the one who was going to kill someone.

"I can't. Not anymore," she had said, not one tear dropping from her glistening eyes. "He's sucking all the air from me. My insides have shriveled into a tiny, hard ball." She folded her fingers in, making tight fists. "There will be nothing left of me." Her voice fading away, I could barely hear what came next. "You are my only hope." She spoke in a strained whisper. "The only way I can get out."

I grabbed her hands and held on to them. Willing her my strength. "Leave him."

"He won't let me do that," she'd said. "He'd rather see me dead." Her whole body trembled. "He'd kill me first." She buried her head in her hands. "I swear!" She sobbed. "He'll kill me!"

But it was she who had the murderous intent.

I met Evie at the Red Door Saloon. She occupied the last seat of the long, oak, L-shaped bar that ended at the wall, pushing her body into it as if she wanted to disappear inside it. Hunched over a drink, it seemed she'd given up and given in, waiting for that dingy wall to suck her through. The rest of her said she wanted to be alone.

So I went over to say hello.

"I've been there," I said as I slid onto the stool next to her. "But I found my way back."

"There's no coming back from where I am," she'd said, not looking up from her drink, the ice tinkling as she stirred it with the little red straw.

"Talking about it helps."

She sighed and pushed herself further against the wall. "Talking is what got me into it in the first place."

"And maybe talking can get you out."

For the first time her eyes met mine. "There's no way out."

I saw it as soon as she looked at me. At least I thought I did. A flicker in her eye. Something lost inside trying to get out. A small glimmer of life. It seemed to be overcome by an emptiness that was trying to consume her.

I thought maybe I could help free her soul.

But it wasn't emptiness inside her. It was a darkness that dwelt in a soulless hole. There hadn't been one spark or measure of anything good.

Nope. I didn't save her that night. She consumed me.

Evie had a small frame, narrow hips but enough cleavage showing in her low-cut shirt to make any man's eye wander. Eyes red from too much drinking or too much crying, I wasn't sure.

"I misspoke," she said, after I'd bought the next round of drinks. "There is a way out." She turned to me and stared into my eyes. "One way."

Now I was on my way to kill her husband.

The roads were quiet, the streetlights dim, casting a glow, giving me direction like bread crumbs along the way. Her house, just a couple of blocks away from the bridge, was a long drive from where'd I'd last seen her. We'd had a drink before I was to go to her house, at a restaurant we'd never been to before. Open spaces. Good food. Lots of people around. Just like any other normal outing. But the familiarity of dinner out with friends made the night's task no easier. She was already there, waiting for me. As soon as she saw me, she waved me over, a smile pressed onto her face. A light turned on inside her.

"Tonight's the night," she cooed as I sat down across from her. She scooted her chair closer to me and placed her hand over mine and leaned in. "You know this is the only thing that will save me, right?"

"I know," I said, seeing a wash of worry cross her face. "I'm not backing out."

"I didn't think you would," she said. She pulled her hand back and picked up her bottle of beer. "And if you had, I would have done it myself. Or gotten someone else." She winked as she clanked the top of her bottle to the one she'd ordered for me. "I knew I could count on you."

She'd downed the rest of her beer in one swig, her eyes then searching for the waitress to order another.

I sat in front of her house and stared at it. I wasn't going to back out. I'd meant that. I wanted to make her happy. To set her free.

I'd been there. Desperate. Seeing no way out. Lucky for me, so far my bad decisions hadn't led me to any criminal enterprise. Well, that is, up until now.

It wasn't that I hadn't caused other people unnecessary pain, or that I hadn't found myself dangerously close to crossing the law. I'd disappointed plenty of people I cared about, given up the one thing I loved most.

But with age comes wisdom and the unfettered need to share what you've learned down that rugged road of life with every tattered soul encountered, even when yours still needs mending.

I'd come back to town to set things straight. If I could. It was the reason I'd been in that bar the night I met Evie.

I thought maybe I could share my wisdom with her.

As our friendship blossomed, it seemed so did she.

We met up lots of times at that old bridge. It was quiet and familiar. Worn and old like me. But still standing.

Like me.

Evie would walk from her house. Always at midnight. And I'd meet her there. We'd sit in my old beat-up convertible, breeze blowing through our hair and we'd talk, laugh and sip wine from paper cups.

"Is Cy short for anything?" she once asked.

"Nope."

"That's all to your name?"

"That's all I got," I said.

"What was your mother thinking about?" she said and laughed.

I smiled at her.

"I know you have a last name."

"I do," I said.

"You gonna tell me what it is?"

"Nope."

"Why? You running from the law or something?"

"I'm not running from anything," I said. "Not anymore."

"I wish I was like that," she'd said. "Not running from anything."

"You're not," I said, and glanced over at her. "Looks to me, you're holding tight in one place."

"You don't get it," she said.

"Explain it to me."

"I don't know if I can." She stared through the windshield. Out past the bridge and into the darkness. "You may not see it, but he has this hold on me. It's tighter than a window that's been painted shut." She was quiet for a while. Thinking it through, it seemed. I waited for her to start back up.

"I got in trouble once. Wasn't my fault," she said.

"What kind of trouble?"

She glanced at me. "It don't matter much now. I should have never been blamed for it in the first place. But I told them that I'd been with him."

"Him? Your husband?"

She nodded. "He wasn't my husband then."

"That wasn't true? That you were with him?"

"No."

"And he backed you up?"

"He's selfish!" Anger flashed in her eyes. "I don't owe him anything, you know."

"He's being selfish for covering up for you?"

"By thinking he can make me stay with him." She spat out the words.

"Oh." I nodded. "I see."

"He didn't have to tell them nothing. I would have been fine." She raised her eyebrows. "And I shouldn't be made to feel like I owe him."

Her leg shaking enough to rock the car, she let out a groan. "Don't you think so?" she said.

I didn't say anything.

"Don't you have anything to say?" She looked at me from the corner of her eye. Shielding herself, it seemed, from an answer she didn't want to hear.

"It's your story," I said. "I'm letting you tell it. Come to your own conclusions."

"It'll be nothing to tell if I don't get away from him."

"Then do it."

"I told you, you wouldn't understand." She turned her back on me.

"I understand that you feel stuck and think there's no way out. But I'm telling you, there is."

"You're right about that." She turned back and eyed me. "There is that one way out."

And that's when she told me what she wanted me to do.

I think she may have been planning to ask me all along. It wasn't the first time she'd mentioned there was only one way for her to get that release she needed.

"You couldn't wake him up after he falls asleep even if you hit him over his head with a sledgehammer," she said. "He doesn't know I leave." I could hear the disgust in her voice. "That's why I wait until midnight. After I know he's out for the night."

"Well, you're out now," I'd said. Her lack of a dilemma didn't seem as obvious to her. "Instead of coming here, to the bridge, you could keep going."

She jerked to face me, her eyes on fire. "Would you want to live always having to look over your shoulder?" She landed a hand on her forehead and dragged it through her hair. "He would find me. Kill me! I've told you that." She grabbed my arm. "There's only one way for me to break free."

Permanently get rid of him. That's what she was asking for. The kind of permanence that comes only with death.

The moon hung low in the sky the night we planned it, like it was listening in. Crickets chirped and the night was particularly still, like everything in it had stopped.

And when it started again, at least for me, it was all a blur.

"Hi. Come on in and meet my husband, Colt." She waved me into her house. Their house. She'd wanted to show me the layout. "In the daylight," she'd said, once I agreed to help. "Because when you do it, you know, *kill him*"—she mouthed the last two words—"it'll be dark, and I don't want you stumbling around. Plus"—she pushed herself into me and nodded her head—"you need to know what he looks like."

Stepping inside, I took in every part of that house. Every part of him.

It was a big house and matched the man I could see him to be. They both had scents that filled the senses. Clean and fragrant. His a fresh-out-of-the-shower, aquatic, citrusy smell.

The inside of the craftsman bungalow smelled of cookies, lemons, and a summer breeze. The house was bright and cheery, as was his smile.

He had a familiar way about him, an easy demeanor. And it wasn't hard to see the love he had for Evie. Evident in the gentleness he spoke to her, the eagerness he attended to her.

It hit me with a whoosh. Standing in that house. Watching that man. Colt. Emotions started swirling, bubbling up. I didn't know if I could keep them hidden. I put my hand on the wall, sucked in a breath, and tried to steady myself.

How ironic, I thought. I'd come back to save my family, and here I was going to tear this one apart.

I collected my thoughts and through the dark night stared at the house. Yep, I memorized the layout just like Evie wanted me to. I knew just how to get to the bedroom where she'd promised I'd find him sleeping. And I memorized him too—the crinkle in his nose when he smiled. The way he rubbed his hand over his low-cut hair when he was thinking. His lopsided smile. I took all of him in—every word, every movement—and hadn't been able to get him out of my mind since.

Not that I hadn't thought of him before. Wondered what kind of man he was. Why it was Evie he had picked.

Now I walked around to the back of the house. The air was so heavy it felt as if it were weighing me down. My shoulders drooped, and a sinking feeling lurched in my stomach. I stopped, sucked in a gulp of air, and closed my eyes just for a moment so I could find my bearings.

Thankful for a light coming from the house on the other side of Evie's backyard, I finished my trek around back and spotted the shed where she'd told me they kept that sledgehammer.

The door creaked open, and a dirt-infused wind gusted up my nose and into my eyes. I coughed into my shoulder and waved away the motes of dust.

The sledgehammer sat in a corner along with a shovel and an ax. All good pickings for the job I needed to do. But it was Evie who had chosen for me. I dragged it out of the shed and across the grass. Heavier than I'd imagined. I had to lift it with two hands so it wouldn't scrape across the concrete patio or bump up the two back steps. I prayed I had enough strength to lug it up the stairs to the bedroom where I'd find him.

Using the flashlight on my phone, I made it up the staircase. Tucking the phone back inside my pocket, I stood in the doorway, holding on to the knob with one hand, the sledgehammer with the other, and tried to adjust my eyes. I replaced the shadows with my memory of how the room looked in the daylight. Blue carpet. Soft blue painted walls and sheer white curtains that had wafted back and forth with the breeze that came in through the windows. Abstract color-coordinated artwork hung on the wall; a Peloton in one corner seemed to be used for hanging clothes instead of toning muscles. The bed was in the center of the room, and off to the right was a chair.

I needed to sit down.

I dragged the sledgehammer behind me as I crossed the room. Sinking down into the chair, I let out a breath I hadn't realized I'd been holding. I swiped the hair that was sticking to my forehead, glued down from the perspiration, and stared at him.

With the glow from the streetlight streaming in through the window, I watched his chest move up and down in his sleep. I could hear him breathe. Slow. Rhythmic.

It had been a long time since I'd done that. Watched someone sleep. Made sure they were breathing. That they were all right.

The last time had been the night I left.

The night I left my little boy.

He'd slept peacefully, with no idea how his world was about to be shattered. How he'd wake up to a whole new reality because of what I'd done. Now I was doing it again.

I'd always thought that when people died in their sleep, they never knew they were dead. They went from one state of unconsciousness to another without ever realizing it.

Wake up dead, my mother used to say.

I wouldn't want to die like that.

I closed my eyes. He'd been too young to know, I'd always told myself. My son. To know how awful the thing I did to him was.

I'd prayed so many times that he'd grow up happy. I reasoned that no one remembers what happens to them when they're three.

But I was never able to shake the feeling that he wasn't all right. That maybe he still needed me.

That's why I'd come back.

To do whatever he needed me to do. To help in whatever way I could. Keep him safe from harm. From others doing what I'd done to him. To make sure he was happy.

I opened my eyes. It was time to get this show on the road. Sliding to the end of the chair, using the sledgehammer for leverage, I pushed myself out of the seat and let out a grunt. I glanced at the clock on the nightstand.

Eleven fifty.

I blew out another breath and figured I'd better hurry if I wanted to get back to the bridge by midnight.

* * *

She popped up off the bench as soon as my car came into view. Running down the broken gravel road, she met me. She made little circles with her finger, wanting me to roll down the window. I did. She couldn't wait for me to stop the car or even get out of it. "Is it done? Did you kill him?" She trotted alongside the car as I pulled up closer to the bridge.

Opening the car door, I swung a foot out, not saying a word.

She stomped her foot and pounded a balled fist on the car. "Is he dead?"

I got out of the car and walked around to the trunk. Clicking the lock, I popped it open. I pulled out the sledgehammer.

"You brought *it* here?" she shrieked. Not out of terror, it seemed; it was more of a gleeful squeal.

"Wait . . ." she said, her shoulders visibly drooping. "There's no blood on it." She looked at me. "Where's the blood? Wasn't there lots of it?" She turned down her mouth and opened and closed her fingers. "Didn't it squirt everywhere?" Her eyes went down to my clothes. "Why isn't there any blood on you?"

"There will be soon enough," I said.

* * *

"Officer. What's going on?" Colt was out of breath, looking around wildly as he climbed out of the back of the police cruiser.

"Took you long enough." Detective Tamarin looked up from the notebook he'd been scrawling in to glare at the uniformed police officer who held the back car door open. "We need an ID so we can wrap this up. Get the body out of here."

"The body?" Colt said, terror ripping over his face.

"We couldn't wake him up," the officer told Tamarin, nodding toward Colt. "There was a light on; we knew somebody was there. It took a while to rouse him."

"Can somebody tell me what's going on?" Colt pleaded.

"Are you Evie Seidman's husband?" Detective Tamarin asked.

"Yes. Yes. I am," he said, his voice shaking. He couldn't keep his eyes fixed. They wandered around the area. "I'm Colt Seidman. Can you please tell me what's going on? Where's Evie?"

"She called us," the detective said, then pointed to me. "You know her?"

Colt squinted and looked my way. Panic in his eyes.

The police floodlights had lit up the area, but still I wasn't sure he'd recognize me. He'd seen me recently only the one time.

"Cy?" he asked.

"Yep. Cy Long."

The detective coughed into his fist. "I'll ask you again. You know her?"

"She knows my wife."

"Yeah. That's what she told us," Detective Tamarin said. "You know anything else about her?"

"No. Why? What happened? Where is my wife?"

"Ms. Long said she came to meet your wife. She said they met here often." The detective seemed to have no compassion. I wished I could wrap my arms around Colt. Help him through this. Tell him everything was going to be okay.

Colt glanced at me, tears streaming down his face. "Did she do something to Evie?" he asked. "Is that Evie's blood on her?" He lifted a limp hand and pointed to me.

"She found her. We're looking into if it was more than that."

I saw his knees buckle as he braced himself by putting his hand on the car. "Dead? Evie's dead?"

I don't think he'd processed what dead meant, or any of the other references to her state Detective Tamarin had carelessly thrown out. Colt's eyes still searched the area as if he expected to see Evie walking around there.

"Yes, sir. Dead." The lines across the detective's forehead relaxed and his eyes softened. "I'm sorry." He closed his notebook and put a hand on Colt's shoulder momentarily, then blew out a breath. "The ME puts her time of death at about midnight." He was back to the business at hand. "I'll need you to identify the body."

"Detective Tamarin?" A police officer walked over. "We've searched Ms. Long's car. It's clean. Nothing's there."

"You checked the trunk?"

"Nothing in there but a spare, a tire rod, and a sledgehammer."

Detective Tamarin nodded at the police officer and then looked at me. "I still don't want you wandering off. You hear?"

I held up my hands. "I'm not going anywhere." I tipped my head toward Colt. "He might need me."

* * *

She'd managed to get away from me when I tried to bash her head in with that sledgehammer, but like I said, it was heavy.

Still, she didn't get far. Fear makes a person unsteady, and the uneven ground didn't help her footing.

She tripped on one of the rivets that had come undone on the planks of the bridge and fell on the steel beam.

It probably wouldn't have killed her. It took a little help from me for that to happen.

She had cried and pleaded with me not to do it. Not so keen about death when it was her own. I'd covered up her blood that had gotten on me by cradling her head in my chest. Good reason for me to have it all over me.

But even if they did figure it out, it was worth it.

I looked over at Colt, bawling his eyes out. He wasn't taking losing his wife well.

If he only knew the truth about her.

Or about me.

I wondered if he'd cried like that when he found out I'd left him all those years ago.

I felt tears coming down my cheeks as well. But my tears were tears of joy. I'd given him life twice now. The nine months I carried him and gave him birth, and then rescuing him from that wretched wife of his. Maybe he'd get over it like he'd gotten over losing his mother and find happiness again.

I hoped so.

It was all I could do for him. Happy I could be there after abandoning him all those years ago.

I couldn't ever tell him who I really was.

I was just grateful that me and that old rusty bridge had saved my son. And Evie was free, just like she wanted to be.

DEAD MEN TELL NO TALES

By Callie Browning

"What do you mean, he's dead?"

"Just what I said . . . he's dead."

"Are you sure?"

"Despite what you think, I'm not so stupid that I can't see he's dead."

They stared at each other for a long moment, both of them gauging if the other was as dim as they claimed to be.

"Lemme see."

Vivian's shapely silhouette slunk along the dimly lit corridor as she led the way through the great house, seemingly unperturbed by the fact that she had killed the prime minister of Barbados. Her steps were even and sure, her silk dressing gown glowing in the darkness and grazing the floor as she walked. Behind her, Annie heaved a big breath that contracted the entirety of her stout frame. She followed tremulously in Vivian's wake, cursing both her curiosity and her trepidation as she tiptoed down the massive wooden staircase. Annie didn't want to see a dead body. Her skin prickled uneasily; the cold of the midnight hour coupled with her anxiety sank into her skin like icy needles.

Annie wasn't sure if she was more disturbed by Vivian not being disturbed about what she'd done or by the fact that Vivian had confided in Annie in the first place. Her mind flitted back and forth over her worries as their bare feet padded gently on the hardwood floor.

It had been two months since Annie found out that Vivian had been having an affair with Ivan Oxley, the newly reinstated prime minister of Barbados. And from the moment she found out, she had known it would end in tears—Ivan's, not Vivian's.

Ivan Oxley was a notorious Lothario with a penchant for dim-witted women with loose morals. But he had gotten more than he bargained for with Vivian Holder, the daughter of poor cane cutters who had clawed her way through life. Vivian had no qualms about conducting business with questionable characters and no compunction about making enemies to get what she wanted. A married lover had funded a small salon to get her on her feet, and ever the prudent businesswoman, Vivian had grown and diversified. Vivian now owned 10 percent of the most prime real estate in the country's capital—a remarkable feat for someone who had neither family money nor bank loans—and a reputation for being shrewd.

Ivan's first mistake was to make himself believe he could bed Vivian without repercussions. His second was being prime minister during their affair. The power he wielded in a small society was enough to make Vivian giddy. She reveled in the luxuries she enjoyed under the auspices of the prime minister's hospitality. So much so that she engaged Ivan in countless nights of blatant debauchery in order to join his political party. The poor man had never experienced—and in some cases, even imagined—the things Vivian let him do to her. Ivan figured no harm would come from letting Vivian do as she liked once it kept the sweet sex coming. Little did Ivan know that it was akin to lighting a match while wearing sulfur gloves—only one outcome was possible. And as sure as night turns to day, sweet sex became Ivan's undoing.

Two months later his deputy prime minister, Arden Welch, died of food poisoning while in office, and Vivian insisted that she be appointed deputy prime minister or she would tell the entire country about Ivan's lurid desires. Feeling like his hands were tied—literally and figuratively—he had installed her as his second-in-command.

It seemed now to Annie that perhaps Ivan should have given Vivian a bit more credit from the very beginning. If he had, maybe Annie wouldn't have been dragged out of a deep sleep to stare at his corpse in the middle of the night.

Damned Ivan and his selfishness.

Annie closed the polished mahogany door behind them when they reached the large open-air terrace. A moment later a dull click sounded in Vivian's hand and a yellow beam of light broke through the darkness. In the silence, the sound of the flashlight turning on was loud as a gunshot. Annie hadn't even noticed Vivian was holding it. She clutched her hand to her sputtering chest as a single tear rolled down her cheek.

The tropical air warmed the garden's flowers, perfuming the night air with the sweet scents of frangipani and amaryllis. Annie barely noticed. Her mind was too preoccupied. In many ways, morbid curiosity filled her; she was dying (pardon the pun) to ask questions. How did he die? Was there a lot of blood? Vivian said they had been having sex . . . was he naked?

On the other hand, she was afraid to find out. Her body had grown heavier, more burdensome as she walked behind Vivian, each footstep more difficult than the last with the realization that they were getting closer to the body. The dark night sky echoed the heaviness inside Anne's heart, and she wondered how even she had let herself be cornered by Vivian's treachery. Every detail was richer and brighter, magnified with crystal-clear clarity under the spotlight of Annie's misgivings.

The beam from Vivian's flashlight bobbed along the dark path that snaked through the gardens around the prime minister's residence. The dew-laden trail was slick against their bare feet as the younger woman led the way to a large baroque wall fountain covered by masses of allamanda vines. The silky blooms were a pale fluorescent yellow under the dusty pallor of moonlight. Vivian pulled aside the thick curtain of vines to reveal a heavy steel door hidden in the stone wall.

This secret underground bunker had been the brainchild of Barbados's last Caucasian governor. He had watched with alarm as political unrest had reared its head in other countries around the world. Fearing a civil war in the years preceding the country's independence from Britain, he was convinced that he would be dragged through the streets and lynched because of "the people's faltering allegiance to the Queen," as he had so delicately put it. He had used his own money to construct this shelter under the guise of a "beautification program." But he hadn't given much thought to how to maintain the secrecy of the bunker. And so the masons, painters, artisans, gardeners, and plumbers who were commissioned to create it spread the word far and wide, rendering it absolutely useless as a safe house.

And then along came Ivan Oxley. While the prime minister hadn't felt the need for a safe room in a paradise like Barbados, he had, being the enterprising visionary that he was, spent thousands converting it to a sex room for his escapades. Had his constituents known of his remarkable thriftiness, they might have found it difficult to understand why he made half the public sector redundant due to "budgetary constraints."

The dull yellow beam from Vivian's flashlight illuminated a flight of narrow stone stairs that led to a cavernous but homey room below. A large cupboard filled with war rations was next to a small wooden sideboard covered with liquor bottles and a large crystal decanter. A large four-poster bed with silk sheets filled almost the entire left side of the room, and the dead prime minister's robust corpse completed the otherwise cozy scene.

Annie's breath hitched in her chest, and she hesitated before she inched her way toward the body. He lay there, still and unmoving, but still she hoped against hope that Vivian was wrong. She had silently prayed that Vivian was overreacting. But there was no arguing with the ten-inch butcher knife that stuck out of his back like a bloody flagpole.

Annie sneaked a glance at Vivian out of the corner of her eye. She was motionless—almost catlike in her stillness—watching Annie intently.

Annie knew Vivian wanted her to break down, to shriek hysterically and sob uncontrollably. But if Vivian was waiting for a sign of weakness, she wouldn't get it. The older woman didn't fool herself about Vivian's ruthlessness, and Annie didn't plan to end up lying next to Ivan to rot in his fancified mausoleum.

"Well . . . what do you want to do?" Annie asked bravely.

Vivian continued to stare at her, holding her gaze while she reached for the crystal decanter and a stout brandy glass.

"I have a few notions in mind," Vivian said lightly as she drained the decanter of the smooth amber liquid. "One, we could just lock him up inside here and leave him. Honestly, Barbadians are starting to hate him, and they will be glad that he went missing."

Annie nodded numbly.

Vivian swallowed a mouthful of brandy. "Or we could take his body up to the master bedroom and put him on the bed. You can 'discover' him in a little bit and say there was a home invasion."

Annie turned to her, eyes wide open and mouth agape. "Why do I have to do it? Can't we leave the body in the bed for the maid to find in the morning?"

Vivian shrugged her shoulders indifferently. "It's up to you. I was just trying to help you out. I just thought it would make more sense for *his wife* to call the police the same night rather than for the maid to call the next morning." She smiled broadly. "But if you're good with that, who am I to argue?"

Annie trembled as cold sweat started to form on her brow. To be in alliance with her husband's killer was a testament to how afraid she was of the other woman. After watching Vivian manipulate Ivan until she had gone from real estate mogul to deputy prime minister, Annie knew she couldn't afford to take any chances with her. She was already distrustful of being inside a soundproof underground crypt with her.

Her mouth grew so dry that her tongue felt like sandpaper that scratched her lips when she spoke.

Vivian eyed her curiously. She could see Annie was trembling. She approached her slowly, sympathetically, and held her by the shoulders as she guided Annie to sit on one of the cheap pine chairs. "I know this is a lot for you to deal with. Believe me, it's hard for me too. I've lost my boss and my lover in one fell swoop. You've only lost a husband. Truth is, you should be comforting me."

Hard for her to deal with? Annie's eyes opened wide and her chest tightened.

Vivian was a lunatic.

*   *   *

Vivian took a fresh glass from the shelf and filled it with brandy using another decanter. She pushed the glass across the varnished surface. It slid easily on the table, bumping into Annie's hand and causing the liquid to swish and swirl around the sides of the glass. Annie eyed it warily. She didn't touch it.

Vivian held her drink aloft and beckoned Annie to do the same. "To the cheating scoundrels: may the gates of hell be thrown open for their arrival!"

Annie looked from the glass to Vivian, her eyes swinging back and forth like a pendulum, her heart fluttering wildly in her chest.

She shook her head nervously. "No thank you. I'm not thirsty."

Vivian shot up from the chair and slammed her glass down on the table with such ferocity that it shattered in her hand.

"*Drink it!*" Vivian shrieked at her. "You're so stupid! Do you think I planned to bring you down here to poison you?"

Annie grabbed the glass quickly and choked down a mouthful of liquor as tears streamed down her face. The brandy burned her throat and left a metallic aftertaste on her tongue. She grimaced.

Vivian stared at the wall, her eyes unfocused and glassy as she muttered, "I didn't *plan* it, but after I got here, it seemed the wisest thing to do."

Annie let out a plaintive wail that filled the cavernous bunker. It was so mournful and hair-raising that it almost roused her dead husband.

"I believe they call it a 'crime of opportunity,' if I'm not mistaken," Vivian said as she wandered past the bed, idly flicking the bloody knife that pierced Ivan's back.

Annie's stomach churned. She bent double over the table, holding her head in her hands, her vision growing blurry.

Vivian was pensive as she cocked her head to one side. "You know . . . I never loved any of the men in my life except Arden."

Annie turned her head in disbelief at the mention of the deceased deputy prime minister. She gulped before saying, "Is that why you killed him?"

Coldness crept over Vivian's face as she met Annie's eyes with a steely look. "Yes. The only thing that could have incriminated me in Arden's murder was security footage from his house. When I went to get it the next day, it was gone." Her smile didn't reach her eyes as she stared at Annie. "Knowing him, he gave you a key to the house. I put two and two together and figured you had the tape."

She wandered back to the table and pressed her bare feet toe-to-toe with Annie's.

"Do you think it's fair that you got a prime minister *and* a deputy prime minister all to yourself? Arden was happy enough to bump groins and do things to me that you wouldn't let him do to you, but it wasn't enough."

Vivian kicked the chair angrily, her body practically vibrating as she glared at the older woman. "No. He loved his fat little Annie. He worshiped every bit of excess blubber on your body, and it sickened me. I gave everything to your husband *and* your lover, and neither of them would leave you. Arden didn't mind sharing you and Ivan was too selfish to share himself.

"I couldn't let you find out the truth. You'd spill the beans. Then I'd be in prison with nothing to show for bending over backwards for these men. Plus"—Vivian cinched her silk robe around her trim waist—"I'm a patriot. I'd never leave Barbados without a leader."

* * *

Vivian quirked her eyebrows as she walked toward the stone staircase, her voice steady and strong. "I took an oath to forsake everything else for this country, and I intend to keep it."

Clattering chairs and a heavy thud behind her were proof that Annie had succumbed to the poison and now lay dead on the floor. A slow, triumphant smile crept across Vivian's lips.

Vivian exited the underground bunker, ripping down the allamanda vines that curtained the entrance and tossing them carelessly aside before she stalked back to her car and drove home to get a good night's sleep.

Two days later Vivian stood alone just off the large sitting room where the swearing-in ceremony was about to start. In just a few moments she would be presented to a throng of reporters, parliamentary officials, and the governor-general to be sworn in as Barbados' second female Prime Minister following the shocking murder-suicide committed by the former Prime Minister's wife.

She smoothed the skirt of her designer suit, admiring the way it held her curves. It was a somber navy blue, a proper color for mourning her predecessor, but more importantly, it did wonderful things for her complexion. Her aide had hastily written a speech the night before. The papers were crisp and smooth in the palm of Vivian's hand. She raised the sheets slowly and mouthed the words. It was a long monologue of random dribble about her profound sadness at Ivan's passing and her strengthened resolve to do her duty to the country.

Vivian wrinkled her mouth in distaste. It was all pointless, and she probably wouldn't mean any of it. She crushed the speech between her hands and threw it in the ceramic bin before tossing her hair over her shoulder and reaching for the doorknob. In her mind, she pictured everyone waiting to greet her when she opened the door, anticipating the moment when she would place her hand on the Bible and take the oath. They would smile at Vivian and thank her for her courage in the face of all of the hardships she had endured. She would return a smile and fill them with false hope through lots of empty promises.

It was miraculous, really. It was so easy to become prime minister, as long as you were willing to sleep your way to the top.

Vivian sighed contentedly and turned the door handle.

That was the last time Vivian ever sighed contentedly. That's because the only person smiling at her when she opened the door was Annie. Vivian's face went white at the sight of the woman she had murdered only two nights earlier. For a moment Vivian thought she was having a nightmare; surely Annie's deathly pallor and the phalanx of police waiting to arrest her could only be a figment of her imagination.

Vivian frowned. She didn't particularly like nightmares, and this one was encroaching on such a good dream. In the blink of an eye, two policemen stepped forward. Cold steel handcuffs clapped on her wrists. Never before had one of her dreams been so vivid.

The placid smile on portly little Annie's face never wavered. The younger woman stared back at her, never once registering the policeman rattling off her right to silence as he led her from the room.

"Wait!" Vivian shouted anxiously. She turned back and advanced toward Annie, her pace so brisk that she dragged the policeman behind her. There was no hiding the bewilderment on her face when she spoke to Annie. "I didn't kill you?"

"Almost." A sly look crossed Annie's face. "Good thing I'm so fat—turns out you didn't give me enough poison to do me in. Or didn't you know that the dosage given must be proportionate to my weight?" Annie cocked her head mockingly to the side and smiled. "Luckily, I'm not as skinny as you or I'd be six feet under."

DOC'S AT MIDNIGHT

By Richie Narvaez

Thirty indoor and outdoor venues on sixteen acres, an acropolis of the arts. Squatting broadly on what used to be called San Juan Hill, where African Americans and Puerto Ricans once tried to live until they were eminent-domained out. A pair of star-crossed fools meet again in misadventure involving blackmail and murder, the continuance of a story that started decades before. The woman limos through two hours of traffic to be here. The man is already there, waiting, ferrying a handcart stacked with boxes of lightbulbs.

When she turns and sees him, nothing happens.

She looks right through him, doesn't register the handcart. She wears a dark-purple trench coat, a black dress underneath, a large quilted leather bag. Her eyes do not want to settle on him. Perhaps she does not recognize him. To be fair, it has been forty-something years since the trial, and he may look a bit different now, thicker skin on the wide, swarthy face he was once both conceited about and ashamed of. But his hair has never been better.

She must be here for the opera. *Eugene Onegin* tonight. She is still *oh so pretty.* How old must she be, he wonders—sixty,

sixty-one? Time has been kind to her. Of course, it would be. She looks polite, refined, well bred, mature. But what is that he sees in her eyes that are looking beyond him? Pain. Expectation. Or is he imagining that?

He must talk to her. He will probably never have this chance again.

Just as he steps forward, some kid, some delinquent, appears from the crowd and grabs her leather purse. She resists, but the kid tugs hard and the purse comes free and the kid stumbles—the bag seems heavy—then flies. A bird.

She screams in agony.

He forgets the handcart and takes off after the kid. He waves frantically at Mr. Bramley, the security chief, who is standing nearby. Mr. Bramley has seen the whole thing but isn't moving. He smirks.

The kid is past the fountain and down the stairs, already disappearing down Columbus Avenue. So fast. Embalao. A rocket in his pocket.

He tries to keep up. He is short but fast. He used to run, dance, fly up and down these streets all day long.

But that was a long time ago.

The last he sees is the kid's red high-tops disappearing into a mob of tourists. Gone.

* * *

He looks at Mr. Bramley, who is still standing in the same place.

"I coulda told you it was no use trying to play hero," Mr. Bramley says. "Especially if you don't fit the part."

"He robbed her."

"If she wants to make a complaint, she can." Mr. Bramley walks away.

Out of breath, he searches for her in the milling crowds.

There she stands by the fountain as if she were its statue. She stares out at nothing, but as he approaches, he sees the recognition (also anger, hatred) in her eyes before she turns away.

What can he do? He just ran for her purse, tried to get it back. He needs to explain, has to talk to her. He stands in front of her and waits. She is silent for a very long minute.

"Chino," she says, spitting it out.

"Maria," he says. "You hurt?"

She won't look at him directly, as if she's not sure what to say. Then she says, "No."

"Sorry. He was so fast." He does not know how to say what he needs to say, so he sticks to practical advice, the first thing he can think of. "You cancel your credit cards, no? That's what you do."

"I needed that purse!" she says. "Not the purse. What was in it!"

"I want to help. Can I help you?"

"I do not want your help."

He sees then that her shin is bleeding. Must have been cut when the kid yanked the purse.

"You're hurt. I can—"

"You don't understand," she spits out. "There was twenty thousand dollars in that bag. Twenty thousand! In cash and jewelry, Chino."

When she says his name, it's like a curse.

"In cash? You shouldn't—"

She sighs. "I don't carry around that kind of money. I'm not stupid. I'm being blackmailed."

"Qué qué?"

"It's none of your business, Chino. Go back to whatever it is you were doing and leave me alone."

* * *

A lifetime ago, he swore he loved this woman. But it has been forty years since he killed the man she loved. He did it to prove he loved her, to show his bravery, and to save her from that comemierda.

In the end it was for nothing.

He comes from a devout Catholic family in Ponce, Puerto Rico, the oldest of ten siblings. His mother was very strict, and when he was bad, she made him kneel on a box grater for hours. Half of the children worked on farms, hard work under a stubborn sun. Then the U.S. came in with their Operation Bootstrap and the farm jobs disappeared. His cousin Guiso went to Nueva York and came back with nice suits and pictures of his gringa girlfriend. So Chino's family put together all the money they had and sent him, seventeen years old, más pelado qué la rodilla de un cabro and thin as a stalk of sugarcane, to the big city.

Taking a plane for the first time, he was so scared he prayed to God that it would crash to ease his panic.

In Manhattan, he stayed with Guiso and his parents in a tenement on West Sixty-Third, above a grocery store. They were nice to him, but he was another mouth to feed and he knew it. He tried every day to find work. But his English was bad and his skin was brown, and he realized fast that no one wanted to hire a boy like that.

And he grew lonely. Guiso, who went out every night (no sign of his gringa girlfriend), told him he was too much of a jíbaro for the city.

One day in front of the luncheonette on the corner, Chino met a handsome morenito named Paco smoking a cigarette. Paco asked Chino if he wanted one and Chino said yes, though he couldn't stand smoking. He just wanted to talk to the boy.

Paco told him about the gang of Puerto Rican boys he ran with. When Chino met them, they all seemed so sophisticated, so sharp. He fell in with them easily. For money, they did gorilla work, shaking people down, sometimes breaking and entering. But they helped him with his English and shared all the money they made on the streets. They ran together, took every meal together, even went to church together. They were just like family.

Then there was the fighting. Growing up with six brothers, Chino knew how to give a punch and how to take one. In San Juan Hill, they were always rumbling, sometimes against the blacks, sometimes alongside them. But always against the white boys. For territory, for pride. If the white boys beat up one of yours, you beat up one of theirs. It they cut one of yours, one of them got cut. That was the law.

Guiso saw him on the street once and tried to call him out, got into his face. "Chino! What are you doing with these degenerates?"

"No me jodas, charlatan," Chino said.

"Sinvergüenza!" Guiso went to push him.

Chino, always small and fast, ducked under Guiso's hands and punched him twice in the gut. He left Guiso spitting on the floor.

He had to find a new place to live after that, ended up staying in a basement in the building of one of his gang brothers. He would stay there alone most times, chain-smoking and listening to rock 'n' roll records. Sometimes Paco would visit him. He would come in disguise so no one would know. Half their fun was in peeling away the layers, smearing his makeup.

The cops called him a delincuente. They made a special example out of him. Maybe it was his size. Maybe it was his brown skin. Big, bad Lieutenant Schrank, who always stank like stale beer and meat, would find him walking by himself on the street, pull him over, take him to the station. There he would be grilled for hours and hurt in places that wouldn't show right away.

* * *

"You're going to bleed all over your nice shoes," he says to Maria. "At least let me bandage that."

She says nothing, ignores him.

Chino decides on drastic action. He stands back and bows dramatically, and as he bows he rips his dark toupee off his head and doffs it like a hat. Cool air on his open scalp.

"It's nice to meet you, mademoiselle," he says.

"Mademoiselle! You're a fool." There is the slightest suggestion of a smile on Maria's face. It disappears quickly, but she is clearly more relaxed.

"Come," he says. "Ven conmigo."

She lets him lead her to a staff entrance and past the costume department, which always makes him think of Paco, and down to the locker room. He gets alcohol and Band-Aids, and on his knees he covers her wounds.

"My husband is a successful man," she says out of nowhere. "A doctor. Mami always said to marry a doctor. We have two beautiful daughters, Natalie and Marnie. One of them is a teacher. She's poor but she's happy. The other one—she wanted to be an actress ever since she was a little girl. She has no luck. Always needs money. She meets these men. For fun. For I don't know what. And one of them, this Mike, he says he took pictures of her doing . . . terrible things. Now he wants money or her life and my husband's life will be ruined. No parent should have a favorite, but Marnie was always his favorite. She can do no wrong in his eyes. And no father should have to see his daughter shamed."

"Where is your husband?" says Chino. "Why isn't he here?"

"He's back home in New Jersey, asleep with his Scotch by this time. Oh, they knew not to go to him. They knew I was the one to deal with."

Chino notices that she is not crying. This isn't the same Maria he knew years ago. She's made of concrete and steel now. Maybe he's the one who did that to her.

"I was supposed to give him the money at midnight, under the highway," she says, "and he was going to give me the pictures."

She tells him she bought a ticket for the opera as an excuse to tell her husband. She doesn't like opera, doesn't like music much anymore, she says, and she has purposely avoided this area of the city since she moved away. She had planned on going to sleep in her seat and then to meet this Mike.

"But now the money is gone. What luck!" she says. "What lousy luck!"

Chino thinks about her situation. He wants to help her, must help her.

"This Mike, it's just him? He has no gang or a crew or the Mafia?"

She laughs at this. "It's just him. He's just a dirty man-child."

"Does he have backups, copias?"

"No. I think he just wants money quick."

"Espera. I have an idea," Chino says, taking her hand. "Arise, Maria, arise!"

Back in the costume department, he sits her down and asks her to wait as he ducks into aisles of robes and capes and dresses.

When he comes out, he twirls and says, "What do you think?"

"Your bra is crooked, and so is your wig. Is this . . . is this what you do?"

"No, but I had a friend who liked to dress up, and that gave me the idea."

"Well, the dress is close to mine. It could work. You need a new purse and something as heavy so that it feels full of money."

"Por supuesto."

"Ay, Chino. How ironic that I would need to turn to you after all these years."

He sits close to her. "All these years I wanted to talk to you."

"There was no point, Chino. I wouldn't have listened. I was too angry."

When she finally looks him in the eye, she is crying. Her expression holds no anger, desire for revenge, or pity. In her eyes is understanding. She puts a hand on his.

Before they leave, he gets her a new coat from costumes and picks up a pointy pair of shears from a worktable.

* * *

The last war council he went to was at Doc's Drug Store, at midnight.

Chino was quiet because he was always afraid the white boys would make fun of his accent. Then that mamabicho Tony came into the store and tried to get them to stop the rumble. They almost started throwing down right there.

He would do anything for the gang, anything for his family. With the gang, Chino felt like he had a purpose, felt like he belonged.

But they would have thrown him out if they had seen inside his heart.

When he first saw Maria, it was in church. She was just fourteen, dressed in blue and white, looking like la Virgen. By this point Chino had his own suits and was going to the local dances, and in time he saw her there, started hanging around her. He liked looking at her, liked dancing with her, being seen with her. It wasn't exactly love, but he felt like she belonged to him.

Then she fell head over heels for that carifresco. That set Chino off. Even if he didn't love her the way he thought he should, Maria was his, no one else's. And then the come-mierda killed their gang leader, and that gave Chino even more reason to make the guy pay.

And one day in the school yard, he did. He shot him.

The last time Maria ever talked to him, she was screaming over the cold body and telling Chino to shoot her too.

He didn't run. Schrank took him away and started beating on him before they even got to the car. Closing an eye, busting an ear. Three other cops had to pull him away.

At the trial, Chino never said a word in his defense. He knew he had to pay for what he'd done.

In the joint, Paco used to visit him, write him long letters. But Chino was stuck with plenty of time to think, too much, and he came to realize his attachment to Maria had been a front, a way of hiding from himself. He hadn't shot the white boy to save her. He'd done it to save himself and everything he was trying to hold on to, the idea that he belonged, that he was one of them. He wanted to tell her that, wrote her letters. They all came back *Return to Sender*.

Chino knew he could never have God's forgiveness for killing a man, but if he couldn't have Maria's either, he'd lost all hope. And then Paco's letters stopped coming, and he stopped visiting. What was there to live for then?

After that, it seemed like he looked for a fight every day in the joint, wearing his anger like a cape, waiting for a shiv to come kill him. But to his torment, he survived. After two dimes and a nickel of time, Chino got out. He had enough of being a delincuente, had no ambitions to be a hoodlum. He never looked up any of his old friends to see if they were alive.

He took low-paying jobs until he lucked out with this maintenance gig at Lincoln Center, and he's had it for ten years. He has a locker in the basement a few blocks from where he used to sleep out on the fire escape on summer nights. They talk to him a lot about retirement, but why should he? What would he do all day? He lives alone in a tiny apartment in Washington Heights, and when it gets hot, he still likes to sleep out on the fire escape. And when he prays, he still kneels on the two box graters, staring up at the Lord and an old picture of Paco.

* * *

Chino normally avoids the West Side Highway. It was industrial, abandoned when he was coming up, a perfect place for the gang's idiotic rumbles. But now, forty years later, the city is finally starting to clean it up, make it decent.

At ten minutes to midnight, he walks in wide, flat pumps under the highway, near Sixty-Eighth Street. In the distance the Twin Towers shine in the dark. He wears a dark wig, heels, and Maria's purple trench coat. He holds a purse that is not as fancy as Maria's but the same shape. Inside are two bottles of cleaning liquid that weigh about as much as twenty thousand in hundred-dollar bills and jewelry.

Chino follows the instructions Maria got from Mike and waits. He has sworn against violence for years, has avoided anything illegal or immoral since he left the joint. Now he knows he might have to go against all the promises he made to God. He crosses himself and says, "Lord forgive me."

Soon, a tall, athletic-looking guy walks into the underpass.

Chino keeps his face in the shadows. The disguise isn't meant to work for long, only long enough for Chino to get close.

This Mike looks like a pendejo from way back. Why did Maria's daughter fall for him? Maybe everyone in the family has bad taste in men.

"We'll make this quick," Mike says. He holds up a big envelope and waves it.

That's when Chino steps into the light.

"What the hell?"

Chino reaches up, grabs Mike by the collar, shoves him down. He is still strong. His body still remembers the violence. Like an old song you never forget.

Mike tries to get up, but Chino chops him in the throat.

He holds the scissors to Mike's throat until there is blood at the tip. "Leave the pictures. Go home alive."

"Where's the woman?" Mike says. His breath smells of beer and meat.

Abby L. Vandiver

Then a voice behind Chino speaks a single word: "Spic." And a bullet rips through Chino's side.

Off-balance, he gets a boot in the face.

Down on the pavement, he sees that the one holding a gun looks like Mike, but taller, more built. Both faces look familiar.

"Where the fuck is she?" this one says, pointing the gun. It is old, a revolver. A Smith & Wesson 28. A police weapon.

"Our plan is fucked," Mike says. "Who expected him to wear a dress?"

"Shut the fuck up!"

The second one gets close. Too close. Chino still has the scissors in his hand, is still quick enough. He whirls and stabs the scissors deep into this one's ankle. The guy yelps like a dying pig.

Mike jumps back up, and Chino kicks him in the balls, sending him down. The gun? It's not in the other's hand. There is too much darkness on the ground to see.

Chino bends, picks up the envelope. It makes him dizzy, but he is smart enough to start moving away, to get out of there. But he checks, and there are no pictures inside. "Carajo!" He moves back, steps on the ankle of the second one.

"The pictures?"

"You stupid wetback," the shooter says. "There were never any stupid pictures."

Chino bends to pull out the scissor. An arc of blood spurts out as the man screams like a pig again.

Chino holds the scissor against the man's side and searches his pockets, finds a wallet.

The driver's license reads *Simon Schrank*.

"You fucked up our grandfather," says Mike. "They threw him off the force because of you."

This is news to Chino. He didn't think to keep tabs on the officer who nearly made him blind. "You're wrong. What he did to me, that's why they threw him out."

"He killed himself! He blew his brains out!"

"With this gun?" Chino says, seeing it now on the edge of the darkness. "But why Maria?"

"Fuck you!" one of them says.

Chino gets on his knees slowly, picks up the gun. He slowly gets back up. It's not easy. He doesn't know how many times he will be able to do that again. "She testified against him. Something like that, right?"

"Fuck you!" says the other.

"You expected both of us. But how did you know I would come?"

And then he sees: outside the edge of the shadows, the kid who took Maria's purse. Red high-tops. In his hand is the quilted leather bag. He drops it and books. Embalao.

"We'll kill you!" says Mike.

"With bottles, knives, or guns?" Chino says, emptying the bullets onto the ground.

He leaves the grandsons there, cringing on the blacktop. Blocks away, he tosses the gun into a recycling basket.

*   *   *

Maria is waiting for him by Amsterdam and Sixty-Second, where there used to be a soda shop owned by a Puerto Rican. Where he once bought her an ice cream float.

He hands her back the light purse. "It's empty."

77

"Que será, será," she says. "Chino, you're hurt!"

"Like old times. I been hurt worse." But he slumps against a lamppost and then down to the ground. "You remember Paco," he says, "from back in the day?"

"Paco? No, it was so long ago. Wait! Yes! Paco. Of course."

"I never saw him again. I think about him every day."

"Oh, Chino. I'm so sorry."

"I'm sorry, Maria. So sorry. For everything."

She touches his face. "We can't do anything about it. It's in the past. Let it stay in the past, Chino."

She says his name with tenderness now, like it's a beautiful sound.

And then the moon veils itself with clouds, and a soft rain begins. Let us no more revisit these streets of sorrow, that is the end of Maria and her Chino.

NIGHTHAWKS

By Frankie Y. Bailey

Eudora, New York
February 1949

Her head hurt.

She touched her fingers to her forehead. They came away wet.

Blood.

She wiped her fingers on her jacket.

Feeling around her throat, she tugged at the scarf Howard had given her for her birthday. When it came free, she shifted until she could reach her coat pocket and stuffed it inside.

She reached up and felt for the key in the ignition. Turned it and got the engine shut off.

Grasping the dashboard, she pulled herself up until she could see.

Her headlights were still working. Spilling white light over frost-blasted cornstalks and, beyond that, leafless trees.

She found her purse as she was crawling across the seat. She dug inside for a handkerchief to press against the gash on her forehead.

She shoved at the passenger door. It wouldn't open even after she remembered to unlock it. She found the knob and rolled down the window. She twisted and turned and got herself halfway out. Then she remembered the flashlight in the glove compartment.

She mumbled a curse and slid back down to retrieve it.

Then she climbed out onto the passenger door and slid down.

She hit the soggy ground and one foot slipped. She felt a jolt through her ankle.

"What else can happen?" she asked the air.

The car was almost on its side because the back wheels were in the ditch.

If her ribs were only bruised and she had only a mild concussion and her ankle could withstand a walk, she would call it a wash.

She couldn't get her nurse's bag out of the trunk because she couldn't climb around the car to get it out. She'd have to hope it would be safe until she could get the car towed out of the ditch and into the village.

Up on the road, she sent her flashlight beam in both directions.

She saw only empty back road.

She heard an owl. And the wind rattling the tree branches, and bushes rustling.

The deer who had caused all this hadn't even stopped to make sure she was all right.

She waited a few more minutes, looking in both directions for headlights. But she was on a side road, and it was late on a Thursday night. The people who worked the night shift out at the factory took the main highway. Almost everyone else would be at home, asleep in their beds or about to be.

Eudora was not New York City. Except for citizens who had insomnia or work to do, the village turned off its lights and went to bed.

If she had been driving, she would have been home in about fifteen minutes.

It was going to take a lot longer on foot, especially when she'd have to stop to rest along the way.

She sighed. "Well, get walking, Jo, girl. It not going to get any better standing here."

She dug into her other coat pocket for her gloves.

By the time she got there, Dempsey would be giving her the cold shoulder. He was tolerating her these days, but not when she kept him waiting for his supper.

* * *

The rain had turned to sleet by the time she got to the outskirts of the village. When she saw that the lights were still on in the Crossroads Diner, she almost wept with relief. She was cold and hurting in multiple places—and she needed to pee.

She slumped against the nearest of the two cars in the rutted parking lot and took a shallow breath, careful of her ribs.

The diner's window glowed with yellow light. The three customers inside looked like characters on a stage, framed in the plate-glass window as they sat at the counter and at a booth.

"All right, get moving, Josephine. You're almost there."

When she stumbled into the diner, the counterman looked up and froze with a coffee carafe in his hand. The woman and man at the counter and the old man sitting in the booth turned to see what the counterman was staring at.

"Hello," Jo said. "I'm so glad you're still open."

"Hello, pretty girl!"

Jo swung toward the croaking voice. She burst out laughing.

"Hello, pretty girl!" the blue-and-gold macaw said again.

He was in a large cage in an alcove near the door and probably not supposed to be in a diner. But he looked like a charmer. He skipped back and forth on his perch, bobbing his head. "Hello, sweetie!"

The counterman called out, "Charlie! Hey, be quiet, would you please." He turned his attention back to Jo. "Sorry about that, miss. He ain't got no manners."

"That's all right," Jo said. "It's nice to be greeted."

The old man sitting in the booth said, "Do you need help, young woman?"

The blond in the emerald-green dress and velvet jacket said, "Yeah, you don't look too good, honey. You're bleeding."

Jo dug into her coat pocket for her soggy handkerchief and pressed it to her forehead. "A deer ran in front of my car, and I ended up in a ditch."

"So that's what happened to your face," the woman said. "I thought you might have run into some guy's fists. Looks like you're going to have a real shiner by morning."

"Did you hit the deer?" the old man asked.

"No," Jo said.

"Too bad. Venison is a delicacy."

Would he have proposed going out to collect the deer's carcass?

But it was probably a matter of not letting good meat go to waste.

She turned to the counterman. "Could I please use your telephone? And the ladies' room. And maybe get a cup of coffee and a hamburger."

He rubbed at his chin with the back of his hand. "Sure, as long as you don't expect cloth napkins and crystal. We don't get a lot of fancy people in here."

So he wasn't counting the blond and the man in the sharp pinstripe suit sitting beside her at the counter. They must be regulars who liked dressing up.

Answering her unspoken question, the woman said, "Except the ones who are looking for Danny to get into one of his poker games."

The man slanted her a look. "Ever heard about talking too much, Velma?"

"Who? Me?"

"Yeah, you."

Velma shrugged. "You're going to mind your own business, aren't you, honey?"

"Sure," Jo said. "Honey will sit quietly and mind her own business until her friend picks her up."

Velma pouted at the man. "You see, Danny. Honey's a well-brought-up young lady. She knows how to behave." She smiled at Jo, her pout gone. "That hall right behind you. The ladies' is next to the outside door."

"Thanks."

"Hey," Danny said. "You know our names. What's yours?"

"Jo."

"I'm Oscar," the counterman said. "You can make your phone call when you get back. I'll start your burger."

"Thanks. I'm really starving."

"I'm Thaddeus," the old man said. "And, if you'll excuse me, I'll get back to my newspaper."

"Sure. Don't mind me."

As she limped down the hall, she heard Danny, the gambler in the fedora, say something in a low voice. Velma burst into a carol of laughter.

That was okay. As long as they didn't kick her back out in the cold, she could handle knowing they found her amusing.

The restroom was painted mustard yellow, but it was reasonably clean. Jo used the toilet, then washed her hands over the sink with the squeaky faucet. She glanced at the cloth towel on the roll and reached for some toilet paper to dry her hands.

Then she turned and looked directly into the mirror.

She had a shallow gash caked with half-dried blood. And Velma was right—the area around her left eye was bruised. She was going to have a shiner.

If she were twelve again and playing softball, she would have been proud.

She pulled some more toilet paper from the roll and dampened it. She dabbed at the gash and wished for her nurse's bag.

Maybe the counterman had an old towel she could rip up and use to make a bandage. During the war, she and the other nurses in her unit had become experts at making do when the supplies were late arriving.

* * *

When she stepped back out into the hall, she heard Charlie squawking. He sounded excited, but she wasn't sure what he was saying. As she stepped in the dining room, she saw.

"Bang, you're dead! Bang, you're dead!"

"Shut up, Charlie," Oscar said. "Shut your mouth."

The masked man with the gun motioned for Jo to come into the room.

"Sit there," he said. "There in the booth with the old man, where I can see both of you."

Jo sat down. She was facing the counter. The clock said 12:02. The witching hour.

And she hadn't had a chance to make her phone call.

Howard would have appreciated being there to get this scoop firsthand. *Ski-Masked Man With Gun Holds Up Local Diner.*

"Anyone else back there?" the man asked.

"No," Jo said. "It was just me."

He pointed his gun at Oscar. "Give me what you've got in the cash register."

"Okay. I'll put it in a bag for you, pal. Just take it easy."

Jo squinted against the light, which was too bright. Not good. She probably had at least a mild concussion.

The police would ask for a description of the holdup man. Focus on that.

Average built. About her height, five foot eight or maybe five nine.

His face and head were covered by a red ski mask and a dark knit cap. He was wearing a heavy jacket and worn jeans. Gloves on his hands.

He sounded southern.

A Negro?

Abby L. Vandiver

In the two months that she'd been the county public health nurse, her rounds had included the village's working-class neighborhoods. She had met colored migrants who had come up from the South during the war to work in the factory.

"Okay, here it is."

Oscar put the paper bag with the cash from the register on the counter. The holdup man reached out to pick it up. Stretching with his left hand. For just a moment his jacket sleeve was bunched at his wrist.

Jo glanced at the others. Had they seen?

"Now we're going to pass this bag around," the man said. "And the rest of you are going to contribute to the collection plate." He held the bag out to Velma. "The bracelet. Then pass the bag along."

Velma took off her bracelet and dropped it in the bag. She held it out to Danny.

"The ring too."

Velma's hand closed around the ring on her left hand. "It isn't worth anything," she said. "I just wear it because . . . there was this sweet guy who . . . he was shipping out—"

"Put it in the bag."

"Please, it really isn't . . . honest, it's—"

"I said put it in the bag. Now."

"Hey, look," Danny said. "Let the lady keep her ring, okay?"

"You got enough on you to make me forget about the lady's ring?"

"Five or six hundred. Better than a ring you'd have to try to sell." Danny started to reach into his jacket.

"Don't try anything." the holdup man said.

86

"I wouldn't think of it, pal. Just getting my wallet."

"Unbutton your jacket so I can see what you're doing."

Danny opened his jacket and took his wallet out by his fingertips. He opened it and took out the bills inside. He dropped the cash into the bag.

"Pass the collection plate on to Pops."

Danny reached over and passed the bag out to Thaddeus.

Thaddeus said, "I brought only enough cash to pay for my meal. All I have is an old pocket watch."

"Drop it in."

Thaddeus unhooked the watch from the chain and put it into the bag.

"You're last, sis."

"I need to open my purse."

"Go ahead."

Jo dropped in the twenty dollar bill she had left after putting gas in her car. "That's all I have." She held out the bag, and he took it.

"I thank you folks kindly. I'm going to leave you now."

The headlights of a car flashed through the window.

A blue-and-white county sheriff's car stopped slightly to the left of the plate-glass window.

Oh shit, Jo thought.

The holdup man had stepped back into the alcove to the side of the entrance.

Charlie, the parrot, hopped over to peer at him. "Treat," he said. "Give me a treat, robber."

"I'll give you a bullet if you don't shut the hell up."

Oscar said, "Wait! Don't do that. I'll move—"

"Are you crazy, man? I got a cop outside, and you think I got time for you to move your damn bird?"

"Then why don't you just leave," Velma said. "Go out the back door."

Danny pushed back his fedora. "You might not get away, but your odds would be a lot better than they are now. Shoot a cop and you're dead."

Thaddeus said, "He's talking on his radio. If you're going, you'd better go now."

"Why you trying to get me out of here with your money?"

"We don't want to get caught in the cross fire," Danny said.

"Or watch you shoot down a cop," Velma said. "So just go, okay?"

"You." He pointed his gun in Jo's direction. "You go out there. While he's asking you about how your face got like that, I'm going out the back way with her."

"With me?" Velma said.

"As far as my car. I want you between me and that cop's gun in case she doesn't keep his attention." He motioned to Jo. "Get out there."

The deputy was standing outside his car with his radio receiver in his hand. He glanced at Jo, sizing her up as he listened to what the person on the other end was saying.

She pulled her coat collar higher, glad she had remembered to put it on.

The deputy replaced his receiver and straightened.

She was shivering as she spoke. "Hello," she said. "I'm so glad to see you. I had an accident back down the road."

The deputy nodded. He looked young and earnest. "I thought you might be the person I'm looking for. Would that be your car in the ditch back there?"

"Yes, that's mine. A deer ran across the road in front of me."

"They do that around here. I was just on the radio with dispatch trying to find out if anyone had called in about it."

Jo looked back at the door. Should she tell him? "I was about to do that. To call."

"Did you get a ride here?"

"No, I walked. It took me a while."

He took out his notebook. "What's your name, miss?"

She told him.

"Do you need medical attention?"

"No, I'm—" A car came out from behind the diner and turned toward the road. Jo let go of the breath she had been holding.

"You're what? It's late to be out on a night like this. Were you on your way home?"

He was beginning to sound suspicious. But the holdup man was gone.

"I'm the county public health nurse. I was out visiting a family, and the mother went into labor. We couldn't get her to the hospital in time, so I acted as her midwife." She cleared her throat. "Deputy, there's something I should tell you. I was supposed to keep your attention."

The deputy frowned. "Keep my attention?"

"A man was inside with a gun. He held up the diner, and he was about to go when you came. He sent me out here to keep you distracted until he could go out the back door."

"Are you telling me that you—"

Oscar came running out. "He killed her! He killed Velma! The black son of a bitch killed her."

"Oh God," Jo whispered.

But why would he do that? When they were helping him get away without anyone getting hurt, why would he do that?

"No," she said. "He wasn't a Negro. I saw—"

"He was wearing a mask. I know a nigger's voice—"

"His jacket sleeve bunched up," Jo said. "I could see a patch of skin between his sleeve and his glove. He was white."

"I know a nigger's voice—"

The deputy held up his hands. "Stop. Wait—let me—the two of you can both give your descriptions. But first I need to call this in. Show me where she is."

"I'm a nurse," Jo told the deputy. "Maybe she's only unconscious."

"And she's going to stay that way," Oscar said.

* * *

Velma's body was crumpled on the ground by the back entrance. Jo sank down beside her to check for her pulse.

She was on her back. Blood had pooled around her head.

"Was she lying like this when you found her?" the deputy asked.

"I pushed the door open when I heard the car leave," Oscar said. "I didn't know she was lying against . . . but she was already dead. I didn't—"

Jo said, "I think she was shoved back against the door and struck her head."

"You two come with me. We're going back inside through the front door, and I'm going to call this in."

Back in the diner, the deputy told them all to sit down, each in a separate booth, and keep quiet.

If the three men were like her, they didn't want to talk right now.

* * *

Another county sheriff deputy arrived. Then two Eudora police officers.

When the coroner arrived, the deputy told Jo she could go out and speak to him.

She had met the coroner several times. All she could tell him was that she had checked Velma's vitals. He nodded, asked Jo what had happened to her head, and then gave her a bandage from his bag.

She said thank-you as he walked away. Then, instead of going back inside, she lingered by the side of the diner to watch what they were doing. There was a certain grim fascination.

She was still there when Eli Gordon, the chief of police, drove up. The diner was on the outskirts of the village but still in his jurisdiction. And this was a murder, not something that happened that often in Eudora.

"Hello, Jo."

"Hello, Chief Gordon."

He had known Jo's aunt, and he knew Jo.

He said, "I heard you were here."

"Yes, but I'd rather not be."

The chief's presence had caught the attention of the deputy who had just arrived. He turned back to the measurement he was helping one of the Eudora officers take.

"Heard about your accident," the chief said. "You want to go to the hospital and get checked out?"

"No, thank you, I'm okay."

"Then—since you don't have anything to do out here— what say we go inside and talk about this?"

"Okay, we can do that."

Thaddeus and Danny were sitting at the counter with the other sheriff's deputy keeping watch over them. Oscar, the counterman, had poured them all coffee. No one was talking.

Chief Gordon asked Oscar, "Mind if we use your office?"

He gave Jo a sour look. "Sure. Go ahead."

Oscar's office was barely large enough for a desk, two chairs, and storage cabinets. There was a pinup calendar and a peg bulletin board on the wall over the desk, and that was it.

Gordon motioned Jo to the side chair and sat down behind the desk. "So tell me what happened here."

"I'm not sure." She told him about her accident and her arrival at the diner. And about the holdup. Sitting down had reminded her that she was aching all over, from her ankle to her bruised ribs to the headache that was getting worse. She knew she didn't sound convincing when she said she was sure the holdup man had been white.

"A white man who was trying to pass himself off as a Negro," Gordon said. "It's been done before. But I hear the other three witnesses are all sure he was colored."

"Or claim they are," Jo said.

"Do you think they're lying to protect a white man who held them up and killed a friend of theirs?"

"No. Or, at least, I don't know why they would do that."

Gordon leaned back in the desk chair. It creaked under his bulk. "You've had a rough night. You might not have been seeing too clearly. When you heard him talking, did you think he sounded colored?"

"I—yes, maybe. But some white people from the South . . . if he was impersonating—"

"Then he was good if he was able to convince all four of you."

He was right about her rough night. So rough that she thought for a moment of shocking his boots off by asking if she looked and sounded white—*all* white.

Or could he detect even a hint of that colored grandmother she'd discovered in her mother's family tree when she went down South after the war?

Chief Gordon said, "You need to get some rest. I'll have one of my men drive you home."

"If a deer hadn't run in front of my car, Velma might still be alive."

"How do you figure that one?"

"Think about it. The deputy stopped here at the diner because he had been looking for the person whose car he'd found."

"He probably would have swung by here before closing time anyway. This diner is one of the places cops on the night shift stop for their dinner or a cup of coffee and a piece of pie."

"But he might not have stopped when he did if . . ." She tried to catch the thought that had flickered and disappeared.

"You think of something, Jo?"

"Yes. But whatever it was, I've lost it now."

"Well, maybe it'll come back to you after you've had some sleep."

* * *

Dempsey, the Maine Coon Jo had inherited along with her aunt's house, was sitting by the kitchen door. He swished his plumed tail and gave her a cat glare. She hadn't taken the time to give him dinner before she left for the Nielsen farm because she'd expected to be back in a couple of hours. None of them had expected the baby to arrive tonight.

"Sorry," she said. "I'm sorry, okay?"

Jo filled his bowl with fresh water and opened the refrigerator to get the shredded chicken she had cooked for him. He waited until she stepped back before he hunched over his plate and began to eat.

Upstairs, she got into her robe and went into the bathroom to rub herself down with alcohol. She cleaned the cut on her forehead and rebandaged it. Then she went back to her bedroom and put on her warm flannel nightgown.

She was staring at the ceiling, her lamp still on, when Dempsey strolled in. Surprised, she sat up. He jumped onto the foot of her bed and picked his way toward her.

He slept on her aunt's bed at night. He had never been in her room when she was there.

But tonight he strolled up to the head of the bed, stretched, and settled down on the other pillow.

"Thank you, Dempsey," Jo said. "I could use the company."

＊　＊　＊

When she woke up, it was daylight. Dempsey was grooming himself, one leg in the air while he licked. When he saw she was awake, he stopped and waited for what she was going to do.

"It doesn't make sense," Jo told him. "Why would he kill her? If he wanted to get away, why would he commit a murder for no reason?"

Dempsey went back to his licking.

"If he'd gone to the trouble to disguise himself—to pretend to be colored, if that's what he was doing—then why do something that would put every police officer in upstate New York on his trail? Did he think they would be more convinced he was a Negro if he killed a white woman?" Jo asked the cat. "And why would he even have been that concerned if they suspected he was white?"

Dempsey stretched and got up. He gave one of his yowls that amounted to a demand for attention—in this case, breakfast. Then he strolled down the bed and jumped to the floor with a thump.

Jo rolled over and sat up slowly. She could almost hear her body creaking like the Tin Man before he was oiled. "Unless it was an accident. Maybe she thought he intended to take her with him and started to struggle—the ring."

Her ankle was feeling better, but she made herself slow down and hold on to the railing as she went down the stairs.

She called Chief Gordon. His wife said he was on his way to the office. Had left a few minutes ago. But he was on his way to his monthly meeting with the mayor.

Jo stood there for a minute, trying to decide what to do. There was no one else who was likely to tell her if Velma had been wearing her ring. Her left arm had been at her side, half under her. Her right arm had been flung out.

Jo had reached for that arm to check for her pulse.

She went into the kitchen to start her coffeepot. She was at the sink when she looked out the window and saw her car.

She grabbed the jacket she always kept by the door and pulled it on over her bathrobe. Sitting down in a chair, she put on an old pair of loafers.

Her battered car was in the driveway. Chief Gordon must have arranged the tow. The deputy wasn't likely to have done it after the trouble they'd probably gotten him into.

She walked around, checking for damage. A twisted front fender and the passenger door dented in. The headlights had stayed on last night, but now she could see that the glass around one of them was cracked. But it looked like she would be able to drive the car. At least until she had time to get it in for repairs.

She went back inside and got dressed. Then she looked in the telephone book. And found what she was looking for—a telephone number and address for Daniel Reece Innis. That was the name she had heard Danny give the deputy.

Danny, the gambler, lived in the Riverview neighborhood—old mansions and family retainers. A woman who sounded like a maid answered his telephone.

He seemed surprised to hear from her. But when she told him she hoped they might compare notes about last night, he said she was welcome to stop by.

The maid who opened the door of Daniel Reece Innis's Victorian mansion might have been the same woman she had spoken to on the phone. She escorted Jo to the "solarium" and went to let Mr. Innis know she was there.

This was stranger and stranger, Jo thought.

Did Innis like to slum for fun as "Danny," or was that how he made his money? It was hard to believe that in Eudora, even high-stakes poker games would allow a gambler to live like this. Maybe he traveled out of town.

"Good morning, Nurse Radcliffe," he said as he came in.

He was clean-shaven and dressed in a dark suit that was more sedate than his pinstripe of the night before. But he had circles under his eyes, as if he hadn't slept well, if at all.

"Were you and Velma good friends?" Jo asked.

"Yes," he said. "We'd known each other for about a decade."

"I'm sorry. I sure it must be awful to lose her in such a way."

Before he could reply, the maid returned. She was pushing a trolley. "I brought both coffee and tea, sir,"

"Thank you, Edith." He turned to Jo. "Tea or coffee?"

"Coffee, please."

When the maid had served their coffee and left the room, Jo said, "If I'm not being rude—do you live a double life?"

"I have some family money. I own an antique store. I also enjoy poker and other games of luck and skill. I may occasionally engage in activities that reformers would frown on, but neither they nor the police have seen fit to pursue the matter."

"Do you think what happened last night might make things awkward for you?"

"I doubt it." He set his coffee cup on the side table. "Chief Gordon tells me that you disagree with the rest of us about the race of the holdup man. Of Velma's killer."

"His jacket bunched up and his wrist was exposed for a moment."

"There are very fair skinned Negroes."

Jo picked up her napkin and dabbed at her mouth.

"That's true," she said. "But if they are so fair that they can be mistaken for white, they probably don't deliberately try to sound colored."

"You mean they're more likely to try to pass as white?"

"From what I've heard, it's more a matter of not correcting assumptions about their ancestry," Jo said. "Like when you don't correct people who assume you make your living as a gambler."

"I was in good company last night."

"How so?"

"What did you assume about Thaddeus?"

"Thaddeus? Nothing really. He seemed a rather nice elderly man."

"Who owns the building in which the Crossroads Diner is located and a number of other more valuable properties in Eudora and elsewhere in the state."

"That's interesting. What about Velma?"

"She was once married. Her husband wasn't particularly faithful, so she got a divorce and alimony sufficient to live on."

"To live well?"

"Well, enough to enjoy herself."

"That ring she was wearing—was it valuable?"

"Very. An emerald ring that she kept as part of her divorce settlement."

"Kept?"

"It belonged to her husband's late mother. He gave it to Velma."

"Was her husband all right with that?"

Danny raised an eyebrow. "If you're thinking that was Jack Lawrence wearing a mask—he's six three and at least two hundred pounds. And he was on his way to DC when Velma spoke to him yesterday morning."

"Of course, if he really wanted the ring back, he could have hired someone—"

"They got a divorce when the war ended. I don't think he'd change his mind four years later. And if he did, he's not the type to hire a thug—colored or white."

Jo nodded. "So whoever the holdup man was, he probably wasn't connected to her husband."

"Was the ring gone?"

"I don't know. I just wondered if the holdup man tried again to get the ring."

"And she was killed trying to hold on to it?"

"Yes. What about Oscar, the counterman—is he what he seems?"

"The only thing unusual about Oscar is his interest in parrots. Charlie has an extensive vocabulary." He glanced at his wristwatch. "I'm afraid I am going to have to cut this short. I had a call from a client who's interested in an item I have."

Jo nodded and put down her cup. "Then I'll get out of your way. Just one more question—did Velma have family? I'd like to send flowers for her funeral service."

"No close relatives, as far as I know. But believe it or not, she and her ex-husband became good friends after their divorce. I'm sure he'll take charge of the service." He paused. "After the autopsy. When her body is released."

"I'll check for her obituary."

"I'll give you a call when the arrangements are made." He picked up a pen and pad from the side table. "What's your telephone number?"

Jo told him.

"I'll be in touch."

Jo gathered up her purse. He escorted her to his foyer and helped her on with the coat that Edith the maid took from the closet.

"Edith, may I have my overcoat too? I'm leaving now, and I'll walk out with Miss Radcliffe."

Innis put on the gray tweed coat that his maid brought him.

Outside, he helped Jo into her car. They said their good-byes.

As she drove away, Jo saw a man in a white shirt and gray uniform pants get out of the sports car he had brought up to the front steps. He held the door for his employer as Danny got behind the steering wheel.

It was as if she had wandered into a play in which no one—including her—was quite what he or she seemed.

* * *

Chief Gordon was in his office when she got to the station. He waved her to the chair across from his desk.

"Did you remember something else?" he asked.

"Not exactly. But I did think about Velma's ring. The holdup man wanted it. She told him it wasn't worth very much. That it was a memento from a soldier she had known who had gone off to war. Then Danny reminded him that he would have to sell it, and he offered him all the cash he had."

"He told me about the cash, but he didn't mention the ring."

"Was she still wearing it?"

The chief reached for a sheet of paper on his desk.

"Emerald ring on left hand," he said.

"But they might have struggled. He might have panicked after she fell and run away without taking the ring."

"From what you said, he wasn't panicking a whole lot. Even when the deputy drove up." The chief tapped his pen on his blotter. "And it doesn't matter why he killed her. What matters is finding him and making an arrest."

"Yes, but there's a different between an accident and a deliberate murder."

"Felony homicide," the chief said. "When someone is killed in the course of committing another felony, it doesn't matter whether it was deliberate."

And why was she arguing for this man? Jo wondered. She was sure he had been white. He could fend for himself.

"But there's something," she said. "Something that still seems wrong. These people."

"What about them?"

"While I was waiting for you to get into your office, I went to see Danny—Daniel Reece Ellis, who has old money and an antique shop and likes to wear pinstriped suits and gamble. And Velma, who was married to a man wealthy enough to give her alimony and his mother's emerald ring as part of a divorce settlement."

The chief nodded. "I have the report on them. Ellis gambles and occasionally runs poker games. But no one has complained. Velma liked having fun. But she wasn't a pros—" He cleared his throat. "I mean . . ."

"I know what you mean. Since the war, a lot of people have been looking for ways to entertain themselves. Do you know about Thaddeus? That he owns the building the diner is in?"

"He told me about that."

Jo sit back in her chair. "I don't know where I'm going with this."

"Neither do I."

"Okay. I'm going home now."

"That's a good idea. Go home and get some rest."

"Dempsey slept on my bed last night."

"So he's warming up to you, is he? I told you he would."

"Maybe Aunt Meg—"

That was it. That was it.

"Charlie, the parrot," she said. "When the holdup man stepped back into the alcove to be out of sight of the deputy, he was standing beside Charlie's cage."

"What about it?"

"Charlie said, 'Treat. Give me a treat, robber.'"

"A smart bird. But—"

"I heard 'robber' because he had said, 'Bang, you're dead.' But what if he was saying a name, not 'robber' but 'Robert'? The holdup man told him to shut up—"

"How would the bird be able to recognize someone who was wearing a mask?"

"I don't know. Something about his voice? The way he smelled or something he was wearing? That was the only time the holdup man seemed rattled. He told Charlie to shut up, and then he looked at Oscar. And that was when Oscar told him to wait a minute, he'd move Charlie. And the holdup man asked if he thought he had time for that with a cop outside."

"Are you saying you think Oscar knew who the man was?"

"I'm just saying you might see if there is someone named Robert. If the others know someone named Robert. Last night, you said the officers on the night shift sometimes stop at the diner for a meal or coffee. But wouldn't they do that at about the same time every night? Wouldn't they be predictable? So the holdup man, if he knew that routine—but last night I threw it off. The deputy came looking for whoever had been in an accident—"

"We thought about that. The deputy said he would normally have swung by a couple of hours later." The chief tapped his pen on his pad. "But with this 'Robert' thing . . ." He dropped his pen and reached for his intercom. "Maggie, put me through to Calhoun or Patterson. I want them to check something on the Crossroads Diner case."

* * *

102

Jo was at home when the chief called. She had been pacing back and forth to keep herself from stiffening up and because she couldn't sit still.

"Oscar has a brother named Robert," he told her. "We picked the two of them up for questioning."

"Have they said anything?"

"Both of them were feeling the weight of a dead woman on their conscience. The idea was that Robert was going to hold up the place and help his big brother get some cash. Thaddeus had told him he was selling the property. The man who wanted to buy it had his own plans for the building. Oscar begged Thaddeus to let him buy the property. He told him that he had been putting aside some money and that he could give him a down payment and then he'd get a mortgage from the bank. Thaddeus wanted two thousand dollars' down payment because the other buyer was ready to write a check for the full amount."

"And Oscar didn't have the money."

"He had about five hundred. His brother suggested a holdup. He said they might be able to scrape up the rest. Especially if Danny was there to contribute cash to the pot."

"Velma—did they struggle over the ring?"

"No, but Velma's ears might have been as good as yours. Or maybe when she got closer to him, something looked familiar. They got to the door and were on their way out. And she grabbed his arm and said, 'Robert?' "

"And they struggled?"

"He says he pulled his arm away and she fell. Hit her head. And he ran. He said he didn't know she was dead."

"But it doesn't matter, does it?"

"No, the boy's in a heap of trouble. So is Oscar."

"Thank you for calling me."

"Thank you for your help, Jo. I should have paid more attention when you told me the holdup man was white. And the parrot thing . . . you did good."

He said good-bye.

She was still sitting there in the hall beside the phone when Dempsey strolled in. He sat down beside her feet and stared up at her. She stared back.

He sprang up into her lap. Jo pressed her face into his neck. "Oh, Dempsey, I'm really glad you're not a parrot. I could use someone to talk to. Cats never tell."

THE SEARCH FOR ERIC GARCIA

By E. A. Aymar

You're sitting at the bar, thinking about choices.

It's midnight, both clock hands raised like cops have guns on it. And even though you want it to, even though the beers you've been downing since eight taste like angels' kisses, you know your night's not ending here. Your night's not ending at some silent bar in a run-down section of Alexandria, Virginia.

Your night's ending the way you planned.

In bullets.

And blood.

Do you choose to:

A. *Order another beer?*
B. *Stagger out of the bar, walk five blocks, and put a bullet in Eric Garcia, the man your wife left you for?*

Option A

You thought Eric would be here, but he's not. Never showed up.

"I think you've had enough," the bartender tells you.

"How 'bout just a shot?"

The bartender stares at you. "Buddy, you need someone to come get you?"

You feel something hardening in your throat, pathetic love rising in your soul because of this bartender's concern, the way a homeless man must feel when someone slips him a twenty-dollar bill.

But you swallow the lump away, slide off the stool, head out the door. Head out into a hot, humid night . . .

Option B

You thought Eric would be here, but he's not. Never showed up.

You slide off the stool, stagger to the door. Push it open and step out into a hot, humid night.

* * *

It's the kind of humid Virginia night when the air feels like you're being humped to death by a sweaty orangutan. You hear someone shouting behind you, not sure if it's some other drunk or the bartender telling you that you forgot to pay. But you keep walking. After all, you didn't forget. You just have no idea where your wallet is.

Emilia told you this would happen.

You're halfway to the apartment, walking up Route 1, the beaten boulevard in Alexandria bordered by shitty strip malls and despair. And you see the store, the discount mattress store where you used to work. You hurry behind it, unzipping your pants on the way. Think about painting your name on the store's back wall with piss. The thought makes you smile.

Emilia told you she needed someone else. Someone like him. Someone stronger than you. The opposite of you.

"Mejor que tu."

Better than you.

She said that, actually said all those harsh, unforgettable words. Words screamed in that mix of English and Spanish she used when she got excited, when the two of you argued or fought or fucked, words like a nail driven into your skin until . . .

Wait.

You finished peeing a while ago. How long have you been standing behind Eric's store, head against the bricks, penis in hand? And when did your pants fall down to your ankles?

And who's laughing behind you?

You turn and see two kids, each standing with a foot on a skateboard, filming you with their phones. The phones drowning your eyes in light.

Do you choose to:

A. *Pull up your pants and shuffle off?*
B. *Chase the kids, grab their phones, and destroy them?*

Option A

You yank your pants up to your thighs, turn, promptly slip in a puddle of piss, and fall.

Option B

"What you want?" you ask the kids, turning, one hand tugging your pants up, the other pressed against the wall for balance.

"What you want?" One of the kids mimics your broken language.

Allusion doesn't work.

"Hey, shut up," you say, and you've had enough.

You yank your pants up to your thighs, turn, promptly slip in a puddle of piss, and fall.

* * *

The kids laugh and film as you flail about.

"Isn't that the dude who used to work here?" one of them asks.

You shake your head, not wanting to admit that the man your wife left you for used to be your boss. Until he fired you.

The kids hop on their skateboards and ride away.

You pull yourself to your feet, buckle your pants.

Spit on Eric's store.

Keep walking.

You wonder if Emilia still has the gun. The tiny .22 you bought to keep her safe when the two of you moved into these apartments a few months ago. She hates guns; the only time she ever touched it was when you took her to that shooting range.

It felt good for you to shoot at something.

Like, for the first time in a long time, you could cast blame somewhere else.

You made her fire at the target, Emilia squinting and wincing as she pulled the trigger. She didn't end up anywhere near the silhouette of a man holding a gun. The whole thing turned into laughter, you two making jokes about what would happen if someone actually broke into your place.

You remember the way the very serious white men at the range watched you.

And it felt like you and Emilia hadn't laughed in years.

You remember that whole day, and sadness fills you. Every type of sadness, you've learned, is some form of longing.

Do you choose to:

A. *Keep trudging along?*
B. *Contemplate the inescapability of sorrow, and whether the human experience is trapped by it?*

Option A

You keep trudging along.

Option B

Yeah, that's not going to happen. You keep trudging along.

* * *

You don't know how long you've walked, but you're sweating. And you're standing in front of the Oasis, the misnamed apartment building you and Emilia moved into months after your daughter died.

After your wife was let go from her job for missing too much work.

After you were fired from the mattress store.

After you found that the only way to move forward was with a blurred image of your daughter Isabella, like an old painting faded beyond recognition.

How long has it been since Isabella died?

A year?

A week?

Was it yesterday?

You're too drunk to remember.

You push open the lobby door, the security keypad broken ever since you moved in, and walk up the stairs because the elevator doesn't work either. The building is trash, but at least your savings can afford it. And it's away from the people who know you, the people who will never recover from what you've lost.

Losing Isabella was something you never thought could happen, even though you worried about it. Worried about it until the worry became habit. But it happened while you were driving through an intersection, three-year-old Isabella babbling in the back while you were texting your cousin about some chick he met at some bar. And then, an instant later, the entire passenger side of your Accord was a crumpled ball of paper.

No one could have told you what you would see when you looked into the back seat, the phone still in your hand.

Everything changed in that second.

You wanted to go to jail for negligence, begged for it, but the driver in the other car was screaming past a red light. He's the one who ended up with the threat of a long jail term, a prominent University of Virginia white boy home for the summer. Everyone made it seem like he was receiving an unfair lifelong punishment for one mistake. He had the grades, the potential, the grief-struck repentant parents who just wanted the best for their son. Had too much to lose.

Most of the articles and news shows, they didn't even mention Isabella's name.

UVA will be okay.

Not like you and Emilia, twenty years of working hard in Virginia vanished. You starting your own business, Emilia working in IT, fields where people don't see a lot of Hispanics (no one gives a shit you're from Panama and she's from Guatemala—you're just "Hispanics"). Moving from an apartment building in Alexandria to a townhouse in Centreville to a home with a yard in Burke. Making enough money to send some back home. Seemingly endless gifts for Isabella under the Christmas tree. White neighbors who'd started inviting you over once they heard how fluently you and Isabella could speak English, once they knew there wouldn't be any problems.

That's the thing that surprised both you and Emilia. The sense in America that life exists without problem. That it needs to. That any disruption to life is catastrophic.

Instead of just being life.

"El sueño Americano," Emilia used to say about it.

You were starting to believe that dream. And then your dream was gone in an instant. Like you were taken from your lives and cast back down.

Everything lost.

You climb fourteen long flights of stairs up the Oasis. Stop once to throw up, your stomach like a snake's body's tightening around it.

On the fourteenth floor you walk down the hall, try the door at the first apartment, realize yours is the fifth. The apartment you shared with Emilia.

The apartment she now shares with Eric.

Do you choose to:

A. *Turn around and go back to the bar?*
B. *Fish your key out of your pocket and unlock the door?*

Option A

You stop at the stairs, at the open door leading back down. Think about choices.

You turn around. Go back to your apartment.

Your key roughly slides into the lock. You push open the door with your shoulder, sprawl inside.

Option B

Your key roughly slides into the lock. You push open the door with your shoulder, sprawl inside.

*   *   *

"Alo?"

No one answers you. But you know Eric's here. He has to be. He needs to be.

This night is ending one way.

No one can deny you that.

Everything else was taken from you, except for this choice.

The apartment has an abrupt disheveled sense to it, like someone left in a hurry. Cushions out of place on the couch, clothes on the carpet, microwave door hanging open.

The mess reminds you of Isabella. You remember that she used to do that thing with her toy bin when she was searching for a toy. Just pick one up and toss it over her shoulder. Such disregard, completely unintentional, and it made you and Emilia laugh. Little Isabella would look back at both of you, confused, and then she'd start laughing too.

Nothing in the world like a baby laugh.

That pure expression—otherwise, it was hard for Isabella to tell you what she wanted. You could see the frustration when Isabella sought words. Emilia taught Isabella baby sign language, so Isabella could bump her little fists together and say "más más" when she wanted more, more to eat or more time to play or more of you tickling her belly with your beard so she could scream in laughter.

Isabella was going to be good. Everyone knew it. So did she. Strangers smiled when they saw her. She knew how to manipulate you and Emilia from birth, and the two of you loved it. The road ahead of her was paved in gold, like she was destined for a crown.

El sueño Americano.

You stagger through the apartment, and Emilia's not here. But you do find Eric.

He's in the bedroom, in front of the closet door with the full mirror, standing in that perfect way he does. The way where he's not you. Eyes not helplessly sad, no belly from too many beers. Brushed hair. Pants held up by a belt. Clean, flossed teeth. He's the works, this guy, the total package. Kind of guy people want to cheer for. As perfect and blameless as an American president.

"I'm just here for a little bit," you say.

Like Isabella, you think. *Only here for a little bit.*

Everything's like Isabella.

Eric sniffs but doesn't stop you as you walk to the closet and pull out the safe. You look down at your wrist where Isabella's birthday is tattooed, slide the numbers in the safe's circular lock to match the date.

You feel Eric watching you.

He must not know about the gun.

The safe pops open. You spin around, the little .22 cold in your hard hand, and stare at him with hate. Sadness. Envy.

You can see why she loves him. Eric has what you used to, that sense of confidence, shoulders back, chin up. The kind of Hispanic that makes people say things like "He's got that hot Latin blood" or "I love his complexion."

Not the kind of Hispanic you are. The poverty kind. The invisible kind.

Eric's not what you became.

The only thing you do have in common is that he's not putting up a fight. He seems resigned to you.

Like he's a sinner and you're a flood.

"She left me," Eric tells you. "And I can't get her back."

"Yeah," you agree. "She gone."

"I miss holding her," he says.

Do you choose to:

A. *Shoot him?*
B. *Shoot him?*

There's a moment of regret when you start to squeeze that trigger, a moment where you wish you could throw the gun away. Run to the cemetery. Pull Isabella's little body out of the ground and hold her to you.

But the bullet enters your mouth like an angel's kiss.

You'll be with Isabella soon.

And really, Eric, what choice did you have?

THE VERMEER CONSPIRACY

By V. M. Burns

The helicopter touched down onto the back of a yacht that, from the air, looked about the size of a bathtub. Up close and personal, it was massive, as far as watercraft go, but I squeezed my eyes shut and prayed that my breakfast would remain inside my body rather than threatening to join the great outdoors as it had been for the last couple of hours.

The pilot landed in the middle of a circular target. I pried my hand from its grip on the dashboard. From the headset, I heard the pilot's garbled voice mention something, but the blood was rushing in my ears and I had no idea what he said. I removed my headset and gave a thumbs-up, which I hoped said *thank you*. Before the blades stopped moving, someone opened my door and helped me out.

It took a moment for my legs to convert from jelly back to their solid form, but the prospect of getting away from the blades of death motivated me. I moved as quickly as my legs would carry me while bent over toward the ground.

My escort ushered me inside the yacht's cabin, where I finally felt safe to stand upright. I straightened my back and hoped my young guide hadn't heard the creaking as I stood.

Whether he heard or not, he didn't let on. He led me through a large living room with stunning views into an office that was larger than my apartment. One wall was lined with floor-to-ceiling mahogany bookshelves. The bookshelves curved around a half wall and framed a massive screen. There was a glass conference table with seats for ten in front of the screen. A sofa covered in butter-like leather and a comfortable chair created a spacious lounge and conversation area. In the center of the room was a circular mahogany desk, which, if the number of monitors, electronic devices, and gadgets was any indication, was where NASA would be launching the next space shuttle. A wall of windows looked out onto the ocean. There was a bar in one corner and every convenience known to man, making the room both functional and inviting.

"Please make yourself comfortable. Mr. Merriweather will be with you shortly." My guide smiled before he turned and left.

Alone, I looked around the grand space. If it weren't for the view out the window, I could have been in any grand office atop a skyscraper as opposed to on a luxury yacht floating in the middle of the ocean. I couldn't believe I was here. Years of hard work were finally about to pay off.

My palms were sweaty, and my heart raced. I strolled around the lushly carpeted room. It was inevitable that my mind would drift back in time to the moment that forever changed my life.

I remembered I had glanced at my watch a few minutes before midnight. I had just turned twenty-one and was still wet behind the ears. *God, it's hard to believe I was ever that young and innocent.*

I chuckled at the memory of my twenty-one-year-old self. Thin, idealistic, and oh so naïve. I was going to be a great painter—an artist. My art would change the world, and just like the painters I admired—Rembrandt, Van Gogh, Vermeer—my art, my name, would live on hundreds of years after I was dead.

I was brought back to the present when Mr. Merriweather rushed into the room. He was a tightly wound ball of energy. He extended his hand. "I hope you had a pleasant flight."

August Merriweather was what my grandmother called *one of the beautiful people*—tall and slim with thick white hair, piercing dark eyes, a square jaw, and blindingly white teeth. He was tanned, and his tough skin looked like leather.

I swallowed several times to generate enough saliva to talk. "Thank you," I squeaked.

He moved behind the desk and sat in the pilot's chair, leaned back, and looked me over. After several moments, he squinted. "Jasper Bland . . . Bland?" He flipped open a folder on his desk. "I've read up on you. Impressive. But why does your face look so familiar?"

He gave me a hard stare for several moments. Eventually, he shook his head; his memory had failed.

I released a breath. It wasn't time. Not yet. Soon, he'd know me. I'd have the pleasure of telling him who I was and what he'd done to ruin my life, but not yet. I'd planned my big reveal for decades. I'd planned each moment of my triumph.

My mind drifted back. As a starving artist, I'd thought I'd hit the lottery when I acquired a job as a security guard at an art museum. I'd laughed at my friends, who were excited to land jobs working in the university dining halls or grading papers for professors, while each and every night I got to spend hours studying the works of the masters, up close and personal. And I did. I stared at the paintings in the Isabella Stewart Gardner Museum, noting each brushstroke, the way the light and shadows fell on each masterpiece. I knew each crack on the face of the dapper, moustached young man in Édouard Manet's *Chez Tortoni*. I knew every lump, bump, and aged dot in Rembrandt's *A Lady and Gentleman in Black*. For the six months that I worked there, I learned more about art than I had in four years at university.

"Mr. Bland?"

"Sorry, I was . . . daydreaming."

His smirk indicated what he thought of people who dreamed. August Merriweather wasn't a dreamer. He was a man of action, a shark. Eat or be eaten. That was his world.

"Are you an artist?" He flipped through the papers in the folder. "I believe you painted . . . once." Recognition flashed in his eyes, and he snapped his fingers. "You're that artist."

That artist. Just another artist whose career he'd ruined. Barely a day had passed during the last thirty-five years that I hadn't thought about how much I hated him. My hatred ran so deep it had seeped into every area of my life. I'd lost jobs. Relationships had failed. If I'd been able to trace its path like a bloodhound, I was sure, the seeds of my hatred for August Merriweather would be found as the basis for the tumor growing inside my skull. Inoperable, the doctors said. I carried that hate-filled August Merriweather tumor with me at all times. I was rotting from the inside out, and he didn't even remember my name.

"I used to paint a long time ago."

"No hard feelings, I hope." He chuckled. "I call them as I see them. I critiqued your work." He leaned back and tilted his head as he remembered. "I believe I made some reference to your name."

Bland is a perfect moniker. It describes not only the artist but the quality of the artwork—bland. He's wasted years of his life studying the masters, and with the skill of a parrot, he mimics the greats but is unable to create anything original himself. "I don't remember. A lot of time has passed," I lied. I doubted his research would have revealed that I had a photographic memory that prevented me from forgetting anything I saw. Few people knew that. It wouldn't be in his folder.

He narrowed his eyes and stared. "There's something else about you . . ." He squinted with the effort of remembering. This time his memory failed again—no sign of recognition.

I held my breath. When he shook his head, unable to recall, I released it.

He walked to the bar, picked up a decanter, and poured himself a drink and tossed it back. Refilled the glass and sipped.

No thank you. I don't want a drink. I've got to keep my head clear.

Merriweather sat on his sofa, crossed his leg over his lap, and continued to sip his drink.

"You gave up painting, and now you're an . . . art detective? How did you manage that? Don't tell me there's a class at Yale that teaches how to be an art detective."

He's done his research. That wasn't in the folder with the carefully arranged history. "I majored in art history at Yale and then transferred to the Beaux-Arts de Paris." *After you destroyed my dreams of creating art.* "Later, I got a master's in art conservation from the Academy of Fine Arts in Vienna.

I've always loved puzzles and mystery novels. I suppose that's why I enjoyed conservation."

He tilted his head. "I don't understand."

"Conservation requires figuring out what the artist had in mind by examining the brushstrokes and the context of the work. You have to put yourself into their head to make sure your restoration is as close to the original vision as possible— you have to become the artist to solve the puzzle. This isn't a case of whodunit, but howdunit. How did the artist want this to look? What story did he or she want to tell?"

He stared at me as though I'd lost my mind. He didn't get it, but that was okay. I was used to that.

"Anyway, spending hours upon hours staring at one inch of a painting with a magnifying glass, you become intimately acquainted with it. You notice the details no one else did."

"Like what?"

"Did you know that Pierre Auguste Renoir had rheumatoid arthritis for the last twenty years of his life? He had trouble gripping a paintbrush. Some even say he had to have it taped to his hand, but I don't believe that. But when you look carefully at his later works, you notice that his brushstrokes weren't as steady. In fact, there are places where you can see the waviness."

"I can't say I ever noticed any unsteadiness in Renoir's works." He smirked.

"As I said, I do spend hours staring at paintings inch by inch." I shrugged. "The same skill that allows me to restore ancient art helps me find missing artwork. I study the crime scene and look for clues that will help me find the thief."

He stared at me for several moments. Eventually, he tossed back the rest of his drink and stood. "Jasper, your reputation is impeccable. I'm going to trust you." He stood and moved to a door at the side of the room that I had barely noticed before. The door had an optical fingerprint scanner as well as a retina scanner. He placed his finger and right eye in place to be scanned. After a few seconds, there were three beeps and a soft click. He twisted the doorknob, opened it, and walked through. When he noticed that I hadn't followed, he came back. "Well, come on."

I hurried to catch up.

The room was dark. At first I thought we were in a closet. However, after a few seconds, my eyes adapted to the darkness, and a few ambient lights came on. That's when I realized he'd taken me into the inner sanctum—his private art gallery. LED light fixtures mounted in the ceiling provided spotlighting for a few key paintings that lined the walls, along with some sculptures. Discreet picture lights as well as floor lights highlighted each object.

Merriweather's eyes never left me as I examined each piece of art. The room was filled with paintings by the masters. Renoir's *Madeleine Leaning on Her Elbow With Flowers in her Hair* started the collection. It was followed by Rembrandt's *The Storm on the Sea of Galilee, View of Auvers-sur-Oise* by Cézanne, and Van Gogh's *Poppy Flowers*, each painting more breathtakingly beautiful than the one before. However, for me, the pièce de résistance was a painting by Vermeer, *The Concert*.

I always carried a magnifying glass with me, and I pulled it out. I examined every square inch of the painting. Time stood still, and I might have been there for hours.

"Well?" Merriweather smiled.

"It's real." I tore my eyes away from the masterpiece. "It looks . . . it can't be . . . but it looks to be real." I ran my fingers through my short Afro. "Dear God, can this be true?"

Merriweather laughed. "It's the real thing, all right. It had better be real. God knows it cost me a small fortune."

"I don't understand. This painting has been missing for . . . decades. All these paintings were reported missing. But the Vermeer—it was reportedly stolen from the Isabella Stewart Gardner Museum in 1990."

Merriweather smirked. "There's no reportedly about it. It was stolen."

I knew it was the real thing. I stared at this painting night after night for months. "You stole it?"

He shook his head. "I did not steal it. Let's just say I know someone who knows someone who can make things happen, if you have enough money, and I do. It took him a while to track down the Mafia boss that had it, but my friend can be very persuasive."

My mind raced back. Midnight. I'd done my rounds. I walked through the museum as usual. My partner stayed behind the front desk. When I returned, we'd switch; he'd walk through the building while I sat behind the desk. But Ralph Scallini wasn't feeling well that night. He didn't mind sitting behind the desk all night. I didn't mind walking around and gazing at the paintings. We made a great team.

Someone banged on the side door of the museum. "Hey, Jasper. It's me. Open up."

I opened the door.

One of the other guards, Donald Terpino, slipped inside. He smelled of whiskey. "Happy Saint Patrick's Day. I forgot my keys. You mind swinging by my desk and grabbing them for me?" He took a swig from his flask. "I'll get sacked if the boss finds out I was here."

I sighed. Terpino always forgot his keys. He'd forget his head if it weren't attached. "Sure, I'll get them."

It wasn't until years later that I realized Terpino had to have been in on the heist too. That was the start of the heist—midnight. Not 1:20 like the FBI thought.

Not long after Ralph left, the security system started acting up. Alarms were going off in rooms, but when I checked, no fire. Eventually, we turned it off, just like when there are dead batteries in a smoke detector.

I did rounds, and that's when the commotion started.

From the security cameras, I saw two men dressed as Boston Police. They pounded on the door and demanded entry. They said they'd had a report of a disturbance.

The events of that night were etched on my brain. Getting tied up and left in the basement for hours while they stole thirteen of the most valuable paintings in the museum. Now, thirty-five years later, here I was, staring at those same paintings.

I stared at August Merriweather. "I don't understand. Why bring me here? Why show this to me?" I spread my hands to indicate the entire collection.

"These are part of my private collection. I keep them here on my yacht in a climate-controlled room to keep them safe and to—"

"To keep them in international waters so the local authorities can't arrest you?"

His eyes flashed, but it vanished quickly. "I wouldn't put it quite that bluntly. I did not steal any of these items. In fact, *if* I were questioned, I would be able to provide an irrefutable alibi to prove I couldn't possibly have been responsible." He flicked a piece of imaginary dust from his cashmere sweater. "Besides, even if I had, it's been more than thirty years, and the statute of limitations has expired. So, even if I had been guilty of a crime, I couldn't be prosecuted."

"True, but you are in possession of stolen property. Which would be taken and returned to the rightful owner."

He frowned. "I pity the fool who would attempt to board this vessel. I assure you that my crew is fully capable of taking down any uninvited visitors."

"Again, why bring me here?"

"Unfortunately, prior to receiving the items, the plebeians who had them didn't exercise the best care. I'm sure you noticed a few areas of damage."

Yes. I'd noticed.

"Your credentials are outstanding."

I made sure of that, but there can always be a slip.

"You've got a reputation for discretion, and the work you did on Leonardo da Vinci's—"

I held up my hands to stop him. "I wasn't—"

He waved away my objections. "I know you can't talk about it, but I found out. Whenever work needs to be done on the great works of art, they call you. The Met, the Louvre, and even the Vatican."

"I can't discuss any of that."

"You studied the masters of the Dutch Golden Age. No one knows Vermeer better than you. No one else could bring it back to its original glory but you. You're the best, and that's what I want. It's what I'm willing to pay for. Your skill and discretion."

The idea of working for August Merriweather, the man I'd sworn my undying hatred for, was butting up against my desire to touch, to restore, work by one of the greatest Dutch artists of all time.

"Vermeer used unique, sometimes expensive materials. Ultramarine from lapis lazuli, madder lake, azurite, vermillion—"

He waved away my objections. "Money isn't a concern. I want to own the greatest paintings in the world." He smirked. "I went to Mauritshuis in the Hague to see the *Girl With a Pearl Earring.*" He snorted. "It's tiny, barely bigger than a sheet of paper. *The Concert* is twice the size."

Obviously, Merriweather was of the mind-set that bigger was better. At five feet eight, I'd found one more reason to dislike him.

"What's the catch?"

He smiled and fidgeted with a ring on his pinkie. "What makes you think there's a catch?"

"I get a telegram saying you need to see me immediately. You have a limo waiting at my apartment. You fly me in your private helicopter to a yacht where you show me priceless works of art and tell me money is no object." I narrowed my eyes. "What's the catch?"

"You're a very suspicious man." He chuckled. When I didn't join in on the laughter, he continued, "The only catch, other than the obvious requirement of silence, is timing. I'm going to be spending the winter in Greece, and I need the painting back in one month."

"A month? Are you mad? There's no way. I need time. I need time to get the materials. I have tests that need to be run. I can't possibly complete a restoration in a month."

He shrugged. "That's the deal. Take it or leave it." He stared at me, confident in his position. Confident that he could dangle the opportunity to work on the painting of one of my heroes in front of me and I wouldn't have the courage to walk away.

Part of my brain seethed. The truth was, he was right. Vermeer was the main reason I'd wanted to paint. He was the sole reason I'd chosen to study in Vienna under the foremost authority on Golden Age Dutch painters in the world. No, I couldn't walk away from this opportunity, and Merriweather knew it.

* * *

Back in New York, I spent hours, days, in my studio. From morning until night, I labored. I worked until my head hurt from the strain. I grabbed a catnap to replenish my energy. My obsession pushed me on. My obsession with Vermeer had caused me to search the globe for the minerals he'd used to create vibrant blues, reds, and yellows that leaped from the canvas. I'd gone as far as bringing water from Vermeer's homeland of Delft, which I kept in my studio, since water from different regions had different mineral compositions. I felt confident no one would ever test the painting to that level, but I couldn't take the chance.

One month flew by at light speed. When the time came, I was ready. Well, as ready as I could be. Painting in hand and doped up on Dramamine, I boarded the helicopter.

August Merriweather was hosting a farewell party, so this time, unlike my last visit, the cabin was filled with people. The crew member who'd greeted me before was dressed in a formal white ship's uniform rather than the shorts and polo he'd worn previously.

I still kept myself bent over until I was well clear of the copter's Ginsu blades as I got myself and my cargo inside.

A waiter handed me a glass of champagne, which I tossed back to help steady my nerves. My heart raced. It was show time, and I was high on adrenaline and the idea that my revenge was near. I looked around for my host and spotted Merriweather talking to two people I immediately recognized. The man was Vincent Hornbeck, a renowned expert on Dutch paintings who had recently denounced a painting widely believed to have been by another famous Dutch artist, Carel Fabritius, as a fake. The Met had paid ten million dollars for the work to a private collector and was now engaged in a legal battle to recover their money. The woman with Merriweather was another highly acclaimed expert on Dutch art, Margaret Johnson-Bland, my ex-wife. I stopped another waiter and grabbed another glass of champagne. I might need a bottle before this evening was over.

She spotted me, and our eyes locked. Maggie was the curator for the National Museum and the only person on the planet who knew as much as I did about the Dutch masters. She was an excellent poker player. I doubted if anyone who hadn't lived with her for ten years recognized the subtle signs of shock. The vein pulsing on the side of her head. The way she licked her lips more frequently than usual or the way she tugged on her left ear. She plastered a big smile on her face and sauntered over. "Jasper, what a surprise. I didn't expect to see you here," she said, for the benefit of anyone listening in.

When her lips were to my ear, she whispered, "What's going on?"

"I'm working. Just a little unfinished business with August Merriweather." I forced a smile that I knew didn't make it to my eyes.

"Bland, I was afraid you wouldn't make it." Merriweather glanced at his watch. "You're cutting it pretty close. It's thirty minutes until midnight."

Fitting. The timing couldn't have been more perfect. This entire thing had started at midnight. It seemed fitting that it would end at midnight.

I held up a case that contained the well-wrapped painting. "I'm ready whenever you are."

He glanced around and caught Hornbeck's attention and beckoned for him to follow. "Let's take a look."

We followed Merriweather into the office. I wondered if he would open the private room, but I guess Maggie and Hornbeck weren't part of the inner circle. Instead, I walked to the desk and carefully opened the case and unwrapped the painting.

Hornbeck gasped. He stared wide-eyed from me to the painting, and then he gazed at the painting. "This can't be . . . but how can it be . . . it can't be."

I handed him the magnifying glass I carried with me and watched as he examined every inch of the painting.

Maggie was just as eager. Up close, I could see the vein pulsing on the side of her head even better. I watched as she clenched and unclenched her fists as her eyes raked over the painting. I knew she was holding her breath. Only when she stood up did she release it. "Where on earth did you get a Vermeer?"

Merriweather laughed. "Ah . . . that, my dear, is for me to know."

"But this is astonishing. It must be tested. It must be examined by the proper authorities. You've found the lost Vermeer," Hornbeck rattled on.

"Ah, no. I'm afraid we can't do that," Merriweather said.

"But how?" She turned to me.

"I commissioned Mr. Bland to do some much-needed conservation work." He looked from Maggie to Hornbeck. "You are two of the foremost experts on Dutch Golden Age Painters. Do you attest to this as a genuine Vermeer?"

Hornbeck stuttered. "Well . . . it appears . . . I mean . . . it certainly looks, but without tests . . . without a lab analyzing the paint mineral composition and the age of the paper . . . how can I be sure . . . but it gives every indication . . ."

"I can assure you, the paint, the canvas, everything is from the seventeenth century. It's even still on the original stretcher that Vermeer used almost four hundred years ago." Merriweather turned to Maggie. "Well?"

"I couldn't possibly stake my reputation on a painting that I've spent less than twenty minutes examining without proper equipment. However, it certainly appears to be a Vermeer."

"Wonderful. That only leaves payment for services rendered." Merriweather moved behind the desk and tapped his computer screen. After a few minutes, he closed the lid. "Done."

My phone chimed. The payment had been sent to my offshore bank account. I'd pulled it off. Midnight. Perfect. I made a few swipes.

There was a knock on the door.

"Go away. I'm busy," Merriweather yelled.

The knocking grew louder and more persistent.

Frustrated, Merriweather marched to the door and swung it open.

Before he could speak, FBI and Coast Guard officials burst into the room. August Merriweather was pushed against the wall and handcuffed.

With the door open, we could hear the chaos as people scrambled to get out of the way. Men and women dressed as waiters moments earlier were now brandishing guns and firing off orders with the quickness of a machine gun.

Merriweather fumed. "Which one of you betrayed me?"

I reached in my pocket and pulled out my badge that confirmed I was a member of the FBI. "I told you I was an art detective. You should have believed me."

We dragged Merriweather to the wall and forced his fingers and eyes to open the scanners. Inside, the team carefully seized all the stolen art. I took satisfaction in watching Merriweather's face and then released thirty-five years of pent-up anger and told him exactly what I thought of him.

Hours later, the guests and the crew had been removed. The last of the art had been packed and loaded onto the Coast Guard ship to be transported back to the U.S.

On the deck, I wasn't surprised to see Maggie hadn't left with the others. She was leaning against the rail of the yacht.

I removed my jacket and draped it over her shoulders.

We watched the waves on the ocean as the moonlight danced across the water.

"What happens now?"

I shrugged. "Merriweather can afford lawyers who'll keep this tied up in court until he's dead in his grave."

"He'll never serve time. The statute of limitations is up. Was this just about revenge?"

I thought I knew the answer to that, but I pondered it. "I've wanted revenge against that man for more years than I can count. I've blamed him for destroying my dream of being a great artist. However, working on the Vermeer helped me come to terms with that. I may not be a great artist. I may not be original, as Merriweather wrote, but words are powerful, and his words had the power to close doors. He took pleasure in being clever and providing a critique that he knew would humiliate another human. So I wanted revenge for the cruel, blasé way he used his words. I wanted revenge for the shame and trauma from the robbery. Thirty-five years of waking up in the middle of the night in a cold sweat—PTSD before anyone even had a name for it. Revenge for the questions that followed me and Ralph Scallini everywhere we went—were the guards involved?" I thought for a few moments. "I think the worse crime of all was the years that he kept the world from seeing and enjoying those works of art."

She bumped me with her hip. "Softy."

I grinned. "I guess I am."

I could feel her gaze on me. "You know, I doubt that anyone else will ever know the Vermeer is a fake," she said. "I only knew it because I looked at it every day for years when we were married. Plus, I know your style. What did you do with the original?"

"It's in my studio. It got damaged. I'm restoring it. He paid me to restore the Vermeer, so that's what I'm doing." We were close enough for me to feel the question welling inside her before she spoke it. "When it's done, I'll donate the reward to a local organization that helps people coping with trauma. As for the Vermeer, I've spent the past month working on it day and night. When I'm done, you can take it and turn it in for the reward."

She stared. "Are you joking? The reward for that painting is ten million dollars."

"It deserves to be restored to the condition it was in when they took it. It deserves to be put back into the empty frame that's still hanging on the wall at the Isabella Stewart Gardner Museum. It deserves to be seen by other young dreamers. Who knows, maybe it'll inspire one of them to do great things. After all, it's a Vermeer. So, anything's possible."

MIDNIGHT CONFIDENTIAL
By Delia C. Pitts

I hiked my bra strap into the crease on my right shoulder and bustled into the precinct interrogation room. I took the aluminum chair opposite my confidential informant, Tubby Rooney. He flinched, his rat-gray eyes diving for the corner. At five eleven, I towered over him. My frame, crammed into dark trousers and a houndstooth blazer, would have earned me the label *burly* if I'd been Danny Barnett. But as Denise Barnett, I got called *curvy* instead. No matter. Tubby cringed when he saw me, as well he should. He owed me. Not as much as the others, but enough.

They all owed me. Every freaking one of them owed me. All the cops who'd insulted me, threatened me, dissed me during my career. They owed me. Big-time.

There were the white ones, of course. The Aryan Nation pledges who hated the idea of a black female classmate in *their* police academy. I'd saved all the miniature nooses they'd posted on my locker: the meticulous ones made of kitchen string; the crude ones in wire and cable cord, even the arty drawing of my head in a rope by some budding Picasso. The genius had caught my likeness pretty well: the thick fringe of lashes over large dark eyes, the prominent teeth and acorn-brown skin. I kept all those nooses under my bed in a pink shoe box marked *Memories.* Even now, fifteen years later, it cleared my head to take a peek in that box once in a while.

There were the brothers too. Black cops who resented a black woman rising through the ranks. They owed me too. They weren't as artistic as their white colleagues. The black cops relied on verbal campaigns to smear me. According to their stories, there were two reasons I had advanced, both located behind the buttons of my uniform blouse. Or maybe the source of my success was between my legs. Hard to keep track; the stories expanded with every promotion. My favorite moment was when Thomas Perkins and Everett Willis, two black cops I'd imagined were friends, dropped their damp towels in the locker room as I dressed after shift. Even semi-erect, Perkins was the more impressive of the two.

I'd made detective first class eight years ago, sixteen months after Tom Perkins was promoted to lieutenant. We got along fine in his precinct. I cleared my cases, rounded up the requisite number of suspects, even pried a few grateful words from grouchy civilians. My numbers made Perk look good, and that's what counted with the brass downtown. Lieutenant Perkins had no problems with me; I'd never held the nudie show against him. But every day I prayed that his bulging eyes and dull skin were signs of an impending stroke.

I had my own way of collecting on the debt owed me. From the start, no one had missed the dime bags of coke I pocketed when breaking corner dope dealers. So, a few years into that petty trade, I'd graduated to lifting bricks of heroin after each major drug bust. The evidence lockup was crowded;

if a few kilos disappeared before I turned in my haul, I was just making more room on the shelves.

I got rich—far from Hollywood rich, but comfortable. Not that anyone noticed. Ten years on the take and I lived in the same one-bedroom walk-up. Drove the same dented blue Honda Civic; wore the same no-name crepe soles from the discount shoe warehouse. No bling on my neck; no deluxe cruises to places I couldn't pronounce. I had bought a full-length mink coat four years ago, but I wore those glossy black female pelts only around my own place. I needed a bathrobe, and the mink obliged. I'd never taken the coat out for a stroll. Not once. I'd spent most of my take putting my dead sister's three daughters through school: one to Yale, one to Meharry Med. The third one had finished a cosmetology certificate program; her gratitude came in the form of a free wash and flatiron press every other week.

At forty-four years old, my life was fine. Crooked but low-key. Until my snitch Tubby Rooney got caught in a street sting the first week of June. Tubby was a brown-skinned squirt who held up lampposts on several busy corners in my precinct. He watched, scratched, hustled, and kept me informed on local transactions—dope, guns, counterfeit purses—often before they happened. Two years ago, thanks to Tubby's tip, I'd helped break up a major smuggling ring that trafficked girls from Central America. Perkins got the commendation in a big ceremony at Police Plaza One. I got a coupon for dinner at Verona's, a tony seafood restaurant downtown. My niece the hairdresser and I enjoyed a great four-course meal on the city dime.

Tubby Rooney shared his news and views with me in return for small cash donations. I also turned a blind eye to his shoplifting and panhandling. Tubby wasn't vital to the success of my secret operation, but he was a key component. I knew plenty about Tubby. But he knew too much about me. About my drug connections and secret sources of income. If Tubby spilled, I was cooked. So, when I read the intake report on Tubby's arrest, I volunteered to conduct the interrogation. I convinced Lieutenant Perkins I was the right officer for the job; I said I could get Tubby Rooney to open up because he trusted me.

Our precinct's interrogation room was a closet with a giant two-way mirror. Its green walls were washed in sickly light from the overhead lamp; halfway down the green paint was overlaid with beige tiles. The piss of a thousand suspects and the sweat of a thousand lawyers speckled the linoleum floor.

Lieutenant Perkins uncoiled his tall frame near the door of the interrogation room when I reached the corridor. "You don't have to do this, Barney." He called me Barney as if we were chums. I hated the nickname in his mouth. But I went along to get along. He glanced at his watch. "It's almost midnight. You can call it a day."

I stared at the shadows spread like bat wings below his eyes. "That's all right, chief. I got this." I grinned and flicked a salute that slid from my brow to my nose. "Piece of cake."

Perkins shrugged and peered through the glass to the interrogation room. His face was hard and scarred like a carpenter's workbench. Muscles along his jaw flexed when he narrowed his eyes. He checked his watch again, then settled an elbow on the ledge below the two-way mirror. "Empty-bed blues again, huh, Barney?" He suppressed the smirk until I touched the doorknob, then let it snake across his face. I rolled my eyes and prayed for a stroke to take him right then. Nothing.

When I barged in, Tubby Rooney was already seated at the dented metal table in the middle of the room. His hands were cuffed and hooked to a link bolted into the table's enamel surface. Like he was a major crime lord instead of a puny scrub. I dropped my blazer on the chair back and sat opposite my snitch.

The air was dense, invaded by early-summer humidity seeping past cracks in the window moldings. A trapped fly rattled in the light globe overhead. Despite the June heat, my snitch shivered, and his fear salted the air. The collar of his orange T-shirt was dappled with sweat. Its wrinkles stuck to the cords of Tubby's scrawny neck. The nickname was a street taunt: the man was twenty-nine years old and thin as a broom handle. I didn't have to look below the table to know he was wearing beltless jeans draped around his hips like a denim tent. His underwear was sooty gray and the frayed red sneakers were his only pair.

In a corner of the room, a junior cop with pie-crust skin lounged against the tile. His eyelids hung at half-mast over green pupils; he was white, tired, and insulted by his current task. Backup for a middle-aged black woman detective wasn't his dream assignment. But his middle-aged black lieutenant gave the orders, so here he was.

I tried to set Tubby at ease by flashing both rows of teeth. "I'm going to tell you a story, okay? You don't have to answer, just listen." I looked across the table to see if my words had landed. His eyes met mine for a brief moment. So yeah, he was with me, sort of. "But I can't tell you the story until you give me your full name. So what is it?"

"Jamal. Jamal Rooney. People call me Tubby. You know that."

"Okay. Good. Mind if I call you Tubby?"

He lifted his chin, and I plunged on. "So. Tubby. Do you know Iraq? Have you been there?"

Sparse eyebrows bounced in his brown face. I'd surprised him. Good. I wanted him telling the truth as much as possible. Even if it was only one syllable at a time.

"Yeah, I know it."

Our voices sounded tinny and alien as they echoed off the tile walls and the filthy linoleum under our feet.

My back was to the blind expanse of the two-way mirror, so I could use my eyes more freely than Tubby could. His face was under scrutiny; his every expression would be examined by Perkins for minute proof of the guilt the lieutenant assumed was there.

My voice could give away the double game I was playing. But I was sure Perk wasn't paying attention to the timbre of my sentences. Any tremors escaping from my undisciplined vocal cords would go undetected in the intensity of the exchange.

Perkins's presence outside the room pressed on me as I settled into my seat. The man was so eager in his convictions, so fervent in his faith in me, that I hoped he could be deceived by a truth I would shape.

I wanted Tubby to look only at me, to never let his eyes flit to the mirror behind my head. I needed him to stay in the room with me no matter what. "My story is about a cop who went to Iraq."

Tubby's eyes flickered. He shifted on the hard seat, tilting toward me.

To my left I caught the quick movement of the young cop slouching in the corner. Navy pants too short, white shirt too tight; I could see a sliver of salmon-pink belly straining at the buttonhole just above his belt.

I wanted him to play a part in this charade too. I needed his honest reactions to attest that Tubby posed a threat to me. So I jerked, as if I were afraid for my safety, despite the cuffs that kept the snitch's wrists shackled to the lip of the table.

I darted my eyes to the beefy guard and offered a wavering smile. He nodded in smug affirmation, and I loosed a small sigh. My relief was genuine. The bit player knew his part; in the corridor, the audience of one was attuned to my slightest gesture. Now I needed my costar to take the stage.

I focused again on Tubby. His arms looked thin and slack in the orange T-shirt, its color casting a sickly spotlight toward his face. The bones of his skull stood in high relief under the skin, the cheeks and eye sockets sunken from dehydration and sleep deprivation. They'd picked him up last night. Twenty-four hours in a shadowy cell had leached the sun from his skin, leaving it muddy and creased. Tiny flakes rising from his scalp caused my stomach to revolt. The hunched shoulders and concave chest suggested abject submission to his predicament. That surprised me. Tubby used to be quite a little fighter.

I needed him to be alert, engaged, and ready to give his heart to this act. I coughed to capture his attention and was reassured when the eyes he raised were clear.

"Now, Tubby, before I begin my story, I have to ask: did you want a lawyer?"

He gulped. "Do I need one?" The handcuffs rattled against the enamel surface.

"Up to you, Tubby. It's your right. If you want one." I knew he'd been read the standard statements at the time of arrest. But I wanted this conversation by the book. Perk was recording it, so I needed everything as clean as next year's model car. No smudges, stains, or scratches.

"That's all right, I'm good. I'll stick it like this for now."

With this cleared, I began my story. "That cop who went to Iraq was me, of course. I probably shouldn't have gone in the first place, leaving my kid sister alone like that. But I thought I could be of service, help my country and the people over there too." I shrugged and raised my eyebrows, inviting a reply.

Tubby stayed silent, but his gray eyes widened with curiosity.

"You ever heard of a sensory deprivation chamber? You know, where you lie in a tub of lukewarm water and they close the lid on you? And it's pitch-black in there? Can't see a damned thing? Can't feel anything? And all you can hear is the sloshing of water at your elbows and your own breathing?"

I thought I might have thrown him with this detour, but he got what I was saying. I knew he'd been there.

Tubby spoke again, his voice spilling like dry gravel in an abandoned lot. "Iraq is like that after a while: everything flattens out, every village looks the same, everybody is the same. Every day the same as the next one." His tone was uninflected, but his gaze was piercing.

I kept telling my story with an eagerness that was authentic. I wanted this connection. "That's right. The same. Except for the day your buddy gets the side of his face blown off by an IED. That day was different."

Tubby grimaced, a wave of twitches rushing over his face. I placed my arms on the table, stretching them across the narrow surface toward him. I rolled up the sleeves of my black shirt, inviting examination of my bare flesh. I flexed my left biceps to highlight a short gray gash carved above the elbow. I knew he'd seen the scar before.

But until now, I'd never told its story. I pointed at the scar. "I got this that same day. My buddy got dead that day, and I got a Purple Heart and a trip home."

"Home." He echoed the word and blinked twice, tears trembling at the edges of his eyelids now.

"Do you want to go home?" I drilled in, sensing the electricity pulsing from Perkins spying behind the mirror. "If you talk with me, I can make that happen for you, Tubby. I can get you out of here. I can get you home. Do you want that?" I bobbed my head, encouraging him like I would a small child caught with shards of the broken vase in his hand. If he would confess now, all would be forgiven, I wanted to say.

Tubby nodded, mimicking my movements. "I—I want to go home!" He wailed then, not really crying, since the tears never fell, but wrenching something from the depths of his soul nonetheless.

I lowered my voice to a whisper. "Then tell me. Tell me your story, and I'll make it all right."

"Okay, I will." His voice was faint, directed toward the table rather than at me. He bent his forehead to the hard surface and rested it there for over a minute. When he raised his eyes to mine, they were dry again.

"Tell me your story, Tubby, the parts you want me to understand about you."

He spoke fluidly now, flinging his words at me with childlike eagerness. "I went to Iraq too. Like you. But when I came back, I didn't know what to do with myself. Booze seemed like a pretty good option, so I tried it out. My dad got tired of me lying on his sofa sleeping off another drunk at two in the afternoon. And drunk all over again by midnight. So he booted me out the house."

Tubby paused, waiting for my questions, but I only nodded to urge him to continue with his story.

"Funny thing was, I was good at math in high school. Liked the business courses I took then. But somehow I couldn't turn any of that into a job. I hit the street and got stuck there. Like a fly in honey." He paused as if he wanted to make me understand. "Math was good to me. No arguments from the numbers, no fight over what they meant, no bargaining with the bottom line. No bullshit. Just the plain truth. I liked that. After Iraq, you know." He looked at me, his soft mouth open, eager for my approval.

I wanted to draw him out further. "Then you met me, right, Tubby?"

He smiled for the first time. "Yeah, I did. I don't know why, but you and me really fit. Like a team. I was good at watching people, getting their trust. Seeing where they moved, what deals they made. I just slid natural-like into the job with you, Miz Barney. Working the confidential informant racket for you used all my skills and kept me on my toes. I even moved back with my dad."

I wanted to lead him to the confession now. "So, tell me what you were doing in the stock room of the grocery store when you were arrested."

"Well, I don't really know. Just hanging like I always do."

"Yeah, I know that, Tubby. But you need to tell me all of it if we're going to get through this." I was pleading now, my voice quavering enough that I knew Perkins could detect my urgency through the glass.

So Tubby wove a complicated story from scraps of insider intel, greed, and deceit. He said he'd been keeping a lookout for a gang that planned to bump off the grocery. The trio of thieves was led by the daughter of the store owner. She knew the cash register held over three thousand that evening. They planned to use the money to finance a drug purchase—pain pills and other prescription meds supplied by a crooked druggist. They would resell the drugs for six times their worth on the street.

At each turn in the account, as Tubby hesitated, I gently prodded. When he paused, I pushed him on. Once, when he evaded a direct question, I raised my voice, the tones swelling to a scream. A passionate tirade escaped my lips. Tubby seemed shaken. I was too. The whites glinted around his pupils like those of a cornered animal. I bit my lip to convey an apology; I knew Perkins wouldn't see the gesture, but Tubby could. That tongue-lashing seemed to spur him, and the next torrent of words continued for several more minutes without stopping.

I was prepared to pound the table if he halted again, but he never gave me an opening for new theatrics.

As Tubby explained it, his part in the scheme was negligible. Not criminal, he wanted me to see. But he knew he was hurting innocent people. He felt the guilt of that violation. His cheeks flushed with shame and his lids fluttered as he tried to hide from my stare. He wanted to set it right, he told me. When he said he was afraid of how his father would react once the truth was revealed, tears pricked at the corners of my eyes.

I swiped fingers across my cheeks so that Perkins would witness the proof of my emotional investment in the story the chained man had told. When he finished, he exhaled as if a huge burden had been lifted from his chest.

"Now, Tubby, you and I have worked together for, what? Four years now?"

"That's right. You always been good to me."

"I'm being good to you right now, Tubby. And I'll continue to help you as long as you keep telling the truth." I squeezed a smile to tighten the connection. "Now I need you to tell what you can about the people you know. The ones you've seen running drug deals in the neighborhood."

Tubby's spine bent under the weight of my question. His hooded eyes rambled across the ceiling, desperate for a way out. None up there. And none in my face either, when he dragged his gaze to it. "Miz Barney, I don't know about that . . ."

"Yes, you do, Tubby."

Another sigh, bigger than the last. Then out with it: "Well . . . I know about Cherise Fulton; she's the daughter of that city councilman. I seen her cruising our block a time or two, looking to score a big haul."

I nodded encouragement. "Okay, that's good, Tubby. You're doing fine."

With the first name aired, the rest of the list flowed: "I clocked one of them big music producers. You know him, with the tattooed head. Four times I seen him. He took teeny bites for chump change at first. But just last week he stepped up big. And two fellas in sharp business suits come around too. One packing heat, the other picking up the score."

He continued for five minutes, rattling through a cavalcade of stars, each name more celebrated than the last.

Politicians and players, pop magazine queens, glam musicians, and sports figures heading to the Hall of Fame. The husky cop in the corner shifted from foot to foot; sweat darkened the armpits of his white shirt. I figured Perkins behind his mirror was sweating too as the high-profile body count piled up. He was personal friends with half the big shots on Tubby's list. And hoped to rub elbows with the other half as his career advanced. Tubby's story was bad news, if it stuck.

I needed to chop the legs from Tubby's account before he got us all in trouble. My choice was risky, but stakes were high, and it was my best shot. "So, you've seen a lot of top people, Tubby." He grinned, his head bobbing in time with his toe tapping below the table. "But who's the big fish? The biggest one you've seen so far? In terms of kilos and dollars, who's moving the biggest take?"

The toe taps stopped. Tubby's eyes bulged. "I can't say that out loud, Miz Barney." His gaze darkened to a warning glare.

"It's all right. You tell what you know. I'll take care of us. Don't you worry." I slid my forearms over the table until my index finger touched Tubby's cuffs.

He smiled, the saddest smile in the world. "If you say it's all right. Then I best spill it, huh, Miz Barney?" Off my nod, he continued. "The biggest fish, the one with the biggest take I ever seen in these past four years . . . it's *you*, Miz Barney."

The white cop coughed in his corner. Then laughter rolled from deep in his belly. First a wet gurgle, then a full galloping bellow. I laughed too, closing my eyes to screen the confusion on Tubby's face. I leaned against the chair back and clapped my hands.

Lieutenant Perkins burst into the room. "I've heard enough here. Close down this bullshit immediately." No verdict yet on our performance. But the impatience in Perkins's voice raked the dank air. "Get him out now."

My champion the husky guard unlocked the cuffs from the hook on the table. With a rough hand under the elbow, he dragged Tubby upright.

Perkins filled the space with his blustery eagerness. "Barney, you did a good job. *Great* job. But I know how wrenching a session like this can be. You got him to blubber that damn fool story. Everything he said was ridiculous. But that last desperate accusation against you took the cake." His voice softened as he bent low over my shoulder. "He must be high as a kite to think we'd buy a BS story like that."

Perk turned when two uniforms barreled into the tiny room. He growled, "Get this son of a bitch out of my sight. He lied about Detective Barnett; he lied about all the rest too. His testimony is worthless. All of it. Push the paperwork. I want him released tonight."

The two officers bookended Tubby and hustled him from the room. Tongue flapping, he craned his neck to catch my expression, but I froze my face until he'd gone.

Perk clapped me on the shoulder as I rolled down the sleeves of my black shirt. "How come I never knew you served in Iraq? It's not in your file."

"Because I never did."

His low whistle pierced my ear. "Okay, then! And the scar on your arm? How'd you get that?"

"Tripped and fell on a sidewalk. Skating with my kid sister when I was twelve and she was eight."

He shook his head. "You pulled that off like a pro, Barney."

"I *am* a pro, Perk." I paused until he dipped his gaze. "I said I needed Tubby to trust me. I knew he'd been in Iraq. That story was the quickest way to get there."

He pursed his lips into a mix of scorn and admiration. With maybe a dab of fright on top. "You need to get out of here. It's past one. I still got sandwiches and coffee from yesterday in the conference room if you're hungry. I'll catch up with you there in five."

"Thanks, but nah. I'll head home. It's been a long day." I lifted the corners of my mouth. A faint smile to indicate I was just doing my job. And I was damned good at it. Then I shrugged to fake nonchalance. And to get his fucking paw off my shoulder.

I was exhausted. And so hungry that even Perkins's offer of stale sandwiches sounded good. Home sounded better. Slabs of colby melted on rye toast. Hot shower, then drop like a stone into bed.

But there was one final step in my plan. The last source of danger to me had to be eliminated. I dawdled at my desk for an hour, punching computer keys, until I saw Tubby's police escort jostle him to the lobby. I followed at a distance, watching as they pushed him through the glass doors. When the cops evaporated, I joined my snitch on the top step. A curtain of yellow light wavered over the chipped cement stairs. Empty black-and-white patrol cars were slotted in the darkness below. Exhaust fumes wafted on humid June breezes coursing down the block.

"You doing all right, Tubby?" I clamped my arm across his neck and squeezed his knobby shoulder. "That was quite a story back there, wasn't it?"

He looked up at me, then wriggled. "Yeah, that was something else, Miz Barney. Something I never expected to see in all my born days."

I tightened my grasp. "Well, you did fine. Just fine." I grinned, my face in shadows. "I told you I'd get you out. And I did it, just like I promised."

"Yeah, just like you promised." A frown gouged the space between his eyes.

"You know what, Tubby?" I pressed my lips against his ear. "I'm going to do something big for you."

"Something big? What's that?"

"Something that's going to make you famous, Tubby. Everybody in the neighborhood's going to know your name."

His eyes narrowed, pupils darting. "But I don't want nobody to know me."

"Oh, yes. Everybody's going to know how you helped me. You're not my only confidential informant, you know. I have a network of little guys scattered across the precinct. I'll tell them how helpful you were tonight. I'll put out the word about you, Tubby. No way you can fight a rumor. The more you deny it, the faster it spreads. Your name's going to be fire."

His head swiveled, gaze sweeping the dark street in front of the station. He smacked his lips to soothe his dry mouth. "You can't do this to me, Miz Barney. I been good to you."

"Tonight. I'll make it happen tonight. I talk with my little guys. They learn you're in bed with the cops. A longtime errand boy for the po-po." My voice slipped into the easy drawl of the street. "And by midnight tomorrow the whole city knows you're a confidential informant."

"But you owe me! You can't do this." Repeating himself, Tubby struggled to slip from my grip.

"You're wrong. I learned a long time ago: I owe myself. First, last, always." I pulsed my fingers around his arm in a final squeeze. "So best get a move on, Tubby. You know how the streets feel about snitches." Sweat from his armpit wet my thumb, and I pulled it away.

I had no illusions about his life-span under the death sentence I'd just threatened. Neither did Tubby. He'd either leave the city, go to ground, or die. Whichever way he went, I was safe.

Tubby skipped to the foot of the stairs, then plunged into the shadows between two patrol cars and disappeared.

Eight months later, Tom Perkins made captain and bounced to a shiny office in Police Plaza One. The batwing shadows under his eyes darkened, but he never stroked out. I quit skimming from the heroin raids; that deal ended the day Tubby Rooney got busted. I had my long black mink bathrobe, and that was enough.

I never saw Tubby again. I never ratted on him. He was right, I did owe him. I hope the little guy made it, that he's breathing safe and happy somewhere. In another city, another life, far from me and mine.

CHEFS

By Faye Snowden

She wasn't the misogynistic representation of the dime store novel femme fatale who corrupted a good man with her bad ways. Johnny wasn't so gone in love with her that he would rob a bank or kill a man. She was only the woman who would sometimes straighten her hair before winding it around her head until the ends glistened in wisps all around her perfectly symmetrical face. Sometimes she would leave her hair natural so he could plunge his fingers through it as they made love, even though all he could think about was her husband the entire time. Yes, he knew what she was. But more importantly, he knew what he was. And what he wasn't.

They were driving past a field of pumpkins on Highway 99 toward Modesto, some so ripe that they had cracked, spilling pulp and seeds onto the curling green leaves. He hadn't talked since Oakland. He took a drag on his cigarette, a long, extravagant drag like they did in the movies when he was a boy. He blew out a stream of smoke and still didn't say anything. He let the hand not holding the cigarette surf the cool air outside the open window, his silver-tipped leather boots cocked on the dash.

Finally, she said, "I asked you a question."

He looked at her. Straightened black hair whipped across her face in the wind coming through the open windows. She smiled, not looking at the road but with her eyes on him. It was a slow, sexy smile full of confidence and promise.

"Ask it again." He took another drag of the Marlboro and turned to stare out the window once again. Late October and time, like the year, was running out.

"I asked if you had talked to him," she said, before turning back to the road.

"No."

"Johnny," she said. "He knows."

Johnny didn't bother to tell her that he had probably always known but had finally been confronted with a piece of evidence he could no longer ignore.

She exited the freeway at Kiernan, and now they were headed down the expressway shooting toward Riverbank. They wouldn't get there. He knew exactly where she would stop. He returned to his thoughts. Her husband had known almost the moment she and Johnny touched. Johnny was sure of it. He knew him as well as he knew his wife. Johnny had grown up with the man he was now betraying, joined the army with him. He had even saved his life once, but that was a long time ago.

"He's coming back tonight," she said as she exited the expressway.

She rolled onto a dirt road and drove behind an abandoned house so no one would see the Ford pickup from the street. She set the parking brake for no reason at all. The ground was flat and dusty all around. He could feel her looking at him again, but he didn't return her gaze. He opened the truck door and got out, the cigarette burned to a shred of tobacco between his fingers. He could see himself mirrored in the cracked pieces of glass that hung loose in the front window of the abandoned house.

He wore a two-hundred-dollar pair of designer jeans and a black T-shirt that cost half that much. As he watched his fragmented image in the mirror, he wished briefly that he had stayed in the car and returned her gaze. Instead of the man with the sagging gut staring back at him in a pair of young man's jeans, maybe he would see reflected in her eyes the hip chef who had served two tours in Afghanistan before returning home to culinary school to open a restaurant in his hometown.

Johnny squatted on his heels and leaned his back against the graffiti-covered wall. She didn't sit down, and he didn't look up. All he could see were her cowboy boots and the hem of her cotton dress, which was covered in a pattern of strawberries.

He tapped another cigarette into his palm. She waited until he had taken a drag and then sat down beside him flat on her ass with her legs stretched in front of her like a child.

She said, "He won't go home first. He'll come straight to the restaurant from the airport. He'll be there around midnight."

"Okay," was all he said.

"He'll be mad."

They sat quiet for a long time, and then she said, "You know how mad he can get."

He had met her in culinary school, a girl almost ten years his junior with a sassy smile and a fascination with cotton country dresses even in winter. They'd paired up on assignments, and she would ask him all kinds of questions about where he was from, about his family, about the war as they learned how to slice carrots and dice onions without crying. He'd catch her giving him sidelong glances in just the right light so that her brown eyes appeared both transparent and bottomless. Together they learned to butcher and cook every part of an animal. And all he'd ever wanted to do was sleep with her. She met Johnny's friend Oscar, who was richer and better looking, before he had the chance.

"We'll have to defend ourselves," she said.

He extinguished the Marlboro next to his black boots. "We don't have to be at the restaurant when he gets there," he said.

She laughed. "We'll have to see him sometime. Or should we run away together?"

He didn't bother to answer.

"He has a five-hundred-thousand-dollar life insurance policy," she said. "Five hundred thousand dollars. We could split it right down the middle."

"He's my best friend."

"He stopped being your best friend the minute you started sleeping with his wife."

"Why not just divorce him and take half?"

He should have left it at that, but then he laughed, roughly and without any mirth. He knew that something in that laugh made her go on.

"Five hundred thousand dollars," she pressed.

He finally looked at her. Really looked at her full in the face. "Don't tell me that you signed a prenup?"

She hung her head.

"Wow," he breathed. "How could you be so stupid?"

"I had to. Couldn't talk him out of it. He wouldn't marry me without one."

He stood up and looked at her bowed head. She started to cry. "He wouldn't marry me without one," she said again, this time running the sleeve of the big green sweater layered over her dress across her dripping nose.

"Well," he said, "I guess that's his bad."

* * *

The restaurant was crowded tonight. It was the annual Anna's Damn Crab and Steak Feed. Fifty bucks a person bought boiled Alaskan king crab from two huge pots on wood fires on the back patio and a T-bone steak cooked as dry or as bloodied as one desired. The waitstaff in white aprons splattered with blood and butter wove among the noisy tables with great mugs of craft beer and jokes that Johnny had heard during every crab and steak feed since he and Anna had started them years ago. The last customer left at half past ten, the last waitstaff close to eleven.

Anna kept looking at him as she loaded the plates into the dishwasher.

"Do you think he'll come?" she finally asked.

Johnny didn't know what Oscar would do. He knew where *he* would be if he thought his wife was cheating with his best friend. He'd be at a bar, a bar in which one could still smoke and no one cared. He'd smoke one Marlboro after the other along with frequent shots of Gentleman Jack. Oscar, though— if he knew him at all, Oscar would be drinking tequila.

Johnny went outside through the back door without answering. The flames beneath the cauldrons were dying down, the coals on the grill dulling to a gray-black cool. He bent to retrieve a set of tongs that had fallen on the patio and felt the Beretta M9 in the holster under his T-shirt. He left the tongs where they had fallen. He leaned against the stucco and planted a booted foot flat against the wall. He tapped another cigarette against his palm. He lit it but stopped before he put it to his lips.

"What the hell am I doing?" he whispered in the darkness.

What had he been thinking on that drive back from the Bay? Yes—he was not so gone in love with her that he would rob a bank or kill a man. He wondered how he had gotten so caught up. And he wondered why people did what they did. Was it because people were no good at their very core? Or was it because he was no good, no good like his father had told him ever since Johnny was capable of understanding speech? He crushed the tiny flame from the cigarette with the tip of his boot and answered his own questions.

He'd considered what Anna wanted because she was the only one who had looked at him like he was worth something in a long time. That and being thought of as a hero helped fill the hole his father had left in his soul. But memories of Johnny's heroism were fading, and Anna was getting bored. He was becoming what he had feared—a no-good nothing like his father had always warned he would be.

He flipped his wrist over to check the time. It was midnight. Time to make a decision. He gazed at the deep-black sky where the hunter's moon sat fat and full and swaddled in a smoky orange mist. No. He wouldn't kill for her. He was a lot of things, but a murderer wasn't one of them. He'd go home and watch SportsCenter, maybe drink a Corona and pretend like he was on the beach just like they did in the commercials.

He was sighing with relief when he heard loud thuds and glass breaking.

"Help! Johnny, help me!"

He ran inside to see Oscar's hand around Anna's throat and the other fisted in her hair. He was pulling and stretching her long hair as if he were trying to decapitate her.

"Oscar," Johnny said. "Let her go."

Later he thought that it would've been all right if Oscar hadn't looked at him. Never mind the knife protruding just below Oscar's shoulder. Johnny knew he could've made it right.

But Oscar did look at him.

And such a look Johnny never again wanted to see on a living person as long as he lived. The gaze exploded with loathing and contempt. It bore through Johnny's flesh and settled in his bones like cancer. He saw in Oscar's eyes the old man in the young man's jeans. He saw the war hero who wasn't a hero for trying to save the lives of others as everyone thought, but the man who was a hero only because he was trying to save his own skinny ass. The people he'd saved, including Oscar, had been positive collateral.

The look in Oscar's eyes said to Johnny, *You will always be what you have always been.* In Oscar's eyes he saw a father's contempt for a son who had disappointed him since the day he was born.

And so Johnny shot him. He snatched the Beretta from its holster and shot his friend between the eyes.

Anna immediately stepped back, sputtering and choking and grabbing at her throat. Oscar lay on the restaurant floor, his eyes still open.

Someone cried out to cover Oscar's face in a desperate litany that crawled up the walls and dripped from the ceiling like a thick syrup.

Anna tugged his arm. "Johnny," she said. "Quiet. Quit it. Get it together. Stop."

Her voice was hoarse and raspy, but the pleas to cover Oscar's face kept coming. She ripped one of the dirty table-cloths from a pile in the corner and pressed it hard over Oscar's face.

"Okay," she said. "He's covered."

She was a mess, the cotton dress stained with blood, the sleeves of her sweater drenched in it.

"Oh God," she said, as Johnny backed away from her. "Oh God."

She drew her sleeve across her nose, leaving a swath of blood on the lower half of her face. Johnny sat down hard in a wooden chair. She got down on her knees in front of him. She placed both hands on his face and held his head between her bloody fingers until he was forced to look into her eyes. Transparent. Bottomless.

"You know what we have to do," she said. "We have to get rid of him."

He was trying to pull away, but she held him. "We have to get rid of him. You know it. We have to get rid of him, and we have to clean this place up."

When he didn't say anything, she nodded, slowly but emphatically, while holding his face in her hands. He stumbled to his feet.

"Go fix the fire," she said.

*　*　*

Outside, the flame beneath one of the cauldrons was still orange but low and cool looking. He grabbed two wooden logs from the woodpile and placed them on top of the embers.

He stood there watching for a while before squirting lighter fluid over the cooling wood. The flames sputtered hot and large. They licked the sides of the pot as if they would be able to sustain that level of passion forever.

He spent a long time outside. The new morning was cold, and the air felt wet on his skin. He looked up at the sky. The hunter's moon appeared to mock him.

The pack of Marlboros in his shirt pocket was both empty and bloody from Anna's touch. He crumpled it between his fingers and threw it into the fire before going back inside. Pieces of Oscar lay on the white tarps that had previously held pounds and pounds of king crab. Oscar simply no longer looked like Oscar. He was meat, something Johnny dealt with every day. Anna didn't seem too affected by it either, though blood matted the cotton dress to her skin and thickened the hair that had earlier been silky as a waterfall. Without a word he helped her carry the meat outside. They heaved the tarp to the lip of the cauldron and emptied the contents into the warming water.

Johnny sat down on a bench by the door. "How long do you think it will take?"

"A long time."

"You got any smokes?"

She plopped beside him and shook her head. They waited. They waited for the water to boil for what seemed a very long time indeed. So long that he eventually laid his head along the back of the bench, and incredibly, he fell asleep.

A sizzling sound together with an unbelievable stench awakened him. The smell drove him to wretch over the side of the bench until his stomach was flat as an empty sack. He wiped the vomit from his mouth with the designer T-shirt and threw it into the bubbling water before going back inside, convinced that Anna had left him there to take the blame.

But she was still there.

She was running around the kitchen wearing one of her husband's white shirts from the luggage he wouldn't need anymore. She had tried to wash the blood from her skin, but instead of removing the stains, she appeared to have rubbed them in deeper so that her skin glowed red. She ran from the fryer to the sink and back to the fryer again, a pair of huge metal tongs in her hands. She was singing at the top of her lungs a loud gospel song that was both hopeless and full of hope. She had a soaring, lilting voice that would have been the pride of any church choir in the valley.

"Anna," he said.

She sang loud and full the words *I told Jesus.*

"What are you doing?"

She sang that she had told Jesus in a larger voice as she skittered around him. Using the tongs, she pulled out a piece of deep-fried meat and placed it in the center of a white plate delicately sauced with pesto and cream.

It was then that he knew he had been wrong. He had no idea who or what Anna was. But he recognized fully what was on the plate. It held Oscar's tempura-fried hand, the slender fingers still bubbling and curled back on themselves. Johnny uttered a wet sound and fell back, every nightmare he'd ever had coming true in that moment.

"Oh, come on," she said. "You know you always wanted to. It's the one thing we've never tried."

MIDNIGHT ESCAPADE

By Jennifer Chow

My Facebook search had succeeded. I'd managed to reconnect with my old high school friend Amanda. After bonding over timeline posts filled with flashing eighties-movies GIFs and cutesy emojis, we'd agreed to meet in person.

Not over Ventis or anything common like that. The thrill-seeking Amanda I knew and admired couldn't settle for anything less than the promise of a midnight escapade.

Exactly at twelve sharp, in the pitch-black, we planned to meet a few blocks from the secret midnight escape room.

I'd finished parking my own beat-up Pinto when a sleek Beemer pulled up behind me. A sliver of a fingernail moon shone in the dark sky. I could just make out the woman's hourglass figure when she glided out of her fancy car.

"Amanda?" My voice came out cowed, a habit I'd developed in high school when addressing the leader of our pack. I cleared my throat.

She whispered back, in that signature husky voice I'd envied and tried to imitate—before I realized it came from her frequent smoking sessions. "Mandy?"

For a moment, the ghost of an image came to me. A slip of an Asian girl with an unnatural perm and goopy electric-blue eyeliner with an enormous collection of tie-dye shirts.

"Yep?" I said as I sidled closer.

Up close, I saw that Amanda wore a velvet tracksuit, clothes she'd thought appropriate for our midnight run, I supposed. I'd gone for the night-running look, black activewear with practical pockets in the slim pants and lined leather gloves to chase the cold away. Her coal eyes assessed me, even in the dark, before giving me her verdict.

She gestured at my body. "Still thin as a pine needle, I see."

My throat felt dry, and I coughed. She didn't have to know how hard I worked to stay this size.

"But when did you get those ugly Coke-bottle glasses?" she asked.

I pushed up the heavy lenses sliding down my nose. "Those nearsighted Asian genes kicked in during college."

"I got LASIK. So worth the money." Amanda pulled out a lighter from her purse and thumbed it on. "Are you sure this is the place?" In the orange flame, I realized the lighter was the same model she'd used decades ago. But the bullet shine had tarnished to mold green.

"This must be it. Checked the Craigslist ad twice," I said.

The neighborhood with its line of cookie-cutter ranch houses didn't seem like an ideal business spot. But then again, midnight escape rooms weren't exactly common—and this one didn't seem official either. But the ad had called the experience "unique and trendy"—and Amanda was nothing if not the consumer of new trends.

"Must be through there," I said, nodding toward an open iron gate.

Amanda nodded and put away her lighter. I glanced over at the darkened residential house as we crept by and around to the back.

This neighborhood must have been built at a time when people hadn't insisted on direct-access garages. "Look at that," I said, pointing to the roof of the garage, where a small gargoyle statue perched, its eyes protruding and tongue stuck out. "Just like the post said."

The detached building had a closed garage door with a pull handle, but the side entrance lay ajar. I pulled on the side door with its keypad, and it gave a whiny cry. "Remember Mrs. R's scritchy chalkboard?" I said.

Amanda giggled, a sugarcoated laugh that I used to crave hearing all the time. Everything about her had come out refined. Even her burps sounded like cute hiccups. "Those were fun times," she said. "My glory days."

I wondered if she missed her former popularity. She'd been nicknamed Miss Hawaii by the jocks, who'd lusted after her generous curves, beach-tousled dark locks, and huge anime eyes. Age had given her a mass of wrinkles and sunspots, but she still dwarfed me with her queenly height of five foot ten and an even larger confidence.

Inside the garage, it seemed darker than the midnight outside. No windows. "There must be a light source somewhere," I said.

Amanda tilted her shoulder, a half shrug that could convey either indifference or contempt, depending on her mood. "You said it was a western theme. No electricity back then."

I employed the flashlight app on my phone to shine its beam around the room. The tiny light showed a drywalled, furnished room with straw scattered all around the floor. It illuminated an array of cowboy hats and saddles hanging on every side except the back wall, which lay covered with a large U.S. flag. A small glass gun case held pistol props.

An unvarnished wooden desk and a chair stood in the center of the room. A small table made from knotted wood held two kerosene lanterns. A box of matches nestled next to them. "Good old-fashioned wicks," I said.

She pointed to the matches. "Mandy, go ahead and light them up."

I shuddered. "Maybe you should use your lighter. I don't touch matches anymore. Not ever since . . . you know."

"What?" Amanda said as she used her lighter to ignite the wick on one of the lanterns.

"You don't remember?"

She lifted the lantern and searched my face with curious eyes.

"The thing that happened to Man?" I said.

"Which man?" She lit the second lantern and handed it over. "So many flocked me in high school."

"Not man. The third *Amanda* in our Triple Threat group."

We'd made up the name for our trio of Asian Amandas, a very popular girl's name back then.

A long pause before Amanda said, "Oh, that's right. Amanda, Mandy, and Man."

Man had been the third wheel of our group, and she knew it. "Man was good as a gofer," I said, "fetching us our favorite snacks, like barbecue Corn Nuts."

"Or ice-cold blue-raspberry Slurpees."

"Right. But she disappeared our senior ye—"

"Aha." Amanda did a jig, a shimmy that reminded me of the backup dancers from an old MTV video. "Found a clue," she said, picking up a yellowed paper from the table.

"Starting the timer," I said, walking to the side door and pulling it shut. It closed with a satisfying click. "We have sixty minutes to escape."

"We'll be out of here long before your watch chimes," Amanda said. She scanned the ancient page in her hand and smiled. "Especially if all the clues are easy like this one."

She showed me the aged paper. It showed cursive handwriting and read,

> *dear fortune hunter,*
> *if it's my bank LOot you want, yOu'll find the Kindest hint in the glass cAse wiTh my BeAutiful worlD-class firearms.*
> *Good luck.*
> *yours vEry truly,*
> *dot holliday*

"I don't get it," I said. "Looks almost like a ransom note with its awkward letters."

"Exactly." Her dark eyes gleamed with triumph. "If you put all the cap letters together, there's a secret message."

Props to her. Since Amanda loved being the leader, I let her step up to the glass case. Replicas of Wild West pistols lay within the case, but on top of the wooden frame, she found a shiny badge. Flipping the thin shield over, she noticed a piece of torn denim fabric attached to the pin in the back. "Bet we have to match the material," she said.

We walked around the garage, and the air felt stifling. Warmer by the minute from my increasing panic and rising body heat, I tripped over a small potted cactus I hadn't seen before. Some of the oil in my lantern splashed out. "Uh, I'm so clumsy. Must be nerves."

I rerighted the plant as Amanda examined the walls. As she stood near the large American flag at the rear, I asked, "Do you think Man left because of the July Fourth thing?"

Amanda moved to the next wall, snatched a cowboy hat, and perched it on her head. "Huh?"

"When we made her spark those illegal fireworks for us?"

Amanda grinned, her smile turning Cheshire-like in the eerie glow of the lantern. "That was a real blast."

"It was fun—until that one explosion changed into a scream." My jaw clenched tight. "Even though we were on the other side of the park for safety's sake, I still heard her cry out."

"I'm sure she was fine. I mean, there wasn't a funeral or anything." Amanda marched back to the desk and yanked open its drawers. All empty.

"I need to sit down and think," she said. She placed her cowboy hat on the desk and pulled the chair away from the table. Then she noticed the jeans folded on the seat. Even from where I stood, I noticed an unusual rectangular shape in the back pocket.

"What's this?" She yanked out a small red carton and squealed. "Marlboros. My fave brand in high school."

Anachronistic to have modern smokes in the escape room. But I guess the Marlboro Man still adhered to the western theme.

"I'm lighting up," she said. "Celebrating our win."

Amanda always jumped the gun. Enjoyed all the highs, skipped over any lows. "But we haven't gotten the code to the door yet," I said.

"This will help me think clearer." She pulled out a cigarette and placed the carton onto the table next to the hat.

Nicotine addict. Figured she couldn't go a whole hour without needing to smoke.

"I miss high school," she said. "Good times. I'm glad you found me online, Mandy. I probably wouldn't have even recognized you on the street."

"The internet's a wonderful place," I said. "Information at our fingertips." My hand twitched.

Amanda started smoking. Pure bliss erupted on her face. She blew a puff of smoke and watched it spiral up to the ceiling.

I frowned. "No fire detector in here."

She lifted her shoulder. "Good. No need for a false alarm."

Holding her ciggy in one hand, she picked up the pair of jeans in the other. She flipped the pants around and pointed out the hole in the front left pocket. It must mean something, the ripped denim.

"Mandy, dig in the pocket while I finish up here."

Of course I did as she asked. I found three dice in the pocket. Placing the cubes on the table, I commented on their odd design. The dots on five of the sides had been whited out. The die faces with six dots displayed a pattern, with only some of the dots erased. Die number one had one dot in the upper left hand corner; the second had a trail of two dots lined up and a third wandering to the upper right; and the third had a pattern of three dots making an L shape:

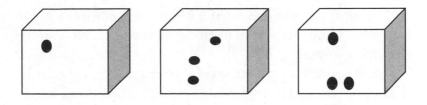

Amanda rearranged the cubes as though playing a shell game with the dice. "What could it mean?"

"Definitely a code of some sort," I said. "Dots . . . could it be Morse?"

"No. That would be dots and dashes."

"Anything else interesting about the dice?"

She held a die in her hand, rubbing the surface with her fingers. "Strange. The dots feel raised, almost like they're filled in with puff paint."

"Kind of like Braille," I said.

"You're right. But how will we figure out the message, then?"

"Let me try. I took a specialized class in college."

"Really?" Amanda stared at me.

"Yeah. Remember I wanted to go into optometry?"

Her eyebrows rose. "Thought you changed your mind senior year when we did that cow eye dissection."

"I gave it a second chance in college. Now, let me see those cubes."

After taking extra time to feel their contours and with some mumbling under my breath, I said, "I think they stand for the letters *A*, *S*, and *U*. What could that mean?"

We both looked around the garage until Amanda drew my attention to the large U.S. flag. "That's got to be it. We just needed to rearrange the letters to get the clue."

Lifting the flag up revealed a hidden door behind it. But we couldn't find any sort of opening mechanism. No handles or locks or anything.

After pounding on it for several fruitless moments, I said, "Did we miss something? Maybe there's something in the other jeans pocket."

"I'll look," Amanda said, as she beelined for the red Marlboro box she'd left on the desk. She made sure to tuck the box in her bag and winked at me. "No one will even notice it's gone."

She took the jeans and examined each pocket. Then she started flipping the jeans inside out. As I watched her work, the lantern slipped from my hand and dropped onto the floor. The hidden door sprang open.

Excited, I rushed through the new doorway and kicked over the lantern. I saw it tilt sideways, spilling out oil before the door closed on me. "What just happened?"

Amanda's voice rose in volume and sounded panicked. "Mandy, where'd you go?"

"I fell through the door. Must have triggered a hidden weight sensor somehow."

"Do you see the bank treasure? That'll be the last clue to get the door code."

"Can't see a thing. I dropped my lant—"

A high-pitched scream came through the divider. "The straw's on fire. Come out and help me."

I made a few ineffectual knockings against the sliding wall between us. Nothing doing. The temperature in the inner area seemed to be growing hotter from the flames beyond the door. But the concrete material of this room should withstand the fire. Peering around, I hurried to the back window and slipped out into the cool night.

Amanda's screaming kept going—until I shut the window behind me. From the outside, no one on the block could hear a thing.

My watch dinged. Time's up.

How would Amanda fare? She didn't have the combo for the side door and couldn't pull open the main entryway. I doubted she could brave the flames and reach the hidden door in the back. And even if she did, she'd need the remote to open it, and the controller lay tucked deep in my pants pocket.

I wondered if the smoke would get to her first. Or the flames. I'd made sure to drip oil on accident all around the straw-covered ground, beyond even the final puddle produced from the dropping of the lantern.

Walking with unhurried steps, I went back to the front of the house and opened the door to my home. I made my way to my bedroom in the deep witching hour.

I'd better get some rest before the firefighters showed up. They'd break into my detached garage and find Amanda ablaze, the traces of cigarettes on her. One plus one, an easy math problem.

When they asked, I would acknowledge that Amanda had been a high school acquaintance. I hadn't seen her since my junior year, when I'd transferred school districts.

Perhaps the police department could try to locate her old BFF, Mandy. After all, I knew there'd be Facebook records between the two, though Mandy had gone online from the comfort of an anonymous internet café. She'd even answered my Craigslist ad from there.

No matter if they believed my story or not, I'd finally get a good's night rest. First, I took off the heavy glasses; my sight had never been the same after the accident. Then I slipped off my thick gloves. For once, I didn't flinch as I gazed on my mottled skin and the burn scars crisscrossing my arms and spidering across my fingertips.

MURDERERS' FEAST

By H-C Chan

Men had been murdered for less. And yet John Manley still lived.

Five days, surrounded by false friends and his truest enemies. Every last one of them cowards.

"They can all get in line for hell." My hand and forehead sweated against the cold glass. From the second story, I'd watched with grasping hope at the drips and drabs of riders returning from their grouse-hunting lesson.

Mag Delana was among the first to return. Bleached blond and pumped full of Botox, she'd literally helped to build this Washington valley—or raze it, depending on one's perspective, turning apple groves into office parks and technology campuses. If anyone could have figured out a discreet vantage point for a hunting accident, it would be Delana. She'd sold Manley this vineyard after he borrowed his first million. In return, he'd driven her twenty-two-year-old daughter into a heroin addiction. The girl drove herself off a crooked curve at 120 miles an hour in his Tesla.

Natomi Hiraku, former billionaire reduced to millionaire as one of Manley's repeatedly duped VC investors, cantered in not long after. Two days ago, as the group foraged for mushrooms, he'd flapped his soft jaws asking a lot of questions when the mycologist tour leader explained how to identify death caps. Six meals and two afternoon hors d'oeuvres later, Manley's bloated gut still hadn't blown up from a bad pick.

Sal Pastor crested the hill. Six lifeless birds dangled from either side of his saddle. Better at birding, he was, than holding on to patents. Mercy Park trotted alongside, her bad-girl tattoos pink and black against hydroquinone-whitened skin. She'd been Manley's college lover, finally pushed out of his bed for good about four years ago by an underage replacement. She could hardly expose him, since the girl had been one of the hundreds of Korean women Park's family trafficked into their massage parlors and nail salons.

But keeping watch stopped mattering once Manley's garish orange cashmere hoodie appeared over Windglass Hill. He bobbed, a comical blob astride an oversized stallion. I knew Manley would've picked Balls to the Walls. Hell, I'd paid for the horse's name change. What else would lure an arrogant prick who owned a gold sledgehammer engraved with the words *Fuck Subtlety*?

The stallion should've thrown and trampled Manley the second they went over that hill. Considering Balls to the Walls' sluggish gait, the bastard had probably doped him up like he did his women.

I backed away. Another second longer and I would put my fist through the window. It took me a moment to catch on that the keening hyena laugh bouncing off the walls was mine. My clenched gut spasmed, doubling me over, wringing out high-pitched staccato giggles.

Five days. Five days at a murderers' feast disguised as an exclusive gourmet retreat, a loudly discreet venture-capitalist gathering hosted by notorious techpreneur John Manley. Snout-to-tail, farm-to-fork, locally sourced agritourism—basically packed to the gills with clichés.

Two hundred people in one place to learn how to sharpen knives, butcher an animal, find fungi, ferment brews, grow mold.

Two hundred fools, waiting for their moment, thinking they could best Manley by being close to the beast, trying to sniff out his weaknesses and swallowing his jizz over and over.

Every last one with motive enough to kill him twice over.

Nobody, much less Manley himself, should've lasted this long. I'd thrown in the grouse-hunting trip as an ironic topper, in the same fingers-up-the-arse spirit as Manley's sledgehammer. I couldn't even fault Manley this time. Venal, preening, noxious, braggadocious, and lecherous, he'd more than lived up to his unwitting role as murder victim, either by premeditation or passion.

Like the first day, when he'd "debated" with Mona Lasher in his fermentation cave. "C'mon, you're supposed to be a journalist," he taunted. "You can't argue with statistics. Every female CEO has failed, pure and simple. Hell, you ripped apart four yourself."

Lasher was little more than a lazy gossip hack, lucky enough to have gotten in early with her tech "insiders" podcast and newsletter and parlaying those modest beginnings into exclusive exorbitant networking lists. She'd snarled back, rhinoceros hide pricked, about glass ceilings and stacked decks, prompting his hideous grin.

"You didn't mind the stacks I gave you for your take-downs," he sneered.

She should have picked up a bottle and brained him. Instead her exit vibrated the shelves of glass bottles—flip-tops bubbling with lemon-ginger kombucha and the air locks with gassy Carolina Reaper pepper–spiked cabbage.

Manley followed in mock pursuit, a grim reaper in an orange hoodie. The exchange spurred a social media storm about payola. The thunderous tapping of thumbs drowned out the bottle rockets that erupted moments later. I'd injected extra sugar and superheated the temperatures the night before to prime the bottles as bombs. Manley was supposed to be in that cave surrounded by weaponized kimchee.

The second day, Manley needled Desi Kapoor at the butchery course. "You know, I admire Indian men's bargaining tactics," Manley told Desi. "Burning brides for dowry is what I call negotiation." Kapoor paled, even more so when Manley told him to hold down the pig. "You're just standing around anyway," he'd said, tying a long-sleeved apron over the orange cashmere.

And Manley proceeded to explain how his "lawyers want to dot every last *i* and cross every last *t*" as the knife sawed and blood gushed over Kapoor's white-knuckled grip. How Kapoor was being the "ace Raj," transplanting his engineering teams' families to one of the most expensive places on earth and holding down a dying pig. "Man, they're not kidding about the squealing. I thought this bitch would've died faster, right?"

If that hadn't been the moment for someone to take a knife and stick Manley like a pig, then when? Some turned away. A few even put fingers in their ears, like mewling kids in a thunderstorm. I'd even hoped that Leslie Ramos, a vicious psychopath who practically blew a wad witnessing this horrific sideshow, would've been inspired to indulge his true self and practice some bloodletting on Manley. Wrong reasons, right act. Didn't happen.

It had come to tonight, to the midnight feast. The sun, still hours from setting, streaked the scudding clouds orange. In these dragging summer days, nightfall didn't arrive until past nine PM. And the festivities would end with a midnight fest.

Or, as Manley insisted on calling it, "Christ, it's the Last Supper." Because even the Son of God couldn't have his final meal in peace.

But at last night did come, as all nights do.

By eleven forty-five PM, all the guests had arrived at a grassy field the size of an airport hangar, shepherding themselves within a perimeter of torches. The past several hours of hot-spring soaks, heated-stone massages, and lava scrubs had made them loose, unsuspecting, amenable to standing next to one of two hundred stones laid out in a massive horseshoe.

Manley stood at the apex of the U shape, a tailor-made backdrop reflecting his hooded swagger.

"I'd thank you all for coming," he said, his voice loud in everyone's earpiece, "but that would mean I got more out of it then you all did." Some tittered, like they were in on the joke and not the butt of it.

"Before this trip, most of you couldn't make anything even if you were handed a hammer, a nail, and a factory of suicidal

Chinamen. For our Last Supper, we're hunting the most dangerous game. But because nobody here's a real man, we had to ship something in."

Manley held aloft the compound bow, looking for all the world like a fanboy who'd bid for the privilege of holding his favorite action hero's prop.

"Here's the dinner plan. Whatever comes our way, you have to stay put. Scream, and he'll come for you. Run, and he'll come for you. Make any sudden movement—well, I can't make no promises. You all should be pretty good standing around doing nothing while someone else closes the deal. That clear?"

"Crystal," said Gwen Fang, who lived on the same dorm floor as Manley and had turned to cage fighting to help earn money for their start-up. She'd lost a front tooth and her founder rights but gained the nickname Fangs. Fangs now smiled, a flash of diamond embedded in a gold tooth.

"That's my girl." Manley saluted her with the compound bow. We stood, murmurs silenced, distrust back at high alert. These were people used to knives in the back and being thrown under a bus. They still wouldn't be ready for what would come. I felt sorry for no one.

Manley handicapped everything to his advantage. The first growl came through our earpieces, faint but so deep throated that my intestines clenched. I could see bodies twitch, a primordial reaction nobody could control. A chain clanged, and a note of fury ratcheted higher with the volume. Two hundred pairs of eyes glittered in the firelight, scanning the open field, the thorny grapevines in skeletal rows, the copse of oak trees a mile away, seeing nothing except one another.

But whatever it was had to come through the opening of the U, the whole point of this treacherous arrangement. The worse kind of conference seating, stones instead of chairs, the wide-open scenery instead of a screen. A succession of low grunts reverberated, a cavernous beast summoning guttural rage.

"Remember what I said about moving." Manley's voice oozed oil but held the sting of a whip. "This is your last chance to arm yourselves and help with dinner."

Mona Lasher was the fastest to pick up her stone, probably at last emboldened to throw it at Manley, and saw the weapon on the grass. People bent to pick up sheathed knives, their undulations like a wave at a sports stadium, except nobody was cheering. Some slipped the sheath back on after seeing the wicked sharp ten-inch blade. Desi Kapoor belonged to the rest who kept their blades exposed. He gripped the handle with both hands that couldn't stop shaking.

The grunts came closer in our ear. Fangs, Sal, and a few others pulled their earpieces out to better hear the thudding earth. A half mile away, the slanting moonlight caught the ivory tusks, curved to vanishing knifepoints.

Manley's fat belly strained with the effort of raising his compound bow. He wouldn't have seen the black raging figure. Any illusion of movement came from trembling oak trees rather than a creature running at full tilt. But the drone above was feeding satellite views to his watch, because Manley was a coward who doped horses and chained prey.

Manley fired his bow.

Everyone strained for the scream that never came. Manley fired another arrow.

The black dot grew into a shape, an impossibly large bulbous shape that had to be a trick of moonlight and torches. Manley lowered his bow, then raised it again. The arrow released with a *thwang*, because Manley was enough of an asshole to add sound effects to the silent compound bow.

The grunts grew loud, bouncing inside our own skulls. Its breathing was the blood rushing to our ears, its hooves our hearts pounding against our ribs. I smelled the sulfurous tang of fear.

The shape took form.

Black needlelike hide covered a rear the size of an elephant's, except no elephant moved at this speed. Its legs, short compared to its girth, galloped with the soundless grace of a horse. In thirty seconds the creature had covered thirty yards, barely hobbled by an iron band clasped around its rear leg, the chain flying straight like a second tail.

"Fuck you," Manley muttered. He let loose four arrows with their *thwang*. One arrow buried itself in a shoulder, another making a shallow hit on the animal's side when it turned from the impact of the first. It stumbled, panting grunts, thirty yards shy of the horseshoe perimeter of human bodies. Knives slipped from the grip of the luckless bastards on the outer edge, but nobody dared move.

The creature's wobble was only momentary. Blood pulsed like a waterfall from its shoulder. It swung its terrible tusks. Someone choked off a shriek. It moved toward the sound, then jerked away as though bouncing off a wall. Its massive head shook, and like a guided missile, it ran right into the horseshoe straight at Manley.

At last. At last.

"Fuck, fuck, fuck." Manley's curses were a chant as he fired off a volley of shots. This time people did drop, curling up to dodge arrows aimed within the horseshoe. Rivulets of blood now sprang from the creature, staining the grass.

When it came within a distance of ten yards, Manley spun around. He cut through the gap between Sal and Mona, then turned to run alongside the perimeter. He was keeping the bodies of his guests and their upturned knives a terrified barrier between himself and his bleeding, monstrous prey.

It turned its head. Those who were still standing dropped to their knees, Manley's instructions and terror still gripping their throats, keeping them silent. The creature pivoted, retracing its path. Above, a drone turned sharply overhead.

"Stop this fucking thing." The grunting pants coming through the earpiece came from Manley. "Bleed the fucker, you assholes."

I hoped there would be takers, fools who would throw themselves at a three-hundred-pound boar with eviscerating tusks and make a human shish kebab. But even if they had tried, the boar would have evaded them. Gotten away from the pungent lion-pee repellent that had been applied during their lava scrubs.

And the boar's single-minded sense of smell, keener than a deer's, would keep on the scent of her slaughtered piglet that lingered on Manley's trademark orange cashmere hoodie, which he'd worn all five days.

The drone fired a bullet between the boar's red-rimmed eyes.

She fell, shaking the earth.

It was the autonomous car coming to save Manley that hit his fat frame and tossed his broken body.

I ran then, out of breath even before I'd taken a step, and reached his side. Blood was staining the grass, slower than the sow's but as relentless. His eyes were fluttering, fighting against the dying light. I knelt, glad to feel his blood slick underneath my knees. I closed my fist over his earpiece and pried it away, shutting out his last words.

"What the fuck," he slurred. I put my face close so he could see me, his wife, soon to be a widow a few days before my twenty-first birthday.

"Thank you for my birthday gift," I said. The shouts were closing in. The beating rotors of a helicopter kicked up a furious wind. There would be first aid and drugs to induce him into a coma. They would try to save him. I covered his body, a supplicant weeping wife, to shield the last signs of life.

"Birthday?" He could barely say the word. Manley always forgot my birthday, maybe the better to forget I'd been seventeen when we married. I sobbed, to stop the burble of laughter.

"Fuck you, Manley. I got my own gift."

The helicopter crew had to take several moments to pry me off before they could airlift Manley's body.

I stood. The guests had left their positions but done little else except wander in stunned shock. Manley was right. They were good at doing nothing.

I walked to the sow. The Samoan pit crew at the ready hadn't moved her, hadn't known what to do either. I put on Manley's earpiece, still damp with sweat.

"Take it to the fryer. Our feast is now a funeral. Let us celebrate Manley's life."

Someone pointed overhead. The first of one hundred Chinese lanterns floated to the sky. Typical Manley: everything had been timed, wildfire danger be damned. I gave no orders to countermand. This was his pyre, although his body would be on ice, for eternal cryopreservation. Or until the Bitcoin payments had been devalued.

We could smell the perfume of the sow's charred flesh before we saw her, wheeled out atop a tray balanced on two more self-driving cars. The skin crackled.

With our clutched knives, we dove into our midnight feast and ate like the animals we were.

THE DIAMOND VANISHES
By Gigi Pandian

"The séance will begin when the clock strikes midnight,"
Sanjay said. The candles flickered around him, casting
violent shadows across his already grave face. "I cannot over-
emphasize the importance of this. Do you all understand?"

Five heads nodded, their faces visible to various degrees in
the shadows, but no one spoke. The only sound was so faint I
couldn't be entirely sure it was real. Floating through the air, a
ghostly violin played a mournful melody that hovered beyond
the grasp of my memory.

I didn't exactly shiver, but in the dimly lit room where
electric lighting was forbidden for the evening, the words
struck me as ominous. I knew it was a performance and nothing more, but I didn't like that I'd been thrust into the situation blind, only an hour before.

"Do you want one of us to set an alarm on our cell phones?"
asked a man who strode into the room, his phone screen shining brightly. "Or will the spirits be offended that my phone
only has a setting for twelve o'clock, not 'the witching hour'?"

This must be Gage Bradford, our host's husband. The harsh
light of the screen and snarky cadence of his questions broke

through the ghostly setting, ruining the carefully crafted experience we had stepped into when we walked through the front door of the Bradfords' home. I was torn between appreciating a break from the oppressive atmosphere and being angry about the disruption of my friend's performance.

Sanjay's eyelids lowered almost imperceptibly, changing his expression from one of measured theatrical authority to that of pissed-off performer. Which, to those who didn't know Sanjay as well as I did, would have been barely noticeable. He was good at hiding his true feelings onstage. Even though we weren't in a theater with rows of seats, that's exactly what this whole house was tonight. At least this wing.

"I'll take care of gathering everyone together five minutes before midnight," Sanjay said, "to ensure we're in place at the séance table, so don't go far. And *thank you*, Gage, for reminding me about cell phones. You can leave each of your phones with the butler now."

The smirk hovering on Gage's lips turned to a frown.

His wife, Anika, laughed and placed a gloved hand on his chest. "You can live without your phone for an hour, can't you, dear? Technology will disrupt the connection with the spirits, remember?" She plucked the phone from his hand. The screen went dark.

Gage eyed the butler, who wasn't a butler at all but their gardener, Marco, whom Anika had hired for added atmosphere for tonight's performance. He'd let us into the house earlier tonight and was now serving drinks in the living room—which we were calling the drawing room for the evening. In about half an hour, we'd be ushered into Gage's study, which had been converted into a conservatory with a round table for the séance.

"Might I point out that there's music playing," Gage said. "Unless you've got a string quartet hidden behind the bar, your little game isn't very consistent, is it?"

"The violin concerto will be finished a few minutes to midnight," Sanjay said diplomatically, "when my own phone goes into the bag with the others."

"Who wants another martini?" Marco the gardener-cum-butler asked. "I'm trading drinks for phones. I make hella good martinis."

Sanjay made a *tsk*ing sound.

"Um." The gardener/butler cleared his throat and continued. "I mean, ladies and gentlemen, may I serve you a drink of your choosing?" He bowed. As he raised his head, he caught my eye and winked.

The guests headed to Marco with varying degrees of enthusiasm. I remained behind in the corner of a room with a grand piano. Although Anika and Gage Bradford didn't actually call their rooms things like "conservatory" or "drawing room," their home really was more of a mansion than a house. Located in the Oakland hills across the bay from San Francisco, the sprawling craftsman was nestled into the hillside. When I'd arrived in the darkness of a moonless night, it had struck me how appropriate their house was for a séance.

I watched the little group from my dark corner. I'd been briefly introduced to Anika and her sister's small family upon my arrival. The thing that struck me most about Anika Bradford wasn't her abundant curly brown hair that reached several inches below her shoulders or the large diamond on her finger, but the prominent dark circles under her eyes. They looked deeper than the work of just a couple of sleepless nights. The makeup she'd used in an attempt to cover them up hadn't been successful.

Her sister Libby had similar curls, and neither woman was much taller than my five feet. Libby's teenage daughter Camden was about a head taller than all of us, as was her father, Luca.

Inside, the house was even more sprawling than it appeared on the outside, and Sanjay had set the scene perfectly. The rooms were illuminated only with candlelight, which served the purpose of disguising whatever Sanjay had in store for the night.

While Marco fixed drinks for the six guests, Sanjay joined me in the shadows.

"I can't believe I'm so broke I'm taking fake séance gigs," Sanjay muttered as he checked the perfectly pressed cuffs of his tux. The living room—sorry, the *drawing room*—was large enough that we had privacy in the corner by the piano.

"Having to fly economy rather than first class doesn't count as broke," I said. "And you promised you'd tell me why I'm here crashing this private party."

"Jaya, you know the Hindi Houdini can't be seen flying coach."

I hated it when my best friend referred to himself in the third person. He only did it when using his stage name, the Hindi Houdini, not his real name, Sanjay Rai. But still.

"Right," I said. "And how many times have you been stopped by a fan on an airplane?"

"A good performer should always be prepared."

"Then why did you invite me at the last minute?"

He sighed. "You weren't part of the initial plan. When Anika hired me, she told me she wanted to invite six people.

With the two of us, that made eight. So of course I told her that was a perfect number of people around the séance table. I didn't count on how seriously she was getting into this. After two of her friends canceled at the last minute, she insisted I find two substitutes. Apparently her friend's partner got freaked out about the idea of a séance happening at midnight, and they had a huge fight about it at dinner tonight. So you and Tamarind are filling in."

"What would you have done if I had other plans?" I asked. "At midnight?"

"It's conceivable."

"Did you?"

"I'm here, aren't I? So I really don't have to do anything?"

"Aside from being a warm body at the séance table, no. I still can't believe Tamarind talked me into this sham spook session. It's embarrassing."

"And very meta. The woman who hired you knows you're a fake yet insists you have to treat this like it's real, even in all of your interactions with her."

He groaned.

"At least it's for a good cause," I reminded him.

"No, it's not." He lowered his voice. "A good cause is the homelessness charity performance you helped me with before. Not helping save the marriage of a wealthy couple by giving them an adrenaline-boosting, 'fun-frightening' experience in a controlled environment. Still . . ."

"Still what?"

"I don't know. There's something odd about this setup."

"Aren't you the one who did this candlelight decor?"

"Yeah, with Marco's help."

"You aren't spooking yourself, are you?"

He grunted. "I've worked for enough rich clients to know they can be eccentric. Tamarind said Anika was good people, though. But get this." He lowered his voice to nearly a whisper. "Anika Bradford even gave me the ghost story she wanted me to use at the séance. She thinks it'll be extra fun, in a watching-a-horror-movie kind of way, because *the history of this ghost is real.*"

I stared at him for a moment, then laughed. "You're good, Sanjay. I know you better than anyone, and I could have sworn you weren't joking."

"Because I'm not. The ghost *itself* isn't real, of course. But the story is. A woman killed herself in this house about a hundred years ago. The messed-up history is true."

It was my turn to groan. "You realize what's happening, don't you? The plan about saving her marriage through an activity that gets them scared together is a ruse. *She believes in the ghost.* In this old house, I'm sure there are all sorts of creaky noises. Didn't you see how nervous she was? And her eyes. She looks like she hasn't slept in weeks."

"Nah," Sanjay said. "That can't be it."

I watched the small group on the other side of the room. Anika and her husband stood at the bar where the butler-bartender was mixing them drinks in a cocktail shaker. Nearby, her sister Libby was talking with Luca. Libby and Luca's teenage daughter stood a few feet away, looking at a painting on the wall. No, that wasn't right. She was only pretending to look at the painting. She was actually watching Anika and Gage. Was that fear I saw in her eyes as she looked at her uncle?

"What are you two kids talking about?" Tamarind sashayed up to us and handed me a martini in an elegant long-stemmed glass. She took a sip from her own glass. In the candlelight, the glass reflected the colors of her red corduroy skirt and purple combat boots. My own black dress and black ballet flats stayed hidden in the shadows.

"Magic," Sanjay said, handing Tamarind a daisy that appeared out of thin air.

Her kohl-lined eyes widened as she sniffed it. "Real. Impressive."

"Did you expect anything less?" he asked. "That's why you recommended me to Anika, isn't it?"

"Yeah, but I wish you hadn't roped me into it as well. I feel like a third wheel over there with her family. Sixth wheel, I suppose, if you want to get technical about it."

"I owe you two," he said. "Thanks for coming at the last minute."

"You're lucky I was having a late dinner at Oeste in Oakland already," Tamarind said. "I didn't have to make a trip across the bridge."

"How exactly do you know Anika and Gage?" I asked.

"You think they don't look like my usual friends?" she asked in a deadpan voice, then grinned and stuck out her tongue at me.

"You don't have a *usual*. You've got the strangest assortment of friends I've ever known anyone to have."

"I'll take that as the compliment that it is."

Tamarind Ortega was a librarian at the university where I taught history. She was brilliant, but she knew she'd also been hired in part for her people skills. Meaning her ability to deal with people in our San Francisco neighborhood who wandered into the library in distress. She had a tough exterior that showed she wasn't to be messed with and not *exactly* a cream-puff interior, but she was good at talking to people across all social strata, from the homeless folks to people like Anika and Gage Bradford.

"I met Anika at a bookbinding workshop," Tamarind continued, after taking another sip of her martini, "at the San Francisco Center for the Book. Oh, you should totally ask her about this rare book in her collection. It's a novel involving the Koh-i-Noor diamond. The book was published in the late 1800s, around when *The Moonstone* came out. *And* it's not in the library system. I checked. If you haven't guessed yet, she's way cooler than her hubby." She lowered her voice. "Honestly, I'm not sure why she's trying to save her marriage. Unless it's so she doesn't lose this amazing house in a divorce. Look at all the built-in bookshelves. Anika constructed them herself. I know she loves this place, but Gage is the kind of guy who'd steal it out from under her. Or bulldoze it down the middle if he failed. This is only like one of six houses he owns."

I followed Tamarind's longing gaze to the handcrafted bookshelves that lined one wall of the living room—er, *drawing* room. The only prefabricated bookcase was a small one in the corner by the entryway, filled with paperback novels and travel guidebooks with well-cracked spines. Filling the rest of the room were Anika's custom-made wooden shelves showcasing books that looked old and full of history, especially in the dim light. I wouldn't be able to read them in this light, even if I had time and permission, but I was especially curious about the Koh-i-Noor diamond book. The diamond, one of the largest in the world, was part of the British Crown Jewels in the Tower of London. It had originally been discovered in India, where it had passed brutally from ruler to ruler— stolen, traded, or given as a gift under duress—never sold for money. From my research on British India, I knew its story well. Including its curse. A twelfth-century legend about the Koh-i-Noor diamond said, *He who owns the diamond will own the world, but will also know all its misfortunes. Only God, or a woman, can wear it with impunity.*

I had to get a closer look. "Want to see if we can find that Koh-i-Noor book?"

Sanjay *tsk*ed, but Tamarind bit her lip and grinned.

We approached the central bookshelf, but it was such a big room that we were stopped before we reached it, as we were illuminated by the light of a large candlelit silver candelabra.

"I don't think you met my husband Gage," Anika said to me. This was the spot in the room with the most light, which allowed me to see the dark circles under Anika's eyes even more clearly. Her figure was also more gaunt than I'd noticed when we'd first been introduced. It hadn't been immediately obvious because she wore a billowing gray shawl over a gray sweater and slacks. All the women in the family were dressed in shades of somber gray, and I was dressed in black as usual. Only Tamarind's bright-red skirt broke up the subdued colors in the room.

"Thanks for rounding out our little circle for my wife's fanciful game." Gage extended his hand to me. "You met the rest of the party? Good. I was otherwise occupied when you arrived. Gage Bradford."

"Jaya Jones."

He frowned. "I know your name."

"Duh," Tamarind muttered.

"Excuse me?" Gage's ears were sharp.

"D'of course," Tamarind said. "That's what I was saying. Of course you know Jaya's name. She's a local celebrity. A history professor who's found hella treasures."

"Oh." Gage gave a curt nod and eyed me skeptically. I got that a lot. People tended to think I was a fortune hunter (which I wasn't) or lived the life of Indiana Jones (which was more true than I sometimes wanted to admit to myself).

"Didn't I read that you laid a ghost to rest?" he continued, leaning forward into my personal space. "Are you going to solve the mystery of our ghost, Miss Jaya Jones?"

That was an odd thing for him to say. Surely he was making a joke.

"Oh!" Anika's niece Camden ran up to us.

"She's way too young to be here," Sanjay whispered in my ear. "I didn't know that when I planned my script."

I wasn't so sure she was too young. It wasn't her height that swayed my opinion, even though she was far taller than her mother. It was the watchful expression on her face I'd noticed. She was an only child, and I bet she'd grown up observing. I guessed her to be thirteen years old. Old enough to separate fact from fiction, even if she hadn't looked more world-wary than she should have at a young age.

"I've read about you," Camden said, openly studying me. "Aunt Anika, you just introduced her as Jaya. Not Dr. Jaya Anand Jones."

"Let's not get distracted, dear," her mother Libby said, pulling Camden back. "Let's get you another soda before we move into the séance room."

"It's a quarter till the bewitching hour," Sanjay said. "Ten minutes to use the powder room and finish your drinks."

191

I followed Camden to the bar, where Marco was fixing her a shaken ginger ale. I was glad her mother hadn't gone with her so I could talk with her on her own.

"Are you sure you want to sit through the séance?" I asked her.

"Are you asking if I know it's fake?"

"Give me more credit than that," I said. "You've got enough common sense to know it is."

She grinned. "Should be fun. As long as I don't have to sit next to my uncle." Her grin faded, replaced by a mask, but the change in expression lasted only a moment before she shook herself and continued. "It's about time my aunt did something sweet with all the old stuff they've got in the house."

"Like these antique books on the shelves?"

"I didn't mean the books. Old books are *fire*. I'm rereading Edgar Allan Poe right now. Have you read him?"

Anika wrapped her arm around Camden's shoulder. "I hope my niece isn't bothering you."

"Not at all. We're discussing books. Tamarind mentioned you've got a rare book about the Koh-i-Noor diamond. I'd love to see it."

Anika smiled. "I think your friend would have a heart attack if I turned on enough light for you to see it properly. But how about a rain check? I definitely want you to see it."

"I'd love that."

The violin music stopped. Sanjay slid his phone into the satchel with the others.

Anika set her half-empty martini glass on the bar, but it was too close to the edge. The glass tumbled toward the floor, splashing the last of its liquid onto an ornate rug. It rolled onto its side with a shard missing.

"Foolish woman," Gage muttered as Anika flinched.

"No harm done," Marco said. "It's a clean break, and I'll clean it up. You can all go inside."

"Wait, I misplaced my handbag," Libby said.

"I'm sure it's fine, Mom," Camden said. "We're the only ones in the house."

"I meant that I wanted my lipstick. My lips are chapped because it's so cold in the house." She glared at Sanjay.

"It's the spirits, madame," he said, never breaking character. "I had no hand in the temperature. But their presence is near. We should go inside the conservatory, where the séance will commence in four minutes—"

"You look out here," Anika said. "I'll check the other rooms for your purse. I won't be a moment."

"A bit of electric light would come in handy . . ." Gage mumbled.

"You could just use Camden's lip balm," Luca suggested to his wife. "The medium looks like he's going to have a conniption if we wait any longer."

"Good idea." She accepted her daughter's egg-shaped lip balm. "But I still don't like not knowing where my purse is. Be a dear and look for just another minute?"

Luca kissed her nose and went to look in the dark corners of the drawing room.

"Two minutes," Sanjay's voice called, but I didn't see where he was.

"Found Mom's purse," Camden called out, lifting a leather handbag from behind the couch.

"Good," Sanjay said, giving me a start as he appeared at my side. "We can delay no longer."

As I stepped into the séance room, my breath caught. There was only one candle burning. It was difficult to see, leaving just enough light to make it feel as if we were stepping into the set of a horror movie. Wild tendrils of ivy crept along two walls. Anika was already seated at the table, her voluminous gray shawl swaying slightly in the breeze that must have come from a window Sanjay had left open to make sure the room was cold. No, that wasn't right. The window wasn't open, and the curtain was drawn.

"Take the hands of the person in the chair next to you," Sanjay said. "Whatever happens, do not break contact."

"What if my nose itches?" Gage asked.

"When the spirits come," Sanjay said, his voice strangely calm, "you won't remember anything about the mortal world. Hurry. There's a chair for each of you." He blew out the candle.

Everyone gasped. Even me. We were in complete darkness.

A clock chimed twelve from somewhere above us. That was why he'd been rushing.

"We're gathered here tonight," Sanjay began, after the echo of the last chime ended, "in this haunted house, to attempt to lay its spirits to rest. One spirit in particular. Most of you know the history of the house. For those of you who don't, as well as to show the spirit we understand her pain, I will share the key details. A woman of singular brilliance once lived here. Gage is one of her descendants. She collected rare books and wrote splendid novels herself, including a Gothic novel about the curse of the Koh-i-Noor diamond. The diamond that has brought death and destruction to many rulers in both India and Britain but brings peace to women.

"But her husband claimed the novel as his own," Sanjay continued, "and she never got the attention she deserved during her lifetime. A lifetime that was cut short when she hung herself in the attic. This very attic directly above us." He shifted uncomfortably, and I knew he was thinking of Camden. I could have told him he needn't have worried.

The faint sound of squeaking, like a rope tugging at a rusty hook, sounded from far above our heads. Around the table, several voices gasped. Luca's hand tightened in my left palm. Sanjay's hand didn't, so I knew it was one of his effects.

"Could that be her?" Sanjay continued in a whisper. "Diana Bradford took her last breath directly over our heads."

A deep voice swore under his breath. "We do not speak her name in this house, Houdini," Gage said, not disguising the rage in his voice. "Anika—you know we shouldn't—"

"*Shh!*" Multiple voices cut him off.

"That's why her spirit haunts this house," Sanjay said. "Her fictitious Koh-i-Noor diamond could not save her from his treachery. Diana! Diana, we feel your anguish descending! Diana, are you with us?"

The squeaking from above grew louder. I knew it was part of the act, but still I shivered.

"Stop that, Gage," Tamarind whispered. "You're going to break my fingers."

The sound changed. It was no longer above us. Now it was *below*. A solid object scraped across the floor. Multiple voices at the table gasped. Both of the hands in mine tightened.

"Diana?" Sanjay said again, now with a slight tremor in his voice. "Is that you?"

Thump. A pause. *Thump.* A pause. *Thump.*

"*Help me.*"

The words were barely above a whisper.

Goose bumps started on my forearms and spread. *That voice.* It didn't sound like Sanjay's. It also hadn't come from where he sat next to me. Where he sat squeezing my hand so hard it began to lose feeling.

I squared my shoulders. I reminded myself he was a master performer. He'd escaped from a coffin at the bottom of the Ganges and performed the fabled Indian rope trick on an outdoor stage in Japan. He could handle setting up and hiding an audio recording in a private home. And acting scared himself would make the performance more believable.

"Diana?" Sanjay repeated, his voice remaining slightly unsteady.

"*My books,*" the raspy whisper croaked. "*He stole my books.*"

A sharp intake of breath came from my right side. I knew that gasp. Sanjay. Why was he gasping?

"*Must take . . .*" The voice was so faint now that I might have imagined it. "*Must take them back. And a friend. Need a friend.*"

"Aunt Anika," whispered Camden. "I don't think this is—"

"*Shh.*"

"She's right," Gage said. "This farce has gone too—" He broke off as the sound of something being dragged across the hardwood floor began again. I felt my skin prickle up to the top of my head.

Thud. A heavy piece of furniture crashed to the floor. A woman screamed. Gage swore and mumbled something about his floor being damaged.

Sanjay pulled his hand away from mine. "Somebody get the lights," he commanded.

"What about disturbing the spirits?" Gage's voice. "If that's all we get for the amount of money my wife paid you—"

"I'm not kidding," Sanjay said. "Can you find the light switch? I've covered it with painter's tape, but if you know where—"

I stood and grabbed at the sturdy table. I couldn't see any better than I had five minutes before. There was truly no light in the room. I flinched as the lights came on. I squinted, forcing my eyes to remain open. Camden stood with her hand on the light switch, a blue piece of painter's tape dangling from the plastic.

I was glad I hadn't decided to make it to the switch myself. An upturned chair was right in front of me. That must have been the piece of furniture that had been thrown to the floor and shocked Sanjay into interrupting the séance. He wasn't the one who'd done it.

"Who fell over?" Tamarind asked, crossing her arms. "No judgment. I nearly pushed myself away from the table too. Come on, guys. Seriously."

I looked from Tamarind to Luca, standing with his wife. Camden still stood at the light switch. She was grinning, and I guessed she wished she had her phone to document the adults who'd been freaked out by a fake séance.

"Anika?" Gage said. "Anika! This isn't funny, *darling*. I know this is your game, but really, disappearing isn't amusing. I've indulged you quite enough."

Tamarind swore. I whipped my head around the room. Unlike the drawing room, Gage's study—er, *conservatory*— was small. We would have seen Anika Bradford if she was in the room. And we didn't.

"Is this part of your little performance, Houdini?" Gage spat out the name.

"Someone," Sanjay said, looking from one of us to the next, "hijacked it."

"That wasn't your voice," I said. Which explained why he'd tensed during the illusion that wasn't his.

He shook his head. "The scraping noises from above and the breeze and knocking sounds inside the room were me. And no, I'm not telling you how I did it. But that voice?" Sanjay shuddered. "It had to be one of you."

"You just admitted you're a fraud," Gage said. "I'm not paying for this."

"I don't care what you do." Sanjay squatted and slid open a wooden box hidden under the table, stood up with a shake of his head, then pulled back the curtains. "As long as you help me look for your wife. This isn't part of the act. Anika isn't hiding. She's vanished."

* * *

Gage yanked open the door. The dozens of candles in the drawing room were still burning strongly. How had Anika opened the door without us seeing the light?

"Where is she?" Gage demanded of Marco.

"Who?"

"Don't be a—"

"My sister," Libby said, stepping between them. "Anika slipped out of the room. That has to have been what happened."

"Nah, she didn't," Marco said. "Sanjay—sorry, I mean *the Hindi Houdini*—"

"Use my real name," Sanjay said. "Show's over. I know it barely started. But something's happened." He ran a hand through his thick black hair and scanned the room. "This is an old house," he said, mostly to himself.

"You're thinking a secret passageway?" I asked.

He nodded.

"You've been holding out on me?" Camden asked, scowling at her parents. "I could have played in a secret passageway when we visited—"

"There are no secret passageways." A vein bulged at the side of Gage's temple. "Marco, turn on the damn lights!"

"No offense," Tamarind said. "No, I *do* mean offense. If you hired someone to sneak into the room and make off with Anika, you wouldn't admit there was a secret passageway."

"Uncle Gage?" Camden gaped at him as her father glared at him.

"Has everyone lost their minds?" Gage shouted. "My wife is unstable. She doesn't sleep. She thought a séance would be *fun*, and she blatantly disregarded my family's wishes of not uttering the name of *that woman*—" He paused to glare at Sanjay. "She's playing a practical joke on us."

"You did this." Libby's voice shook. "What have you done with my sister?"

"Don't be ridiculous," Gage shouted. "I'll call her on her—damn." He felt his empty pocket. "Marco, where are our phones?"

"In that bag on the shelf . . ." Marco's voice trailed off as he reached an empty space on the shelf.

"Where?" Gage barked.

"I swear it was right there." Marco lifted several books and a potted plant. "I really don't know where it could have gone."

For the next half hour we searched the sprawling house. All of us except Marco, who stayed at his post outside the séance room. We found no sign of Anika and no evidence of secret panels or passageways. The bag of cell phones never showed up either.

"I'm telling you," Marco said, "it's impossible. I was here in the living room the whole time you were in that séance room. Nobody came out."

"I'm supposed to take the word of a gardener who never finished college?"

"Hey, I've got an MFA. But what the hell does a degree have to do with trusting me?"

"You don't have to take his word for it," I said. "Though I do believe him. If anything in that room opened—the door or the window—we would have noticed the light."

"Diana's spirit," Libby whispered. "It said it needed a friend."

"Maybe Anika is still hiding in the room," Tamarind suggested. "That table and bookshelves are really sturdy, and Anika is a little tiny thing."

We rushed back into the room. I stepped around the fallen chair. It was a heavy chair like the kind you'd set at a dining table. Seven of the chairs matched, but one was a folding chair.

"Did you break one of the chairs in your set?" I asked Gage.

"You owe me a new chair, Sanjay Houdini." Gage stuck his finger at Sanjay before picking up the overturned chair. He looked almost disappointed when he said, "It appears fine. That's why buying high-quality furniture is important." He righted it and looked at the floor for scratches.

Tamarind snorted. "I can tell how concerned you are about your wife."

"I wasn't talking about *that* chair," I said before the two of them began fighting. "I meant that one." I pointed at a flimsy folding chair.

"Anika is careless," Gage said. "She must've broken one of the set and not mentioned it to me."

"Do you have a landline?" Sanjay asked.

"Of course not," Gage said. "But I doubt she'll answer her cell phone if we call her."

"That's not what I meant," Sanjay said. "I think we should call the police. Your wife might have been kidnapped." He pointed to something none of us had noticed before. A small streak of something that looked like fresh blood, about the size of my little finger, stretched across the windowsill. How had we missed that?

Sanjay slipped on thin cotton gloves from his pocket that he often used in his act and pushed on the window. It was locked and didn't budge. He unlatched it, and it squeaked loudly in protest as he edged it open a few inches. He inspected the window pane itself for a few moments, then turned back to us and shook his head.

Gage threw his head back and looked toward the ceiling. "Has everyone gone mad? She hasn't been kidnapped. That's food coloring or something. She's playing a joke on us. On me." He stormed back into the living room.

"That's weird," Tamarind said. "Not the part about Anika wanting to play a cruel joke on Gage—that's totally understandable. Laudable, I'd argue. But the books. Look. Now that the light is on in the living room, I can tell something is weird about the books."

"Someone moved the books?" Sanjay asked. "You think the shelf slides . . ." He inspected the wall behind the shelves.

"Not moved the books," Tamarind said. "Messed with them."
"I don't see—"
"Trust me. I'm a librarian."
"You're right," I said, touching the spine showing *The Koh-i-Noor Disappearance*. Something was off about the antique book. As I lifted the book from the shelf, it vanished in my hands.

* * *

The book didn't disappear completely. But the spine crumpled inward in my hand, because the inside was completely hollow. A hiding place? No, it was too flimsy for that.

"What the—" Tamarind picked up the book next to it. "Empty!"

"These aren't real books?" Camden picked one up.

"Stupid girl." Gage yanked the book from Camden's hand. "This is a rare book that needs to be handled—aah!" He dropped the book as if it were covered in spiders.

"Don't you touch her," Luca said, shoving Gage away from his daughter.

Gage hit the floor—next to the frame of the book. "Where did they go?" He scrambled to his feet, ignoring Luca in favor of his collection of rare books. "Gone." He squashed the casings of another book. Then another. "They're all gone!"

"The spirit of your ancestor," Libby said. "Do you remember what she said?"

Gage's face was pale. "No," he whispered. "It can't be."

"She said she wanted a friend," I answered, "and that she was going to take her books back."

"The ghost has taken my sister and her books."

* * *

None of Gage's neighbors would open their door at one o'clock in the morning for him, so we resorted to driving down the hill to a convenience store to use a phone to call the police. The police weren't much help, because Anika had been gone less than an hour, and what could a reasonable person do with the ghost story they'd just been told? They were more interested in Gage's temper and the blood on the windowsill.

We found the bag of cell phones, including Anika's, inside the bureau next to the front door of the house. There was no trace of Anika herself.

When I woke up the next morning, a text message from Sanjay informed me that Anika hadn't reappeared. I'd gotten only a few hours of sleep, but Sanjay promised strong coffee if I came over before I had to be on campus.

"You don't think Sanjay really conjured the spirit of the woman who killed herself a century ago, do you?" Tamarind asked. "You saw how scared Gage was. He tried to cover it up with gravitas, or whatever the jerk version of that is, but he believed in Diana's ghost."

Sanjay, Tamarind, and I were sitting next to one of the full-length windows of Sanjay's San Francisco apartment, watching the rain beat down outside from a storm that had blown in overnight. In the daylight, as I savored a cup of strong, sugary coffee with friends, the events of the night before felt otherworldly.

"I didn't conjure any spirits." Sanjay fiddled with the rim of his bowler hat. "But . . ."

"Are you telling me that the great Hindi Houdini hasn't figured it out?" I asked.

Sanjay gripped the rim tighter. "You know where she is?"

"I don't know exactly where she is," I said, "but I think I know how she did it."

"*The ghost?*" Tamarind whispered.

"Not the ghost," I said. "Anika herself."

"You suspect that too?" Sanjay asked.

"What are you two talking about?" Tamarind looked back and forth between us.

"It was a good plan," Sanjay said. "Using me as the distraction."

"She wanted to get away from her abusive husband in a way that cast doubt about what happened," I said, "giving her time to get away. He was physically abusive too. The dark circles under her eyes had makeup on them, which I assumed at the time was a poor attempt to cover dark circles from sleeplessness—but I think what was really going on was that one of them was *painted* on. She wasn't able to fully cover up a black eye with makeup, so she essentially gave herself two, so they'd look like dark circles with poorly applied makeup."

"Shut. Up," Tamarind murmured.

"And she took a bookbinding class with you," I continued.

"Oh my God." Tamarind's eyes grew wide. "She made those fake shells of books!"

I nodded. "She got the real books out of the house before the séance. No doubt with whatever else she wanted to take with her, but the empty shelves would have been an obvious giveaway that the books were missing."

"But you two are forgetting," Tamarind said, "that she disappeared from a room that was essentially sealed by light and sound. We would have seen if she slipped out through the door and heard if she left through the window."

"You're right that it *looked* impossible for anyone to get out of that room," Sanjay said.

"But it wasn't if she was never in the room in the first place," I said.

"Of course she was." Tamarind scowled at me. "We saw her in there—"

"We saw a woman from the back with similar hair and gray clothing."

"Her sister," Tamarind whispered.

"Remember all of the confusion right as we were taking our seats?" Sanjay said. "There were two distractions as I was trying to get everyone together. First, Anika spilled her drink and broke a glass. Second, Libby couldn't find her purse. Marco went to get something to clean up the mess, and everyone was running around. Nobody can swear where anyone else was at a given time. When we finally went into the séance room, a woman with curly brown hair, dressed in flowing gray fabrics, was already seated with her back to us, in dim light. I'd created that lighting to hide the details of what I had in store, and Anika used that to fit her plan.

"What I haven't put together yet," Sanjay continued, "is that as we sat down around the table together, everyone was holding each other's hands. There were no extra chairs. I would have noticed."

"Maybe," Tamarind said, "she had an automaton version of herself that combusted and left no trace except for the chair. When it combusted, it knocked over the chair. Huh? That could be it."

"The chair is key," I agreed. "Remember one of the chairs was a folding chair."

Sanjay swore.

"You see now?" I asked.

He nodded. "Only *seven* of us sat down at the table. Not eight. The eighth chair, the folding one, was folded up under the big table."

"By Anika's accomplice Libby," I said, "when she slipped into the room during the distractions."

"Groupings of seven and eight people are similar enough that it's easy to assume what you're expecting to see," Sanjay said. "I've used a similar misdirection in one of my stage acts, so I should have seen it sooner."

"I'm glad you didn't," Tamarind said. "This way she gets away from her abusive husband with her books and whatever else she planned to take with her."

"They planned it well," I said. "Anika never came back after she went to look for her sister's handbag."

Sanjay shook his head. "She and her sister are better at misdirection than I am."

"Out of desperation," I said. "You do it for entertainment. They did it out of necessity."

* * *

Three months later, a rare edition of a nineteenth-century edition of *The Diamond Vanishes*, a novel about the Koh-i-Noor diamond, was donated to a local museum. I received an invitation to attend the opening reception of the rare books exhibit where it was being featured.

I wasn't worried about running into Gage Bradford. Ever since the police had discovered that it was indeed Anika's blood on the windowsill and that a large chunk of money had been paid from Gage's private bank account the week before to an untraceable account, he'd been staying out of the public eye. Based on the strength of his team of attorneys, he hadn't been formally charged with a crime, but he'd moved into one of his other houses in a more secluded area away from prying eyes and given the Oakland house to Libby and her family. Most people thought it was a public gesture of goodwill, but I wondered if it was because Gage truly believed in the ghost of Diana Bradford.

The theme of the museum's event was unsung heroes of history. New historical documents showed that *The Diamond Vanishes* had been written by nineteenth-century local philanthropist Diana Sosa, not her husband Grant Bradford.

I spotted three familiar faces in the crowd before they saw me.

Libby and Luca were deep in conversation, but their daughter Camden saw me and ducked away from her parents.

"I'm glad she donated it," I said. I had a feeling that when Anika had told me I'd definitely get to see the book, this was what she'd known would happen.

Camden gave me a hesitant smile. "Thanks for not saying anything."

"She's all right?"

Camden grinned. "Better than all right. She's away from Uncle Gage for good. I got a passport this year. I'll see her on vacation this summer."

"Is that safe?" I asked. "A man like Gage has money and connections."

"Mom says he's also the same type of bully as some of the boys I know at school," Camden said. "He's just a frightened little boy who's mean to hide it. Uncle Gage isn't looking for Aunt Anika—he thinks the ghost of his wronged ancestor took her."

"Even with the donation of *The Diamond Vanishes*?"

"That's the best part. You saw that it was donated by a rare-books dealer who said she only now realized what she had? It's a woman my aunt had worked with before who'd also had a bad marriage. Her statement said she had a dream the same night my aunt disappeared, about the book's true author appearing to her. She said she'd forgotten she had the book until that 'dream.' "

"Let me guess," I said, "the book dealer said she had her dream just after midnight."

CAPE MAY MURDERS
By Tina Kashian

Voices woke Sona Simonian at midnight. She didn't believe in nonsense such as haunted houses or ghosts, but nonetheless, someone was whispering outside in the hall of their rented room. Then, just as suddenly, the whispering ceased, and she heard a thump, then a moan.

The hair on her nape stood on end, and she sat up in bed. "What in God's name was that?"

She turned to her roommate, but Priya Patel's bed was empty.

Where was her friend?

Had Priya slipped downstairs because she couldn't sleep?

It wasn't unusual for Priya to seek out the kitchen for a cup of tea. Sona knew Priya had trouble sleeping, of course. They were longtime friends and had met at a playgroup for new mothers at a local hospital. Even though they were from different ethnicities and religions—Priya was Hindu Indian and Sona was Christian Armenian and Lebanese—they had shared their cultures and had instantly bonded over motherhood. Their children—both girls—were now four years old. After a bit of cajoling from their husbands, Sona and Priya had traveled to Cape May at the Jersey Shore for a much needed moms' weekend.

They'd lucked out by finding a vacancy at a lovely Victorian bed-and-breakfast aptly named the Sea Goddess. The house had been built in the early nineteenth century and had a magnificent view of the Atlantic Ocean. The establishment was owned by two fiftysomething refugees from corporate Philadelphia life, Mr. and Mrs. Smith.

So where was Priya now? Was it insomnia that had driven her out of bed? Or had Priya left the room because she'd heard the noises?

Another moan sounded, fainter this time.

Sona slipped out of bed and reached for her robe.

What if someone was hurt? Trying to call for help but unable to do so? Was it Priya?

A cold knot formed in her stomach. Sona hurried to turn the dead bolt and opened the door.

She looked both ways in the hall. Nothing. The other guests were all in their rooms. The newlyweds' door was closed, as was the Axlerods'. Sona knew Mr. and Mrs. Smith had their bedroom at the far end of the hall, and she couldn't see their door from her own bedroom. The moaning had ceased, but then she heard the creak of the staircase floorboards.

"Is anyone there?" she whispered.

Silence.

"Priya?" she whispered, a bit louder this time.

No answer.

She tightened the belt on her robe and headed for the landing, her footsteps silent on the Oriental carpet runner. The faint light of a wall sconce cast an eerie glow on the flocked paper covered walls. Her heart hammered foolishly.

Priya had told her some believed the Victorian-era home was haunted. "The former proprietor died after falling down the winding staircase three decades ago," Priya had said their first day here. "The young newlywed couple next door, the Robinsons, said some believe he was pushed to his death and his spirit haunts the old house." Priya had swallowed and rubbed the elephant-head Hindu god charm of her necklace between her thumb and forefinger, a sure sign that she was nervous. It had been given to her by her husband when they'd gotten engaged. Sona had never seen Priya without it.

Sona had wrinkled her nose and dismissed Priya's concerns. "People always make up stories. It's more likely he had one too many drinks and stumbled," she'd told her friend.

But now, after hearing the strange sounds, Sona wondered if there was a note of truth to Priya's story.

Sona shook her head. *Haunted house be damned. There is no such thing.*

She made it to the top of the staircase, then froze, her hand grasping the banister.

There, at the bottom of the long flight of wooden stairs, a body sprawled facedown. His arms were flung wide and his head was bent at an unnatural angle. As Sona hurried down the stairs, she recognized Mr. Smith, the proprietor. One of his fists was closed tightly around something.

A beam of moonlight from an overhead window reflected off the object, and Sona gasped as she recognized the charm of Priya's necklace.

She placed two fingers to Mr. Smith's neck. There was no pulse.

She screamed.

* * *

The house came to life.

Priya was the first to appear. She ran around the corner, then halted at Sona's side. Her eyes widened as she took in the scene, and her hand covered her mouth. "My God. Is he dead?"

Sona nodded. "I heard whispering, then moaning. I thought someone needed help, and I came to the top of the stairs. That's when I saw him. Where were you?"

"I couldn't sleep. I was in the kitchen fixing myself a cup of tea."

"Did you hear anything?" Sona asked.

Priya shook her head. "No. The kettle started whistling. I only heard your scream."

Doors opened above, and the remaining houseguests for the week, the Axlerods and Robinsons, rushed down the stairs. Amy Axlerod clung to her husband's arm as Samuel Axlerod called the police on his cell phone.

Jim Robinson dropped to his knees by the body. "I know CPR."

"Don't touch him, man!" Samuel shouted. "Can't you see it's too late?"

Last to come down was Mrs. Smith. Her shrill cry made Sona's nerves tense all over again. She clutched the banister as she descended the stairs, her eyes glued to her dead husband. Collapsing by the body, she touched his chest, then began shrieking hysterically.

It took both Jim and Samuel to pry her away. Within minutes, the local police and paramedics arrived. Mr. Smith was declared dead and the county coroner was called.

Priya took Sona's arm and led her away. "Are you sure you're okay? You look deathly pale."

Sona rubbed her temples. "I'm fine . . . just shaken up. I've been to several funerals, but . . . but I've never seen a dead body that wasn't lying inside a casket." She knew she was blabbering, but she couldn't seem to stop.

I must be in shock.

"Slow down and take deep breaths." Priya led Sona away from the gruesome scene and into the kitchen. She pulled out a chair and sat her at the table. "I'll turn on the kettle." She reached for a mug from the cabinet and ripped open a bag of chamomile tea. "My mother always told me that herbal tea calms the nerves."

Sona twisted her hands in her lap as she watched her friend. Priya had dark, straight hair that reached her waist and dark eyes with thick lashes. In contrast, Sona had curly light-brown hair that brushed her shoulders and hazel eyes. "Priya, did you notice that Mr. Smith was clutching your Hindu necklace?"

Priya's hand flew to her neck, and she gasped. "The clasp must have broken."

"You didn't notice it missing?"

"No. I had it after dinner. It must have fallen off sometime last night."

"Why would Mr. Smith have it?" Sona asked.

"I have no idea. Maybe he found it and was planning to return it before he fell."

Their conversation was cut short as the houseguests shuffled into the kitchen and huddled around the table.

The Robinsons, a couple in their early twenties from Philadelphia, were schoolteachers with college debt who could afford only a short trip to Cape May for their honeymoon.

A businessman, Samuel Axlerod was accompanied by his wife, Amy. Sona thought they were the most unlikely couple. Samuel was in his late fifties, with gray at his temples, and Amy appeared to be in her twenties. Tall, thin, and platinum blond, she looked like a fashion model. She raised her teacup, and Sona glimpsed an enormous diamond ring.

Gad! The rock must be at least three carats.

It wasn't the only piece of jewelry the woman had on. An emerald necklace and matching bracelet caught Sona's eye, as did square-cut emerald earrings. The woman was wearing thousands of dollars' worth of gems. Had she slept with them on? Love might be blind, but Amy Axlerod was pretty enough to attract anyone, Sona thought. She couldn't help but wonder if Amy was after Samuel's money.

"The police have secured the scene. No one is allowed in or out of the house," Jim said.

"The head detective is questioning everyone," Samuel said.

"Do you think it was an accident?" Lyn Robinson asked as her husband placed an arm around her shoulder. Of average height, she had short brown hair and brown eyes and wore tortoiseshell glasses.

"What else could it be?" Amy Axlerod asked.

Sona stayed silent. She'd heard voices. Someone had been talking to Mr. Smith before he ended up at the bottom of the stairs. Was it his wife?

Just then, Mrs. Smith appeared in the doorway. Her eyes were red and swollen. Her dyed-auburn hair was mussed as if she'd repeatedly run her fingers through it. She must have dressed quickly in her usual style, as she wore a bright yellow-and-blue Bohemian dress and gladiator sandals. She'd told Sona and Priya that she'd been a corporate lawyer and would be happy if she never had to wear a business suit or pair of panty hose again.

Mrs. Smith's gaze passed over each guest at the table. "I locked all the doors in the house last night, and no one tampered with the locks. My husband was *not* clumsy. Someone in this house pushed him to his death."

* * *

Everyone waited anxiously in the kitchen as the detective questioned the occupants of the house one by one. To everyone's relief, Mrs. Smith remained with a female officer in the parlor.

The kettle was reheated, and a pot of coffee was started. Priya found scones that Mr. Smith had baked—sweet orange, tart lemon, and savory blueberry and cranberry. They weren't dry as expected but moist and delicious. Mr. Smith had been the cook and baker. His wife took care of the rest of the guests' needs. The group nibbled on the pastry and sipped hot beverages around the kitchen table.

Lyn Robinson broke the silence. "Mrs. Smith believes one of us is responsible."

"Nonsense. She's just in shock. It was an accident, nothing more," said her husband, Jim.

"Everyone's vacation is still ruined," Lyn said.

"Vacation? I'm here on business," Samuel Axlerod said.

"What type of business would bring you to Cape May in the summer?" Jim asked.

"Real estate is my livelihood, and I'm in town to acquire a piece of property to build a motel," Samuel said.

"A motel? Is there a need for another one?" Sona asked. She was no expert, but Cape May had its fair share of summer rentals and bed-and-breakfasts.

Abby L. Vandiver

Samuel helped himself to another scone. "During peak summer season, it's hard to find a vacancy in town. It's a good investment, and I have several prospective properties in mind."

"Do you accompany your husband on all his business trips?" Priya asked Amy.

Amy lowered her teacup. "No. He snores even worse when we travel."

Rather than being insulted, Samuel gave his wife an amused look as he took a bite of blueberry scone.

"This trip is special," Amy said. "I adore the Jersey Shore and plan to sunbathe on the beach while Samuel conducts his business."

Priya sighed and set her spoon on the edge of her plate. "I wish my husband traveled for work and I could go along."

"What does he do?" Amy asked.

"He's an accountant. He never travels," Priya said.

Amy turned to Sona. "What about your husband?"

"He's an engineer. He travels occasionally, but wives never get to go," Sona said. "Plus, I wouldn't want to. He goes to Montana and Idaho in the winter. Too cold for me in January."

Amy leaned across the table. "If this trip goes well, we hope never to travel again."

"You'll stay permanently in Cape May?" Priya asked.

"I hope to. Wouldn't you if you could?"

Priya's answer was cut off when Samuel reached across her for his third scone. "It's a shame the man is dead. He certainly knew how to bake."

* * *

"You found the body, Ms. Simonian?"

216

Detective Birmingham was a burly, middle-aged man with a wiry moustache and a bloodhound expression.

Sona straightened her spine as she sat across from the detective at the dining room table. He'd summoned her and Priya for questioning. "Yes. I heard whispering, then a thump, and then a moan. I left my room and saw the body at the bottom of the stairs. I still can't believe Mr. Smith is dead."

The detective flipped open a notepad and reached for a pencil behind his ear. "You didn't bother to wake your roommate when you heard the noises?"

Sona shot Priya an anxious glance. "She wasn't in the room."

"Oh? Where were you, Ms. Patel?"

"I was in the kitchen preparing a cup of tea," Priya said.

The detective arched a dark eyebrow. "In the middle of the night?"

Priya swallowed. "I couldn't sleep. Herbal tea helps."

He scribbled in his notebook. "Did you hear anything?"

"The kettle was simmering, then whistling. I didn't hear a thing other than Sona's scream."

He reached for a paper bag, slipped on a glove, and held up the Hindu elephant necklace. "Is this yours, Ms. Patel?"

Priya nodded and reached for her necklace. "Yes, thank you. I lost it."

He pulled it out of her reach, his gray eyes flat and unreadable as stone. "Are you aware it was found in Mr. Smith's grasp?"

"He must have found it and planned to return it."

The detective leaned forward. "Or maybe he grabbed it as a last-ditch attempt to save himself when you pushed him down the stairs."

Sona gasped. "Pushed him? Are you saying Mr. Smith was murdered?"

The detective met her gaze straight on. "That's exactly what I'm saying."

* * *

"The detective thinks I killed Mr. Smith," Priya said as she rubbed her temples.

"We're all suspects," Sona said.

"But everyone claims to have an alibi, and Mr. Smith was clutching *my* necklace. It looks very bad, doesn't it?" Priya asked, her voice filled with anxiety.

It was the following morning, and they were sitting on wooden rocking chairs outside on the veranda with a magnificent view of the Atlantic Ocean. The Smiths had painstakingly refurbished the Sea Goddess to its former glory. It looked like an elaborate dollhouse, with blue-and-white gingerbread detailing and a wraparound porch with a breathtaking view of the beach and ocean. Seagulls squawked as they circled above, and a breeze blew the loose curls at Sona's nape that had escaped her ponytail.

But Priya was not finding the view relaxing today. Sona didn't blame her. Her own thoughts were churning away.

"I have an idea," Sona said. "But I don't want to talk about it here. Let's go to our room."

The two women climbed the steps, crossed the porch, and entered the vestibule. A sparkling chandelier illuminated gleaming hardwood floors, red-painted walls, and high arched windows. The parlor was decorated with elaborately ornamented wood-trimmed furniture, and leather armchairs were arranged around a fireplace with a marble mantel.

Thankfully, they made it to their room without running into anyone. Fishing in her bag for their room key, Sona opened the door.

Everything about the Sea Goddess was lavish. The room was decorated in the Victorian style with two twin cherry sleigh beds, dainty end tables with hand-painted glass lamps, and a private bathroom with a claw-foot bathtub.

Priya sat on the edge of the bed and blew her nose in a tissue. "That detective thinks I pushed Mr. Smith to his death. Me! What am I going to do?"

"You mean, what are we going to do?" Sona leaned against the windowsill and tapped her chin with a forefinger. "I say we help Detective Birmingham by finding the real murderer."

Priya lowered her tissue and stared at Sona. "You mean investigate on our own?"

"That's exactly what I mean. There were seven people in the house that night. Seven suspects. We just need to narrow it down by finding out who had the strongest motive," Sona said.

"As far as I can tell, no one had motive for murder. Samuel Axlerod is here on business and scouting for properties. His wife is tagging along and enjoying the beach. Other than a huge age difference between them, they seem like a normal couple. They went to bed and didn't leave their room. They are alibis for each other. So are the newlyweds, the Robinsons." Priya's voice broke, and she choked on a sob. "Unfortunately, I don't have an alibi. I was in the kitchen making tea. Why did my necklace have to be in Mr. Smith's hand?"

"There must be an explanation. Like you told the detective the clasp probably broke, and Mr. Smith happened to find it. He was most likely going to return it."

"But if Mr. Smith was pushed at the top of the stairs, wouldn't he reach out to grasp the railing? Even if he missed, he wouldn't hold onto my necklace as he plummeted to his death."

"You're right," Sona said. "Which means the murderer put your necklace in his hand *after* pushing him down the staircase. You were framed."

Priya's eyes welled with tears once more. "This is awful. Who would want to frame me?"

Sona left the windowsill to sit by her friend's side on the edge of the bed. "We aren't going to let that happen. I've been going over everything in my mind, every little detail. Do you remember Amy Axlerod complaining about her husband's snoring when we were in the kitchen eating scones?"

"How does that help us?"

"My mom used to complain that my dad's snoring often kept her up all night. He slept like a baby, but she was the one who suffered. She'd often end up in the spare room and return in the early morning, and my dad would have no idea she'd ever left his side. My point is that Amy could have left the room and Samuel wouldn't have heard it."

"You think Amy slipped out of the room, pushed Mr. Smith down the stairs, then returned to bed without waking her husband?" Priya asked.

"It's possible."

"How could we prove it?" Priya asked.

Sona sighed. "We can't. But the one thing I know for certain is that I heard talking that night. Someone in this house was up and speaking with Mr. Smith right before I found him at the bottom of the stairs." A shiver traveled down Sona's spine as she recalled the gruesome image.

"It's a brilliant theory except for one problem. Motive. Why would Amy Axlerod murder the owner of a bed-and-breakfast?"

Sona bit her bottom lip. *Why indeed?* Amy wore thousands of dollars' worth of jewels. Her engagement ring alone was worth a small fortune. Money couldn't be the motive. Detective Birmingham would ask the same question. They were no closer to finding the truth.

"The answer is not in our room. We need to keep our eyes and ears open."

They left the room and quietly shut the door behind them. When they were halfway down the hall, Amy appeared around a corner.

"Hey, where are you two headed?" Amy asked.

Sona smiled, trying to appear as if she hadn't a care in the world. "We're going downstairs to find something for breakfast."

"Good idea. I'm hungry. I'll join you soon," Amy said with a jaunty wave.

They waited until Amy closed her bedroom door behind her before letting out deep breaths. "That was weird. It's like we conjured her presence by talking about her," Priya whispered. "I almost wanted to confront her right then and ask if she left her snoring husband's side that night."

They continued down the hall and were about to pass Lyn and Jim Robinson's room on the way to the stairs when the unmistakable sound of Mrs. Smith's voice stopped Sona in her tracks.

"What's Mrs. Smith doing in the newlyweds' room?" Sona whispered.

"Maybe she's asking if they need anything?" Priya offered.

Sona looked at her incredulously. "After her husband was murdered?"

Mutual understanding passed between them, and they pressed their ears to the door.

Jim's voice carried through the wood. "Uncle Henry gave me his portion of this house in his will. I want to run it differently."

"I won't let you do it. I'll sell my share before I allow you to turn it into a freak show." Mrs. Smith's voice was laced with indignation.

"We can capitalize on the ghost stories. If we advertise it as a haunted bed-and-breakfast, we'll be booked solid not just for the summer season but through October and Halloween."

"Think of the money to be made!" Lyn said.

"I won't agree to it. I still own half the house," Mrs. Smith said.

Jim laughed bitterly. "It may take time, but with my uncle dead, you'll have no choice but to do things our way."

*　*　*

In the kitchen with the door closed, Sona and Priya hashed over what they'd learned. "Mr. Smith was Jim Robinson's uncle. No wonder the Robinsons honeymooned here. It was either for a reduced rate or free," Priya said.

"With Mr. Smith dead, they will inherit half the house," Sona said.

"But half may not be enough for their plan to advertise it as a haunted Victorian house." Priya collapsed in a chair. "And what about Mrs. Smith? Don't the police always suspect the spouse?"

"The detective probably does consider Mrs. Smith a suspect," Sona said. "But if he had sufficient evidence, he would have arrested her."

Priya's face fell. "I fear he's focused on me instead."

*   *   *

The next day passed slowly. Detective Birmingham had "strongly" requested that no one leave Cape May. Because it was the height of the summer season, it was nearly impossible to find lodgings, and they all remained at the Sea Goddess. If it hadn't been for the absence of Mrs. Smith, who stayed in her room, it would have felt like a continued vacation. Except they were no closer to finding additional clues. Priya's stress level had increased, and she was convinced the detective would show up at any moment with handcuffs and start reading her Miranda rights to her.

After eating a breakfast of scrambled eggs and rye toast, Sona and Priya decided to sit outside on the wide porch. As they made their way from the kitchen to the front door, a masculine voice sounded from the parlor. They peeked inside to see Samuel Axlerod sitting on a red velvet sofa studying papers while talking on his cell phone. His briefcase was open on a dainty end table. His tone was businesslike, and Sona assumed he was speaking with one of his contacts. "Business must go on." His tone turned a bit harsher and he abruptly stood, a cigarette and matches in one hand and the cell phone in the other. He left the parlor to step outside and shut the front door. He never saw Sona or Priya where they were standing.

When opportunity knocks, don't waste it. Sona glanced at her friend. "Are you thinking what I'm thinking?" Perhaps it was desperation, but Priya must have shared her thoughts.

Priya's dark-brown eyes widened. "We have to be quick," she whispered. "That cigarette won't last long."

They sprang into action and rushed into the parlor. "You look," Priya said. "I'll keep watch." With her back to Sona, Priya stood to the side and peered outside the parlor. She had a view of the front door and part of the staircase.

Sona scanned the parlor, and her gaze rested on the mahogany coffee table. Samuel's briefcase was open, and a document sat beside it on the table. She hurried over and picked it up. "My God. It's a contract for sale of the Sea Goddess to the Axlerods. It lists owners Mr. and Mrs. Smith at the top of the document, but Mr. Smith's name has been crossed off in black ink."

"The Axlerods are planning on buying the house? That's crazy," Priya said.

Sona pursed her lips. "It's also motive."

Priya began to frantically wave her hand. "Quick! I hear something!"

Sona returned the document to where she'd found it, and the two women stepped out of the parlor just as the front door opened and Samuel stepped into the vestibule.

He halted, his brows level. "Good day, ladies."

Sona's heart pounded like a drum inside her chest. "Good afternoon."

Priya smiled and nodded.

Samuel stepped back into the parlor. The scent of lingering cigarette smoke wafted to Sona's nostrils. She prayed she'd had enough time to put all the papers back in the briefcase exactly as he'd left them.

Once they reached the porch and were certain no one was about, Sona collapsed on one of the rocking chairs. "From no one having motive, now they all do."

"With Mr. Smith dead, the Robinsons inherit half the house and plan on capitalizing on the haunted history. Mr. Smith's murder will only add to the creepy theme, and the inheritance will certainly help with their student debt."

"But half may not be enough," Sona said. "They don't know Mrs. Smith may sell her share to Samuel Axlerod. He's looking for investment properties, and this beautiful Victorian must be worth a sizable amount. Plus, his wife said she loves Cape May and that she hopes to live here permanently."

Sona sat forward in the rocking chair and gripped the armrests. "But what if Mr. Smith had refused to sell Samuel Axlerod the Sea Goddess? What better way for Amy to get her ocean-shore home than to get rid of the obstacle? Amy couldn't have known that Lyn and Jim stood to inherit half the home," Priya said.

"Maybe we should enlighten her."

*   *   *

That night they all gathered around the dining room table for dinner. Sona had pizza and sodas delivered, and rather than eating on fine china, everyone used paper plates. Mrs. Smith didn't feel up to joining the group, and Priya had two slices of pizza brought to her bedroom.

Sona took a sip of soda from her can. "Everyone knows the police believe Mr. Smith was murdered. That means someone in this room is the murderer."

Silence reigned.

Jim Robinson finally spoke up. "You conveniently heard noises and discovered the body, and your roommate's necklace was found in the victim's fist. I think *you're* accusing *us* to take the blame away from yourselves."

Sona was prepared. "Funny you should point the blame when Mr. Smith was your uncle and you stand to inherit half of this house."

"You're Mr. Smith's nephew?" Samuel Axlerod said, glaring at Jim. "You never said a word."

"What's it to you? Why else would I choose to have my honeymoon in this old house?"

Samuel slapped a palm on the table. "Because I plan on purchasing it."

Jim's face darkened with fury. "Purchasing it! Did my lousy aunt agree to that? She can't. We now legally own half the house, and we have plans to market it as a haunted B and B. I won't agree to any sale."

Amy Axlerod pushed back her chair and tossed her fair hair behind her shoulder. "All this talk has made me lose my appetite. Let's go, Samuel."

Samuel reluctantly stood, then departed with his wife.

Priya whispered in Sona's ear. "It's time. Make the call."

*   *   *

"I've been waiting outside. What took you so long?" Detective Birmingham said.

Priya and Sona stepped onto the porch. "We apologize for the wait, but we promise it will be worth your while," Priya said.

"Well? Are you going to confess?"

"Not here," Sona said, glancing around. "Please come with us upstairs."

The detective grumbled but followed the women into the house and climbed the stairs. They stopped outside the Axlerods' room. The couple's voices were loud enough to hear.

"This can't be happening!" Amy Axlerod shrieked. "You promised *me* this place. You said it would be mine. *Mine!*"

"That was before Mr. Smith couldn't be persuaded to sell, remember?" Samuel said.

"I remember. I took care of him for you," Amy said.

"What do you mean, you took care of him for me?" Samuel asked.

"What do you think it means? Mr. Smith is out of the picture. Mrs. Smith can't run this place on her own. She would have been easy pickings if it wasn't for those newlyweds."

"Amy, did you push Mr. Smith down the stairs?"

"I tried to talk some sense into him, but he was a stubborn old fool. Yes, I ended up pushing him. I found that Indian woman's necklace and planted it on the body. I thought all you had to do after that was seal the deal and I'd have my house. How would I know the Robinsons inherited half the place?"

"My God, Amy."

Outside the door, Sona looked at the detective. "Do you have what you need?"

"Sure do." Detective Birmingham nodded, then threw open the door.

Amy's mouth gaped as she glanced from the women to the detective, then back to the women.

The detective reached for the handcuffs at his waist. "Amy Axlerod, you're under arrest for the murder of Harold Smith."

Realization struck, and Amy took a threatening step toward Sona. "Bitch! You set me up," she shrieked.

Detective Birmingham blocked Amy's path and grasped her arm. "Not so fast," he said.

As Amy was led away, Sona turned to Priya. "This was one weekend getaway I'll never forget."

Priya gave her a faint smile. "The only thing more challenging and exciting is motherhood."

Sona agreed wholeheartedly with her friend. "You're right. So, should we plan a vacation for the same time next year?"

CHANGE OF PLANS

By Elizabeth Wilkerson

"We only have what you see." The floor clerk lifted an arm in the direction of the wall display. She turned her back to Kamilah and busied herself punching buttons on her handheld computer.

Kamilah was at the mother ship—Itoya's Ginza headquarters in Tokyo. Over a century of artistry and commerce dedicated to stationery. Itoya was the place where she could get everything she needed. Tomorrow was going to be a new day, a new month, a new year, and a new her.

But she needed pages for her planner. Paper size B5, which was common in Japan. And she needed one calendar week printed across two pages so she could easily add the pages to her planner binder. That kind of weekly page layout was standard in the planner community. Kamilah didn't think it was a tall order, but the store clerk said they didn't have it. And if Itoya didn't have it, nobody would. And she was screwed.

Kamilah ground her teeth at the thought of starting the new year without her planner in order. She'd check the store shelves again. Maybe she'd overlooked something. With her limited Japanese—*Learn a new Japanese word every week* was one of her yearly goals—it would be hard for her to ask another store employee for help.

She just needed a few planner supplies. The weekly pages, some fun stickers, and maybe a new pen or two. Or three. It was so much better to write in a new planner with a new pen for the new year. And Kamilah was determined to make the new year a better year. This year had really sucked. She was glad that in just a few hours, the year would finally be over. But the dwindling hours also meant she had less time to get her new yearly journal prepared. If her planner was all set out, organized, lined, and decorated before midnight, next year would be a good year. She was sure of it.

Despite the electric excitement in the air on New Year's Eve, the shoppers standing in front of the planner refills studied the wares with a quiet gravity. Kamilah edged to the front of the crowd and removed a packet of planner pages from the wall display.

She studied the contents to see if the page had everything she needed for her new year. Was there space for a to-do list? Goal setting? Blank space for free writing, doodles, and stickers?

And what about the paper? Were the lines close enough together? Were they too far apart? Would her writing bleed through the paper if she was using her favorite pen, a Sakura Pigma Micron, 0.2 mm? That was her favorite pen today, anyway. Who knew what it'd be tomorrow?

The new year presented so many decisions. So many ways to make it turn out perfect. But also, so many ways to fuck it up. Her heart raced with excitement and dread.

Her doctor had said she shouldn't worry about things she couldn't control. But that was just the point. Kamilah could control her planner, and her planner was her life. Crossing items off her to-do list reduced her stress. Stress reduction would be another yearly goal she'd add as soon as she could put together her yearly planner.

Kamilah checked her watch. Itoya had let her down, didn't have the preprinted pages she needed. But she might still have enough time. If she could stay focused, she could do it. She could make her own planner and begin a happy new year.

The train back to her apartment was already full of high-spirited revelers. Probably people on their way to visit a temple or shrine for good luck in the new year. A rowdy group of college-age guys pushed onto the train just behind Kamilah. The acrid smell of beer wafted through the crowded train car. New Year's Eve had a certain universality. A boozy start to a new day.

Kamilah understood the urge to slide through the disappointments of one year and ease into the new. After all, what was she going to do? If she didn't get her planner set up before midnight, it was certain to be unlucky. She'd start the new year off on the wrong foot, under a rain cloud, and the catastrophes that had plagued her this year would follow her across the turn of the calendar page like dog shit on a shoe. Her stomach tensed.

Back at home, she sat at her desk and pulled out her empty new planner binder. She didn't have everything she wanted, but it was time to get ready for the new year.

She opened the translucent lilac cover of her binder—size B5—and slid open the rings. She hadn't seen the B5 notebook size before she moved to Japan. It was smaller than the 8½ by 11 everyone used back in the States, but not as small as the half-size planners that had gotten popular in the journal community.

Planner mania had taken over in the States, judging from the number of YouTubers and Instagrammers who featured planner unboxing and journal setup. When she visited her family over the summer, she'd seen planner inserts, stickers, pens, and even Japanese washi tape at the local Walmart. She wasn't the only one who understood the importance of a carefully curated schedule. Her doctor didn't get it. Another yearly goal: find a new shrink.

From the cabinet at the end of her desk, Kamilah pulled out twelve pieces of B5 paper, all punched with the twenty-six holes needed to fit her binder. The dot-grid pattern on the pages made the next part easy. She got out her clear plastic ruler, her Pigma Micron pen, and her Zebra Mildliner double-headed brush pen.

She opened the Spotify playlist she had created to listen to on days she'd be adding new pages to her planner. SZA, Nao, Esperanza. She'd made the playlist just for herself because it added another dimension to the pleasure of creating the perfect day, month, year. The playlist had twelve followers. People who wanted to live the perfect life because of careful planning. Her tribe.

At the top of the dotted B5 paper, she wrote *January* using the brush pen. Some might call the next part of her ritual tedious, but she found it relaxing. And with the proper background music, it was almost meditative. She set down her brush pen and picked up her Micron and the ruler.

Count six blocks over, put a dot. Count six more blocks and put a dot. Count four blocks down and put a dot. She connected the dots, forming a rectangle. The ruler edge guaranteed perfection. Every line was just so. And at the end, she would put in her headers and the days of the week, and she'd have the start of a calendar. Day by day. Sunday to Saturday—not Monday to Sunday—because weeks started on Sunday. That was the correct way, the way it should be.

She glanced at her watch. Laying out a planner page had taken longer than expected. She had fifty-one more weeks to go. And the pages were going to take a long time because she had to do it all herself. Fifty-one weeks, 102 pages. Itoya had really let her down.

Kamilah took two blank pages of B5 paper from her cabinet and laid them side to side. Her gaze drifted across the paper. She blinked, her eyes not finding a focal point in the absolute blankness of the pages. She didn't know where to start. She had no template, just some ideas. There was no way she could get her planner ready, not in time. Not before midnight. The year hadn't even started, and she'd already fucked it up.

Kamilah went to the kitchen and poured herself a glass of shochu. She added an umeboshi pickled plum. Grabbing a chopstick, she stabbed at the plum's tender pink flesh until it broke apart.

She'd been sure that Itoya would have everything she needed for her planner. Itoya had everything. Even things she never knew she needed, things she didn't know existed. Itoya had it all. But not today. Kamilah took a big gulp of shochu, fished the plum pit out of the glass, and popped the umeboshi into her mouth.

Itoya didn't have what she was looking for, but maybe another store did. Kamilah remembered creating a Pinterest board of planner page designs she liked. The board was a collection of websites where designers sold planner page templates you could download, customize, and print out. Why hadn't she remembered her Pinterest board?

Kamilah got on her computer and navigated to her Pinterest board "Cool Planner Printables"—thirty-seven followers—and checked out some of the planner page designs she had pinned. The templates offered an array of tantalizing ways to create the perfect life. The downloadable and print-able templates included meal-planning pages, habit trackers, books to read, movies to see, and—most important—calendar pages. Calendar pages for a month, a week, or a day. Jackpot. Seeing the variety of choices, Kamilah's shoulders relaxed. She was still under the gun, but maybe she had some help. Things were looking up.

She clicked through the websites on her board. One shop—LesIsMore by Leslie Gant—included B5 printables. The home page for the online store had a clean look, a minimal design. The template pages Leslie sold were simplicity itself and included a line of inspiration, or "inspo," as the Insta-gram planner community called it.

Your useless crap is holding you back.

Simplicity is sanity.

Kamilah chuckled at the designer's humor. *Les is More.*

Kamilah liked Leslie's no-bullshit attitude, and she loved all of that wide-open white space on the template page just waiting for Kamilah to add her stickers and washi decora-tions. The page layout was sparse, and Kamilah liked it that way. There was plenty of room to add a personal touch to make the planner her own.

But time was running out. What Kamilah needed now, before the new year, was weekly pages so that her planner would be ready. And "LesIsMore" Leslie was her last hope. If the designer didn't have the pages, Kamilah would have to hand draw fifty-one weeks with her Micron and ruler. She probably wouldn't be able to do it. At least not in a way that would be poetic and pretty. Kamilah wanted it perfect for the new year. She needed it perfect for the new year.

Kamilah held her breath and double-clicked on the weekly pages in LesIsMore's template gallery. All she wanted was a weekly spread that started on Sunday and ended on Saturday. There wasn't much time. Finding the right template was a long shot, like learning a new Japanese kanji character every day. Kamilah doubted she could do it. And her failure to plan meant that next year was going to suck.

Slouching over the keyboard, Kamilah scrolled through the images in the template gallery.

Wait a second—what was that? A monthly calendar with Japanese holidays! That would be so convenient. She wouldn't have to write in the Japanese holidays as well as the U.S. holidays. But it was a monthly calendar and not the weekly pages she needed. Close, but not perfect. Maybe the designer could help.

Kamilah started a "convo"—online conversation—with Leslie, the designer of the journal template pages.

> *Hi Leslie! Your bujo planner pages are super cute. ☺ I need B5 two-page weekly page spread, starting on Sunday. US holidays and Japanese holidays like in your gallery template #18. And I kinda need it ASAP. For the new year. I'm in Tokyo so that's pretty soon.*

Would the designer get back to her right away? In time for Kamilah to get her planner prepared for the new year? If Leslie was in the States, it would be morning. Leslie probably started her day by checking her online convos and overnight orders, Kamilah guessed, but she couldn't know. Unless

Kamilah heard from the designer, she was on her own to finish the planner.

Kamilah took out a fresh piece of dotted B5 paper. At the top she wrote *February*. Before she could finish counting the dots—six blocks over, four blocks down—she had a reply from the designer. Her customized pages were finished. An image file and an invoice were attached.

Kamilah opened the file. The designer had been blazing fast, and everything was exactly as she had requested. The designer had even added the dates for each day of the year. That would save Kamilah a ton of time—she wouldn't have to go through the planner and hand letter every day of the week for twelve months. She hadn't even asked the designer to add the dates. It was a nice touch. Kamilah would definitely leave a great review for the designer. She printed out the first month and got to work.

She reached for her Mildliner brush pen in Mild Citrus, which she had decided was going to be the year's color theme. She was poised to embellish the page with some stars and flowers when she noticed. Shit. Shit. Shit. Kamilah pounded the table. The weekly spread started on Monday, not Sunday. That wouldn't do. Weeks started on Sunday. Everybody knew that.

Kamilah was positive she had requested a Sunday start. She wouldn't make a mistake like that. She hoped the designer would be quick to reply again. She was losing time in getting her planner ready for the new year.

Hey Leslie. Thanks for getting back to me. But I wanted the week to start on Sunday not on Monday. Can you correct and resend?

Surely the designer would want to make that quick, easy correction. Kamilah held the power of the review, and every online-store owner wanted to have positive, happy reviews. A one-star review could effectively tank a shop owner's sales.

Kamilah was right. Within minutes, an alert went off on her computer. The designer had delivered the corrected pages. With a note.

Sorry. I was trying to get this to you fast. I've corrected it.

People made mistakes. The designer had been rushing because of Kamilah's bad scheduling. She couldn't blame the designer. The job was a custom order at the last minute. Easily worth the price.

Kamilah opened the file and reviewed the pages on her screen.

Sunday start. Check. Kamilah flipped forward to the month of May, one of the months that had both Japanese and U.S. holidays. Memorial Day was noted, but no Japanese holiday. Not a single day of Golden Week, the almost week-long back-to-back holidays celebrated the first week of May in Japan. Shoot. The designer hadn't gotten all the specs straight.

Hi again. It's me again. I don't see any Japanese holidays. In my original request as you can see I had wanted planner pages based on your template with US & Japanese holidays. And I really appreciate your working fast but can you fix it? All of your reviews say how great your work is.

The sound of lively conversation and laughter wafted up from the street. Kamilah looked out of her window and saw groups of pilgrims heading toward the nearby temple to make wishes for the coming year.

On New Year's Eve, Times Square had a falling ball, but Tokyo had temple bells. The low tone of the bell at the nearby temple thundered through the air. It would ring 108 times, with the last bell, the 108th, sounding precisely at midnight. The bell ringing took a couple of hours, but if the monks were already ringing the bell, Kamilah was down to the wire.

The beep of her computer snapped Kamilah back to her task at hand. This time there was no convo. Just an alert that the designer had sent a file.

Kamilah sighed. If this template wasn't right, there wasn't any time to change it. She was destined to have another fucked-up year. Kamilah opened the file.

The weekly pages looked promising. She scrolled to May. Golden Week was there as well as Memorial Day. Just to be sure, Kamilah fast-forwarded the year on the screen to November. The weekly pages showed Thanksgiving and Culture Day in Japan. All good.

She was going to pull it off. She was going to be able to print out her pages and finish setting up her planner on time. She opened to the first week, and her gaze zipped to the lower right corner. She slumped in her chair and cradled her head in her hands.

How had she missed it? The font was small, and it was positioned in the corner, but how had she not seen it? Words of inspiration at the bottom of each week.

Inspo wasn't part of her custom order. Her shrink offered her more than enough inspo.

Kamilah printed out a couple of pages as samples.

Examining the blemish, she considered covering it with washi tape or Wite-Out. She reached into her supply drawer of washi tape and cut a piece to cover the unwanted text.

Kamilah closed one eye and tilted her head, trying to decide if the patch bothered her. It did. It meant she wouldn't have a perfectly beautiful planner for a perfectly beautiful new year. The Wite-Out didn't yield better results. Something just didn't look right. She would begin each week knowing there was a problem she needed to cover up. It wasn't how she wanted to start the year.

The booming gong of the temple bell sounded. Was that the second ring or the third? Kamilah had already lost count. Shit and double shit. She needed help.

> *Leslie, this is my fault. But I didn't notice the inspiration text you have on the pages. I didn't want that in my spread. This is the last change, I promise. Can you delete the text and resend?*

* * *

Leslie returned to the table she had commandeered and sat down with her oat-milk honey latte, her second of the morning. This customer in Tokyo had been particularly whiny, but Leslie would be more than happy to help her delete something.

Leslie had a special file to send. A special file she kept for special customers like this one. And this file wasn't just a planner page template; it included a special surprise. Just for her most deserving customers. She replied to the customer.

> *NP, I'll create a new file. I want to make sure that the format is right. Are you Windows or Mac?*

Leslie didn't know why people called it malicious code. She'd be more than happy to have this high-maintenance customer out of her life. *Happy, not malicious.*

Leslie happily added an innocent-looking piece of code in the weekly planner document page. The customer wouldn't even know it was there. The customer wouldn't suspect that when her computer crashed and burned, it was because of the planner file she'd downloaded. From a total stranger.

The customer was in Tokyo. Leslie set the timer embedded in the file. The fun would begin at midnight, Japan time. At midnight, the code—Leslie couldn't call it malicious—would activate and proceed to wreak havoc on the whiny customer's computer.

Erasing her computer hard drive would set the customer back, for sure, but the customer used a planner. A good old-fashioned, offline, pen-and-paper planner. She'd be okay. And she would be out of Leslie's inbox. *Happy, not malicious.*

Leslie convo'd the customer that the corrections had been made and the file was ready for download.

Before Leslie finished her latte, her computer beeped. The customer had installed the latest file. It would be just a few more minutes before the fun began.

Leslie opened her planner and turned to the weekly page spread. At the bottom of her to-do list was her inspo challenge: *Eliminate something that no longer serves you.* She uncapped her Artwin double-headed pen and checked the box.

It was going to be a good year.

*   *   *

Kamilah downloaded the updated file. It had been really nice of the designer to work so quickly and make the revisions.

Even though most of the needed changes had been the designer's fault, Kamilah would leave a good review anyway.

She printed out the pages and inserted them in her binder. With her yearly planner set up complete and perfect, she closed her binder and poured herself another glass of shochu.

The temple bell rang. Kamilah had tried to keep up with the bell count. Maybe this was number 107? The last bell, number 108, would sound at exactly midnight.

It was going to be a great year.

THE BLACK WIDOW OF OSHOGBO

By Stella Oni

Lara watched as Dr. Chen prepared to cut the dead man with the deep chest wound lying on the stainless-steel gurney in his high-tech lab. The man was stocky, with the well-defined muscles of an outdoor man—maybe a farmer or laborer? His face was forever frozen in the terror of whatever had overtaken and killed him. Lara had seen a lot of bodies blown to pieces while in action in Afghanistan. After all, it was a thin divide between life and death.

Naked you come to the world and naked you go, she thought.

Dr. Chen continued to chat to her in Mandarin, which Lara had taught herself years before. He expertly opened the man's belly to expose the content of his stomach.

"Last meal pounded yam and egusi," he said with satisfaction. "A good meal to have." His dark eyes glinted with mischief. "Here is a man gone to his death with a belly full of food."

"What killed him, Doctor?"

Chen pointed to the chest wound. "Single stab to the heart. But see this?" He turned a powerful torch light onto the back of the man's short, muscled leg. "You make a cut to the Achilles' heel, and that effectively cripples you. He would have bled a lot and without help was game for the killer to do whatever they wanted.

"But this is where the killing became bizarre." He pointed to the man's groin area. "Come closer and see this." The torch blazed on the man's private part. "What do you see?"

"I see a well-endowed man," said Lara, amused. Her voice became serious as she continued to stare. "I also see deeply indented marks."

"Yes," said Chen as he turned off the light. "Those are teeth marks. The killer bit our man whilst his lifeblood was pumping out of him." He took off his gloves. "What time is it?"

"Time to be going home, Doc. It's past midnight. Why do you work so late?"

Chen laughed. "Why are you here with me?"

Lara smiled, crossed her arms, and said nothing. She was tall, lean, with a scar across her face that made one think of a coiled cheetah. She had gotten it surviving a car accident at ten that threw her through the windscreen and killed her parents.

She loved their word games.

"The midnight hours bring more from the dead than you realize. I am a man of science and spirit. When you cut the dead in the night, they reveal more secrets to you."

"So, why did you call me here, Doc?"

Her eyes flickered around the vast space, which contained immaculate stainless-steel drawers that housed the dead in this busy laboratory and autopsy facility. Possibly the largest in Africa. A lucrative partnership between the Nigerian government and a private Chinese company. Dr Chen, as director of operations, had a whole team of experts working under him and therefore liked to pick projects that interested him.

Dr Chen went to a large stainless-steel sink to wash his hands.

She knew he was now ready for home.

He and his staff lived in a gated compound next to the large building and had guards to keep them safe. Lara felt sorry for Chen's driver and guard, both waiting for their employer to finish.

"I was not the one that called you here. Your old SSS boss is waiting outside for you."

Lara's eyes widened. "The secret service? This must be serious."

"It is. That man is the third case I have had in the last three weeks. It seems we have a serial ritual killer in the town of Ilaje in Oshogbo!"

* * *

Chen was right, thought Lara as she stepped out into the lab's vast compound, illuminated by floodlights that pushed back the encroaching darkness of surrounding trees and bushes. Crickets and other creatures sang their night songs and reminded her that it was time to be home.

Mr. Odun was leaning against her old Mercedes. Moses, her Congolese assistant of all trades, was stretched out comfortably on the driver's seat.

He straightened as Mr. Odun, a tall, thin man in his fifties, welcomed her with a smile.

"You still haven't replaced this old car. I thought the wealth from your detective agency would buy you a snappy one."

"Hello, boss. No kidnapper or armed robber would want to steal this. I prefer not to be troubled. Not that Moses and I can't handle them."

Mr. Odun decided not to think too deeply about what she'd said. If he knew Lara, she was armed to the teeth with unlicensed weapons and would fight to the death with an attacker.

"Can we not talk in the morning?" she said.

"This is urgent. You saw what we're dealing with in there?"

"Ritual killings of village men. What is new about that?"

"The town of Ilaje sits on the biggest tranche of the country's tantalite supply. Their Oba is not happy."

Lara laughed without mirth. "I should have known there was money behind it."

"They have the Ilaje festival in a week, and he wants the killings to stop."

"What is CID doing?" Lara shook her head. With limited resourcing and lack of equipment, criminal investigation was a source of frustration for law enforcement. "Forget I asked, boss."

"You know, we try as much as we can with the resources we have," he said.

She'd worked with him for only a year but had no patience with the intelligence service and had set out to work on her own. Her detective agency had become extremely busy because of its success rate, which was one hundred percent.

"We will not even quibble over your enormous fees."

"I feel like doubling it, boss. We have to drive through hazardous roads to reach that town, and a week slumming it in some village doesn't sound like fun."

"I owe you."

"I'll remember that."

"I will email all details to you tonight."

"I'll expect the info, boss." They parted ways.

* * *

Lara was happy to get home and eat the grilled fish and salad left for her by her housekeeper. She poured herself a large glass of wine and was almost tempted to curl up in her comfortable settee and read a book, but she knew Mr. Odun would have sent his email. She loved his work ethic and wished it were appreciated by the government, but he loved his job, and that was all that mattered.

She walked to her large home office, comprising desks and laptops. A smart screen dominated part of her wall. In a corner was a glass cabinet that housed her server. She went to sit behind two large flat-screens and put on her earphones.

She needed to catch up with her contacts around the world. She was part of a smart hacker team and loved to exchange juicy information with them within their secure site. She powered up her computer and printed out Mr. Odun's email.

His report was detailed and covered salient points.

The town of Ilaje had a population of twenty thousand residents.

Their Oba, Ileja of Ilaje, came from a long line that had reigned for over two hundred years. It was a rich and tight-knit community because of the tantalite.

They pretty much kept themselves apart and were committed to their traditional festivals. The biggest one was the Egu Ilaje masquerade to herald the harvest of crops.

The killings had started precisely three weeks before, and it had been one man a week:

Mr. Lekan Omole—thirty-two years old, farmer
Mr. Kolade Balogun—twenty-seven years old, farmer
Mr. Bolaji Elegede—thirty-five years old, farmer

All killed the same way. Strong men in excellent physical health who would have fought back. That told her the killers wanted the ritual to be without struggle. A deep cut to the Achilles' tendon to bring the man down, a sharp stab straight into the heart, then biting down on the private part. Lara winced.

The men would have been terrified at the onslaught of trauma as they bled to death. It could only be ritual killing, she thought. She sent off a quick text to Edith, the only other female member of her team of four. Edith was on the ball when it came to investigations and was an intelligent analyst. Jonathan and David, her other team members, were busy with cases. She and Edith would set off for Oshogbo in the morning, and she would fill the other woman in on the way. She was personally interested in the case now. She forwarded all the notes for the analysis to Edith.

Mr. Odun, in his precise manner, had also provided a map. It showed the distance between where each man had died and the nearest houses. They had found bicycle track marks beside each body. The question was, why had each man been out on his farm after midnight?

Edith replied immediately, and Lara shut down her computer and drained her glass.

* * *

Edith joined her for breakfast at seven the next day. She was the offspring of a Chinese father, long gone to China, and his Nigerian house help. Her hair hung in a short bob around a softly pretty face and wise eyes.

"How do you want us to approach things, boss?" she asked Lara.

"Moses will be driving us down. It will allow us to move around the town quickly." Moses had been a mercenary in Congo. "The detective inspector in charge of the case will be meeting up with us at the hotel, along with Oba Ilaje's chief of liaison."

"That's some red carpet, boss." Edith grinned, revealing a capped gold tooth.

"Mr. Odun felt that help from them might allow us to solve the case faster. I am not convinced. The police would be resentful that a private detective was deemed better than them. As far as the liaison, I don't trust anyone."

Lara stood up and pulled at her small suitcase. Edith did the same.

Moses was waiting at the door and immediately took the cases from them and stowed them in the back of the agency's Range Rover.

They set off. From Lagos to Ilaje would take them about four hours. Lara hated to travel to Nigerian towns or villages because of the hazardous roads.

Moses maneuvered the vehicle as it absorbed the terrible shock of numerous craters and potholes. Edith power-napped, and Lara stared at town sellers and hawkers of cooked food and agricultural produce. They stopped at a small petrol station, and hawkers crowded the car like a swarm of flies.

Moses ignored them and coolly filled the tank. Just as casually, he stopped and bought some bread and fish. Lara wasn't taking any chances with street food and had brought some snacks for herself and Edith.

A dusty signpost that reminded her of the inner American towns in movies announced that they had arrived at Ilaje. Moses saw an old man ambling along the dusty road and slowed the car to ask for directions to their motel.

The Yoruba dialect the man spoke was as close to Russian as it was to English. She shook her head at how Moses understood. He was a man of many talents. He started up the engine again and drove into the compound of a sprawling bungalow that impressed Lara with its perfect flowers and inviting entrance. It was an unexpected welcome. Her lips twitched as she watched Edith's puzzled look.

"This is what a rich town looks like. Moses, don't you wish your hometown was swimming with a mineral demanded by the world?" asked Lara.

Moses grinned, revealing large brown teeth sharpened like a crocodile's. He had been a Congolese child soldier, and one of the initiation ceremonies was the filing of each tooth. Moses had said it was a painful job but allowed the children to quickly become a lethal weapon. They knew how to fell their enemies with a quick bite.

Much like the case they were investigating.

He rolled their suitcases out as Lara and Edith approached the small reception desk, staffed by a young man in a white shirt and black trousers.

"You're booked for room sixteen, madam." Lara had insisted that she and Edith share a room. It wasn't safe to sleep separately in a small town.

Moses was next door in room seventeen. He could quickly become useful if they required it.

Lara also ordered food for later—rice and goat stew with fried plantain. Ilaje was famous for its goat meat stew, which was cooked in a particular way that Lara had only experienced in Chile. The goat was first roasted and then stewed. She had had Ilaje stew in Lagos and was glad to be eating it in the town itself.

She noticed the young man stealing glances at Edith's curvy body.

A porter appeared and led them to their rooms. Their first appointment with the detective inspector and Oba's liaison was in less than an hour.

The room was large, with windows that looked out into the flowered garden. The single beds were separated by a lamp table.

Edith bounced on her bed. "You better not snore, boss."

Lara grinned. It was Edith who snored like a trooper. She walked to the large mirror and nearly winced at her rough appearance.

Her scar stood in relief against her face. She had packed her dreadlocks in a bun to ensure they wouldn't fall over her face.

She went to the toilet to freshen up, and her phone rang as soon as she came out. Edith was applying fresh makeup.

"Yes?" said Lara.

"Madam, you have some people that want to see you," said the young man at the reception desk.

Moses came out of his room as soon as he heard their door opening.

They approached a slim man wearing sandals and baggy native, top and bottom. The other, a tall, thickset man with broad shoulders and a strong face, was in full police uniform.

"Good afternoon, Madam Lara," greeted Oba's liaison man with a small smile. "I am Mr. Ola, and this is Inspector Jide."

"Very nice to meet you both," said Lara. She was aware of the policeman's eyes on her scar. "This is my colleague, Edith."

She saw the usual mix of desire and skepticism as they took in Edith's figure and delicate features.

They sat on the motel's comfortable chairs. "I am told that a killing might happen tonight unless we prevent it," she said.

The inspector's face was stony. "Yes," he said. "I have men staking out the farms, but we don't have enough."

"We will be taking you to visit the Oba, who wants to see you, and then you can follow the inspector to go around the farms," said Mr. Ola.

"We were happy to know that you have a good record of the citizens of the town," said Lara.

Mr. Ola nodded happily. "The Oba insisted that the count of all citizens be updated every year. It is a way to ensure that our brightest student gets their scholarships to study abroad."

Lara turned to the inspector. "I was told that your men have already done door-to-door searches. Anything interesting?"

He shook his head. "Sadly, nothing. We are working on the distance between the houses nearest the farms where the killings took place. I think if we brought you to the crime scene first, it would give you a better idea."

Mr. Ola stood up. "Shall we, then?"

As they rode in the inspector's car, Mr. Ola explained the protocol of greeting the chief. Edith stifled a giggle, and Lara gave her a warning look.

"You are visitors, so just bend your knees slightly. Usually, men prostrate and women kneel."

They approached the sprawling palace within ten minutes and were waved through an ornate gate by uniformed security men. The inspector parked by a set of expensive cars, including a Rolls-Royce. Mr. Ola sprang out and led the way through a calm, lushly carpeted hallway and into a vast open space with scatter rugs. A handsome young man decked in a white embroidered traditional robe and brown leather sandals sat on a massive, intricately carved wooden throne and watched as they approached. The group of people surrounding him went quiet and followed his gaze. When Lara and Edith got near enough, they bent their knees as instructed.

"Welcome to Ilaje, Madam Lara. I have heard a lot about you," said the Oba in a deep, strong voice. That surprised Lara. "You come well recommended. Our festival is coming up in a week, and these killings have to stop. It is an abomination to the celebration of a new harvest and will bring a curse to the town."

"I will try my best, Your Majesty," said Lara.

"The police have questioned many people but have no evidence. We don't want to start punishing innocent people. But we have a few people here and there that we believe might be capable of this."

"Have you got their names, Your Majesty?" Lara was annoyed. Inspector Jide hadn't mentioned that they might have some suspects.

"Inspector will give you the names that we passed on to him."

The inspector looked uncomfortable. "Your Majesty, we agreed that we will not bias Madam Lara's investigation."

"She will need help to start. Give her the names, Jide."

The inspector drove them back to their hotel in silence.

He turned to Lara as they parked at the front of the motel. "We don't like to assume people are guilty until proven."

"It would have been good to know, Inspector."

"We are the police. Maybe detective agencies work differently, but we follow due process no matter how slow. I will give you the names as commanded." He rooted around in some folders and gave Lara a piece of paper. "These are names of people who have had some disagreement or another with the dead men."

"Thank you," said Lara.

"I will come back for you at eleven thirty PM. I hope we can catch the killer tonight. We have imposed curfew, so there should be no man about. All the same, we will take precautions." He drove off.

Lara and Edith ordered more food, and she perused the inspector's paper.

A name jumped out at her that connected all three men—Chief Jinadu. His listed profession was *herbalist*. He had had land disagreements with all three.

That was too much of a coincidence.

Edith showed Lara her analysis. "I think the killer lives within a twenty-mile radius of the farms. The street maps are not so well defined, so it will be challenging to work that out," she said as she frowned at her screen.

"The inspector could do a house-to-house in that radius," said Lara. "Included will also be people who own bicycles, which is how most of the farmers get around.

"We will go and have a chat with this herbalist who seemed to have had a fight with each man. There is a village native doctor, whom the Oba uses, and this herbalist. Maybe it's a simple case of rivalry and sabotage," she mused.

"Also, the inspector writes about an old woman in the village who claims to know what's going on," Lara said. "He said she didn't make much sense. Let's go visit both of them."

"Another angle," Edith said as she sat, her glasses perched on her nose. "Could it be a crime by a woman? I had a quick chat with that young man in reception." She grinned. "They're calling the killer 'The Black Widow of Oshogbo.' They said it's a witch taking revenge on the village men."

"It will have to be a powerful woman to fell able-bodied men. Continue your checks and see if you can segment by age, location, opportunity. Let's see what the perimeter visualization tool brings up."

Their food came well prepared—steaming rice, excellent brown plantain, and the Ilaje goat stew.

Lara and Edith dived in and ate.

* * *

The inspector came for them promptly at eleven thirty.

"We will visit farm areas where we've got the men stationed."

Lara noted that the town's tantalite money didn't stretch to streetlights as the car's headlight sliced through the deep darkness. The inspector had introduced the small man with a beard as his driver. Moses was driving behind them. Lara had wanted them to have their own vehicle but also wanted to chat on the way with the inspector. Edith was with Moses.

The driver guided the car expertly through the shadowy, hulking bushes that seemed to take on a life of their own.

They emerged into farmland, where policemen were camped around a bright fire and talking quite loudly. All stood up as their superior approached—curious hyena-like eyes lighting on Lara and moving to Edith, who had followed them.

"I take it all is well so far," said Inspector Jide.

"Nothing, sir," said a portly policeman who looked like he would be more at home at a beer parlor than staking out a serial killer.

Lara didn't like their setup. It would be difficult to catch a killer if the rest of the farms were policed like this.

"Try to keep the noise down," said the inspector. "You cannot catch a mosquito with this level of noise, let alone a killer."

They left, drove to the next farm, and were met with more noisy officers having a good time. Lara was irritated, and her mind turned to the possible suspects. It might pay her and Edith more to go talk to them than to engage in this comedy.

They arrived at the fifth farm to the sound of a man's loud, agonized scream. All ran in the direction far left of the farmland, which was shrouded in darkness. Lara streaked ahead, officers pounding after her. She had her torch out of her small emergency rucksack and pointed it forward. She saw the victim immediately. He was a well-built man lying still and looking quite dead. She leapt to his side and felt his pulse. Nothing. She shined the torch on him as the policemen arrived. He was wearing a dirty white T-shirt blooming with blood and a pair of shorts that hung around his ankles.

Red bubbled the ground around him. She didn't miss the fresh teeth marks.

She shined the torch on the ground and saw the fresh tire track of a bicycle. The fourth dead man, and right under their nose.

The inspector glared at his men as he spoke into his phone. "Call all the men to Ikere farm." He described their location. "It's freshly done. If we work quickly, we might catch the killer. It is a cyclist, so look for a lone rider on the road."

"I'll come with you," said Lara. The inspector looked as if he was about to refuse when he saw that it was not a request but a command. He nodded.

Lara looked at Edith. "You can stay back with Moses. We should be back soon."

Edith nodded. Running through bushes full of night creatures wasn't her idea of fun. She had her laptop and could use it to run scenarios on Perimeter for their investigation.

* * *

"We will spread out in a chain and see if we can trap this killer," said the inspector as they entered the bushes. "The men are covering the road. I think we might have a chance." He sounded more excited and optimistic than he had previously.

Lara was thankful for her thick jeans and heavy work boots. She doubted they would catch any killer tonight but pressed on with the others.

They combed the farmland and saw the bicycle tracks weave in and out. That raised their hopes, but then the tracks disappeared into denser bush.

"Very clever," hissed the detective. "We can't do much in the bush at this time of the night. This killer knows their terrain well. I'm calling off the search."

The men looked unhappy to hear this.

"We will come back here in the morning."

Lara didn't want to say that they had trampled all over vital evidence, and the inspector hadn't mentioned bringing in the crime scene officers. The Oba could certainly afford to police his town more effectively.

Moses looked like he had dozed off but instantly woke up as he heard her approach. Edith was engrossed in her laptop and looked happier than Lara. "I have narrowed it down to even fewer addresses," she said.

Moses started the car as Lara saw that Edith had created a 3-D modeling of the houses within the radius and then used the tool to include and exclude.

Lara grinned at her assistant, whose gold cap shone back. "Good job. We will start our questioning without the added burden of the inspector and his men. This is where we part ways.

"Better still, as the town is now preparing for the festival from midnight onwards, we could do our questioning without raising much suspicion."

"Are you saying we can rest during the day, boss?"

"No such thing! Let us have our good night's rest and use that to improve your analysis. If we play our cards right, we might be able to reduce the ten houses to five."

* * *

They woke up early, had a hearty Ilaje breakfast of akara and pap, and began their work.

"We have this house in proximity to the farm. Perimeter is saying that they have occupants in there that fit our demography." said Edith.

"How do you know they own a bike?"

"I don't." Edith shrugged. "We will ask when we get there."

"So, we appear as visitors when the midnight feast begins and then do quick questionings. We should be able to cover all five houses in a couple of hours."

"So, boss, we are no longer questioning the original suspects?"

"Let's follow Perimeter's direction first. It takes so many things into consideration that we should consider these five suspect families. On the other hand, it doesn't hurt to go and visit the old woman who claims to know it all and that herbalist."

She called Moses, and they decided to visit the herbalist first.

After obtaining a flurry of directions from passersby, they found a neat house painted a cool green.

Lara and Edith knocked on the front door, which a young man opened. "We came to see Chief Jinadu."

"Wait," he said, and disappeared back inside. He returned almost immediately.

"Please come with me." They followed him through the house to the backyard. Chief Jinadu sat on a mat under a tree, pounding something in a small mortar. He was broad, with a shiny bald head and a face scoured by tribal marks. His eyes flickered over the women like a lazy lizard's.

"Sit down," he said, pointing to some chairs around him.

This must be like a backyard consultation spot, thought Lara.

He carefully set down the mortar and pestle. "I know why you young ladies are here."

"You do?" said Lara.

"Yes, I had a fight with all three dead men."

Lara hid her frown. One of the inspector's men had snitched on them. This was going to be a waste of their time.

His eyes flicked rapidly. "If you ask more questions, you will realize that I have quarreled with half of the men in the village. I own lands and like to buy more. Not everyone is happy to sell."

"Do you own a bicycle?" asked Lara.

The man laughed. "I own lands and bicycles. Which one do you want me to show you?"

"Why did you quarrel with the men?"

"Most of these men are pretend farmers. The Oba gives them a big subsidy to fund their farmlands, but all they want is tantalite money to waste at the beer parlor. That is what easy mineral stone does to able-bodied farmers. I did not kill anyone."

"Thank you for seeing us," said Lara.

"You should be talking to the churches, not herbalists. They are farmers too!" He sniffed.

They left him.

"I still don't trust him," said Edith.

"Same," said Lara.

They drove to the residence of the old woman known as *Iyagba who sees angels.*

Hers was a little mud house, with a yard swept so clean that there was not a leaf in sight. They knocked on ancient wooden doors, and a wizened old woman with filmy eyes covered in cataracts opened one of the doors and peered at them.

"The angels said you would come," she said in a cracked, ancient voice.

Lara didn't want to guess how old she was. A hundred?

"Come in." She turned back into her gloomy entrance hall and led them to a small sitting room with wooden stools. "Thank you for coming to see me. Ilaje town should not be doing this native worship. The demons are killing able-bodied townsmen."

Lara had to strain her ears to hear Iyagba's whispered conversation. The woman had no teeth, and her voice was muffled.

"You have two churches in this town, and how many of these men attend?" Lara asked.

"They prefer to gather at the beer parlor," said the old woman.

"Do you know any of the men?"

"I know every man in this town. I say sin is killing them. That is what the angels told me."

They couldn't get much more out of her than that and left her muttering to herself.

"That's why I don't want to live beyond a hundred," Edith giggled as they got outside. "All those long-held memories."

She stopped laughing as she saw Lara's expression.

"We have missed a very vital clue that has been looking us in the face all along," said Lara.

"What, boss?"

"I'll explain it later."

They went back to the motel. Lara pulled out her computer and looked at Edith's analysis on Perimeter. She saw how they had missed the signs.

"I think I have just narrowed our search to two places. We will be visiting both tonight."

Edith didn't ask any more question.

* * *

At midnight they left their room, and the excitement was palpable in the motel as guests trooped out to mini ceremonies leading to the main festival.

"Drive us to the beer parlor," Lara said to Moses.

She knew he already knew where it was. Moses always made it his business to know the character of a town.

"This place kept getting mentioned in all our investigations, and we didn't think to visit it."

"An obvious place that all the men have in common," said Edith quietly.

The parlor was crowded and full of jolly men drinking. There were a few women. Eyes followed Lara and Edith as they entered the joint. It was a large space with wooden benches and tables that stank of palm wine and beer.

The waiting staff darted from table to table taking orders or delivering steaming bowls of pepper soup and palm wine.

Lara and Edith sat down at a small table in the back of the room.

A plump, cheerful woman came to take their order. Her curious eyes darted from Lara to Edith.

"We want fish pepper soup and palm wine," said Lara. Also, we want to speak to your madam."

Madam Beatrice owned other establishments like this around the town, but this one was within their radius—information supplied to Edith by the motel receptionist.

"Madam Beatrice is very busy, ma," said the woman.

"Tell her madam Lara."

The woman almost curtsied and left them.

The waitress came back. "Madam said you should follow me."

She took them to the back of the building and to a small room where a large woman with a stern face sat before piles of money. She came out to them and carefully closed her door.

She greeted them with a grim face. "I don't like police people coming here. It is not good for business."

"Tell us what we need to know, and we will go," said Lara.

"Like what?" She towered over them with elbows akimbo.

"Give me the names of your staff."

"For what, madam?"

"All the men that died passed through here."

The women seemed to collapse. Then, "I have not seen Morenike for a week."

"Who is she?"

"She came from another town. She said she is a widow. She was a good worker and very pretty. The men liked her."

"And?"

"She changed and became very quiet a couple of months ago."

"Did you ask her why?"

The woman hung her head. "She complained about the men."

"The three men?"

"Five men."

"What did she say?"

The woman's defiance came back. "I cannot believe a beer parlor girl over long-running customers."

They waited.

"She said they raped her. She liked to go to church in the night to pray. She said they followed her and raped her."

"Four of those men are now dead. Why did you not go to the police?"

"I did not think it was possible. Morenike is a tiny woman and very meek. She cannot have killed those men, but she has disappeared."

"Madam, the police will come back."

Tears streaked down the woman's face. Lara imagined they stemmed more from the madam's loss of income than they did the destruction of a woman and the killing of four men.

"Let's go to church," said Lara.

On their way, she called Inspector Jide. He said they would find the fifth man. Lara told him they were nearly at the church.

"Wait and don't enter. We will be there in a few minutes," he commanded.

"Why the church?" asked Edith.

"She'll be there. That's where it happened. Remember, not a lot of this town attends church. It's her hiding place. Moses, you'll follow us in. We have no idea what to expect."

The church was a small building with a cross. There were no lights, and it was deathly quiet.

"How could men not be afraid to desecrate a house of God?" whispered Edith.

Lara shrugged. "Evil men are not afraid to desecrate anywhere," she said. She didn't believe in God, and this meant nothing to her. She saw Edith shiver. Her assistant definitely believed.

They approached the door, and Lara pushed. There was no way she was obeying the inspector. It opened, and they stepped into darkness. She brought out her torch. The interior was filled with about fifty wooden chairs that cast amplified shadows on the wall. At the front sat a still, small figure.

The woman didn't even look back to see who had entered. She finally turned as they neared, and Lara shone the torch on her small face, tiny mouth, and big dead eyes.

"Men are so foolish," she said quietly. "It was too easy. I assisted my dad, who was a bonesetter. He taught me the human body from when I was a child. They destroyed me in the house of God. A place of love and solace. It was easy to lure them to the farm and to disable them. It is not about strength but cunning."

"I'm sorry about what happened to you," said Lara.

"*They* are sorry. I sent them to hell."

Lara looked back as the inspector and his men noisily entered the church.

THE WITCHING HOUR
By Marla Bradeen

The grandfather clock in the corner chimed once, twice, twelve times, sending a shiver down Joan Nguyen's spine. It was now officially the witching hour.

She knew she shouldn't believe in that stuff, but she also couldn't deny a lot of bad things happened during the hour between midnight and one AM. Take the time six months ago when she'd caught a flight home a full day earlier than planned and discovered her boyfriend in bed with her cousin. Or her father's death, the reason she was currently lying on this old ratty couch in her aunt's drafty house. The arson investigator had estimated the fire in his living room had started not long after midnight, the result of a match he'd dropped when trying to light a cigarette. And given the amount of booze he'd spilled on the sofa cushions . . .

Howard Nguyen had never had a chance.

Joan sat up, pulling her knees to her chest and wrapping the blanket Tam had given her around her body. She could use a drink herself right at the moment. Except five days ago, the day the arson report had come back from the Seattle Fire

Department, Tam had announced her home was now an alcohol-free zone.

An unexpected burst of light burned Joan's retinas. She had the urge to pull the blanket over her head, but her aunt would no doubt view that as antisocial behavior. And Joan would never do anything to intentionally hurt Tam's feelings. In some ways Tam was more like Joan's mother than the woman who had birthed her and then died in a car wreck thirteen years later.

"You awake, huh?" Tam said. "Wishing you had gone back to Eastside and own bed?"

"No, I'm glad I crashed here." After the funeral, Joan hadn't felt up to facing the trip back to her apartment. She might live only fifteen miles away, but bridge traffic often made the drive feel interminable. "And I doubt I would get any sleep in my own bed either."

"Thinking about your Ba, no?"

Joan's gaze drifted toward the grandfather clock, her eyes landing on the tacky dust ruffle her aunt had fashioned around its base. "I can't get over his death. The *way* he died. How could his drinking have gotten so bad and I never knew it?"

"You young, think you should know everything about everybody." Tam plopped onto the couch next to Joan, the disruption forcing Joan to brace her hand against the cushion so she didn't tip over. Both Tam and Joan were about the same size, but somehow Tam seemed larger, more commanding. "Everybody has secrets."

Joan stared at her aunt, wondering what kind of secrets she harbored. Could her secrets end up killing her one day too?

"You look blue," Tam said.

266

"Do I?" Joan didn't know if Tam was referring to her coloring or her mood.

Tam pressed a warm, papery palm against Joan's forehead. "You cold, eh?"

Joan hugged her legs closer. "A little."

"You want, I make you some phở."

Joan's stomach rumbled, which was all the encouragement Tam needed. She popped off the couch with a spryness that belied her septuagenarian status. Her shoulder-length hair, now more gray than black, bounced around her face.

"You come," Tam said, patting Joan's upraised knee. "Keep me company in kitchen. I tell you stories about your Ba."

Joan wasn't sure she wanted to hear any more stories about her father. Every old tale, faded album photo, and resurfaced memory had the same effect on her. They ripped off the scab she wanted so badly to harden around her wounded heart.

But what choice did she have?

"Did you know your Ba obsessed with boy?" Tam asked as she pulled a carton of broth out of the refrigerator.

"Uh, yeah."

Growing up, Joan had been acutely aware of how badly she'd disappointed her father by being born female. When one of the leading local technology companies had hired her on as a sales consultant right after she graduated college, she'd thought her father might finally realize she could be just as successful as any man. She still remembered how her insides bottomed out when his only response to her announcement had been to say, "So you're a salesperson now? I put you through college so you could end up like that car dealer next door?" Joan still felt the heavy weight of failure pushing down on her shoulders whenever she recalled his words.

Was being disgraced with a daughter part of what had led him to drink?

Tam unhooked a pot from the rack above the stove. "One time, before you born, it was all he talk about. Boy this and boy that. Drove everybody bananas. Even the dog. He run away that year."

Joan eased onto one of the counter stools. "Cô Tam, maybe we could talk about something el—"

Tam banged the pot onto a stove burner, shutting down Joan's protests. Joan listened to the tick of the gas starter, feeling out of place as a circle of blue flames flickered to life.

Tam adjusted the heat level, then pivoted around to look Joan in the eye. "Your Ba, he escape Vietnam on boat, you know?"

"Yes, I know."

"Sometimes people fall off boat, drown."

"I know. Dad was lucky."

"Yes, your Ba lucky. His wife, the first one, not so lucky. His son, your brother, also not so lucky."

Joan felt the room sway. She gripped the edge of the counter, blinking rapidly as if the problem lay with her eyes and not her ears.

"Yes, that right," Tam said, her tone so matter-of-fact she could have been relaying tomorrow's chance of rain. "Your Ba, he once had a son. When the witches come, he go overboard. Same with the women."

"Witches?" Joan whispered.

"Eh, not witches." Tam pursed her lips. "What the word?"

"Pirates?" Joan ventured, feeling sick to her stomach.

"Yes!" Tam bobbed her head so hard Joan could hear her teeth knock together. "Pirates. They the ones. Kill your brother."

* * *

After she finished making Joan's phở, Tam announced she was going back to bed. Then, without another word concerning the bombshell she'd just dropped, she scuttled upstairs, leaving Joan all alone.

Joan sat there at the counter, watching the steam rise from the hot broth in front of her. She couldn't seem to shut off her mind. She lifted the bowl to her lips once, only to set it back down without taking a sip. She had lost her appetite.

Her thoughts were all over the place. Here she was, thirty-eight years old and discovering for the first time she'd had a brother. Did she still have a brother? Tam couldn't know for sure that he'd died. Maybe one of the women who had jumped overboard to avoid the pirates had rescued him. What if he were out there somewhere right now, wondering about her as she was him?

She glanced at the digital clock on the microwave: 12:17. An image of Taylor sitting in the darkened den of their old apartment, his face illuminated by his laptop monitor, flashed through her mind.

Her gaze drifted toward the living room, where her cell phone rested on the coffee table. She knew Taylor was awake. He rarely went to bed before two or three in the morning. But people who had once shared an intimate relationship didn't make calls to their ex at this hour unless they hoped to rekindle the romance. Then again, he was the one who had told her to phone anytime, day or night. He was the one who had insisted they could remain friends.

But right now, Joan had zero interest in striking up a friendship with the man who had shattered her heart into a million pieces. Right now she wanted answers. And Taylor just might be the person who could help her get them.

She strode into the living room, snatched up her phone, and scrolled through her contact list until she found Taylor's entry, all the while wondering if she was making a huge mistake. Then, before she could talk herself out of it, she stabbed the call button.

"Joan?" He answered on the first ring, almost as if he had been waiting for her to phone.

Joan dropped onto the couch, the sound of his voice triggering an unexpected pang of longing. "Yes, it's me."

"Hey. Hi. How are you?"

"Okay, I guess. Look, the reason I'm calling . . . I mean, if you have your . . ."

The word *laptop* died on Joan's lips as it occurred to her that her mental image of him in front of a computer might not be an accurate reflection of his current state. Maybe nowadays he preferred less wired midnight activities, such as canoodling with her cousin.

She shuddered at the thought.

"I'm not with Viv anymore," Taylor said, as though he could read her mind.

Joan didn't reply. She didn't want to talk about Vivian.

"Getting together with her was a mistake," he went on, eliminating any chance he might possess mind-reading powers. "It's just that you were gone all the time on business, and she was here . . . And, well, and I guess she reminded me of you a little bit."

Something inside Joan hardened. "Vivian and I are nothing alike."

"I know that. But you have to admit, you share some similarities."

"So all of us Asians are interchangeable, is that it?"

"What? No! But you're more than both Asian, right? I mean, she might be a distant cousin, but you two still—"

"Stop talking. Please."

"Okay. Okay."

Joan closed her eyes, using one hand to rub her temple as she gripped the cell phone with her other. "I didn't call to talk about Vivian. I called because I need a favor."

"For you? Anything."

"Remember that DNA kit you gave me for my birthday last year? The one that registers you with some commercial ancestry site?"

"Yeah, sure. You said it was a waste of spit. I had to convince you to do it, and even then you didn't want to be bothered with the results."

"That's the one. I need my account info and password."

"Oh."

Taylor's voice had dulled, evidence it must finally be sinking in that she hadn't reached out with the goal of getting back together. Joan felt a burst of self-righteous satisfaction before the guilt crept in. She should have waited until morning to make this call. That would have been the fair thing to do.

"You ready?" Taylor said.

Joan scrambled for the pen and notepad her aunt kept on the coffee table. "Ready."

As Joan jotted down the information, she felt a spark of excitement in the pit of her belly. Other than glancing at the mostly expected breakdown of her ethnic heritage, she had never paid much attention to the results of her DNA analysis, going through the motions mainly to humor Taylor. But now, assuming her brother had lived, perhaps he too had an entry within this very database.

"Thank you," Joan said when Taylor had finished.

"Sure. Anytime." He paused. "I heard about your dad. I'm sorry. I wanted to call, but . . ."

"It's better you didn't call." Especially since he had probably heard the news from Vivian.

"I did some searching afterward," Taylor said.

"Searching?" Joan pictured her ex crawling around on his hands and knees in search of the soul he'd lost when he took her cousin to bed.

"On the internet. About your dad. Hey, did you know he used to play in some recreational baseball league? I found an old picture of him with his team. You would have been around two when it was taken."

It was a small thing, but it made her wonder. Did everyone know more about her father than she did? Exactly how much of his life had he kept hidden from her?

* * *

Joan practically had to hang up on Taylor before he would let her off the phone. But by half past midnight she was on her laptop, logging in to her account on the ancestry website.

She held her breath as her profile popped up on-screen. Did she dare dream that her brother might be in the system? She knew the odds were slim, but nonetheless she found herself crossing her fingers as she hunted for the listing of people who shared her DNA.

She found it halfway down the page. And there, at the very top, sat a name that sent a shock wave through her system.

Vivian Keystone.

Joan knew she really shouldn't have been surprised to see Vivian's name. They were related, after all. But according to the analysis, they shared almost a full quarter of their DNA. That would make them half sisters, not distant cousins like she'd always believed. How was that even possible?

She hunched forward, her brain struggling to make sense of the data in front of her. Had this record been here last year when she'd first sent in her DNA sample? She was fairly certain she would have noticed, even if she had only been half paying attention.

That meant Vivian must have submitted her own sample sometime within the last twelve or so months. Had Taylor gifted her with a testing kit too? He would have seen the results if he had, unless the two had broken up before Vivian's information made it into the database. Did he know Joan and Vivian were sisters? He hadn't said anything on the phone, and she didn't think he would keep something this big a secret. Then again, she'd never thought he'd cheat on her either.

Joan mentally slapped herself. Who cared whether Taylor knew? As far as she was concerned, he was persona non grata.

On the other hand, she and Vivian shared a bond not so easily ignored.

With shaking fingers, Joan dug deeper into the results. She breezed by the site's cautions that DNA analysis relied on more than simple science and how probabilities and factors like age were taken into account to provide a best guess as to one person's genetic link to another. She didn't care about that. She only wanted to know whose side of her family tree was responsible for this connection.

She didn't have to search long to find the answer. According to what she was seeing, the same man who had fathered Joan Nguyen had almost certainly also sired Vivian Keystone, a woman Joan had always believed to be related to her through their mothers.

Joan collapsed against the back of Tam's sofa. Her head was reeling. Did Vivian know about this? If she did, she hadn't shared it with Joan. Of course, the two hadn't exactly been on speaking terms during the past six months. Joan had seen Vivian only once since the night of the regretful return flight—at her father's funeral yesterday. Vivian had studiously avoided her, hunching down in a back-row pew, her oversized sunglasses eliminating the risk of making accidental eye contact.

Joan had been perfectly happy to give Vivian whatever space she wanted. In fact, she had never intended to ever speak to Vivian again. But this changed everything.

Although news this big merited more than a few typed words, Joan didn't plan to make the mistake of phoning anyone at this hour again. And she didn't think she had the patience to wait until morning. So she shot off a quick text message to Vivian, asking if she realized the ancestry site had established a strong biological link between the two of them. Short, sweet, simple. Just enough for Joan to feel as if she'd fulfilled her moral obligation to the woman who had destroyed the most serious romantic relationship of her life.

Now it was up to Vivian to investigate further and, if she so desired, reply.

* * *

Vivian did more than reply. Ten minutes later she texted Joan that she was standing on Tam's front porch. Joan didn't know how Vivian knew she was here. She must have overheard her asking Tam if she could spend the night after the funeral.

Joan braced herself as she approached the door. She wasn't sure she felt up to the task of finally facing the woman who had ended her relationship with Taylor. And she was doubly sure she wasn't emotionally stable enough to comfort Vivian if she turned out to be a weepy mess. Joan just had to hope the truth about her parentage had left her more upset and dismayed than destroyed.

But Vivian didn't appear to be any of those things. She stood on the other side of the threshold in stoic silence, her eyes almost as black as her hair. Soulless eyes, Joan thought, remembering how those eyes had locked gazes with her when Joan had walked in on Vivian and Taylor six months ago. She remembered thinking then that Vivian looked unapologetic, almost defiant.

The look on Vivian's face now wasn't so different.

Joan felt a chill unrelated to the outside temperature as Vivian pushed her way past Joan and into the house. Vivian circled around the coffee table once, then came to a stop in the middle of the living room.

"So, you know," she said.

Joan took longer than necessary to secure the front door, buying herself a much-needed moment. "The DNA site said results aren't always conclusive."

"The results are correct. Howard Nguyen was my father too."

"He must not have known, then," Joan surmised. "Why else would he never have told me?"

"Why indeed?" Vivian rolled her eyes. "You're so naïve, Joan."

"What's that supposed to mean?"

"It means you're going through life with blinders on, always thinking the best about people, taking everyone at their word. Well, I've got news for you, *sister*. Most of your fellow humans don't give one whit about anyone but themselves."

Joan stared at the woman in front of her. She had thought Vivian might be upset upon discovering the true identity of her father, but this went beyond anger. The venom in her tone penetrated all the way to the marrow of Joan's bones.

"How long have you known?" Joan asked.

"About a week."

So Vivian hadn't learned the truth much earlier than Joan. Did that mean she would have reached out eventually, attempted to make amends so they could do their best to form a true sibling relationship? Or did Vivian feel she had burned that bridge when she slept with Taylor?

Vivian walked across the room and leaned her back against the wall. "I was hurt when I first found out, but the more I think about it, the happier I am that I didn't grow up with Howard. I saw the way he was always talking down to you, punishing you for being a girl. He really did a number on your self-esteem, didn't he?"

"I don't think he meant to hurt me." Joan's perspective had started to shift the moment Tam told her about her brother. "In fact, I think he may have been afraid to love me too much." *In case he lost me too,* she didn't say.

Vivian snorted. "There you go again, thinking the best about him. Wake up, sister. Our dear old dad was a selfish bastard. He didn't care about me, and he didn't care about you either. I did us both a favor when I set that fire."

Time seemed to stop. Blood roared through Joan's ears, and her vision winked in and out. She stumbled farther into the room, barely making it to the couch before her legs gave way.

"What did you say?" Joan's throat had started to close up, and the question came out as more of a croak.

"You heard me."

"But . . ."

Vivian sighed. "I went over to Howard's house as soon as I saw your name on my DNA report. I told him I knew he was my father. He didn't deny it. He even answered some of my questions before he shut me down the way he always does, by drinking himself into oblivion."

An ache bloomed in Joan's chest. She wished she had known the severity of her father's addiction earlier. Maybe she could have helped him.

"You can imagine how I felt," Vivian said. "I'd seen him dismiss you many a time too. Maybe not with alcohol, but with his air of superiority. But I'm not like you. I wasn't going to stand there and put up with it."

Joan's hands trembled as she folded them in her lap. She wasn't sure she wanted to hear what Vivian had to say next. If the reality was anything like the image her mind had conjured up, the nightmares might haunt her for years.

"I yelled at him, told him he was weak and spineless." Vivian stared at the far wall, her eyes unfocused. "I don't know how long I berated him before I realized he had passed out. In the middle of lighting up a smoke, no less. Seeing him like that, so oblivious to anyone's pain but his own, enraged me. So I grabbed a few of his precious rum bottles from the kitchen, emptied them all around him, and lit a match. Then I hightailed it out of there. One of the neighbors almost spotted me when I was jogging down the street toward my car, but luckily I was dressed in black and could fade into the shadows."

"Like a witch," Joan whispered.

Vivian smirked. "If that helps you come to terms with it. But if you ask me, my mother was the real witch."

"What do you mean?"

"Our dear old dad, before he passed out, confessed that my mother had told him about me several years ago. I gather she wanted to settle a few things before the cancer took her." Vivian scoffed. "Too bad she didn't feel the need to include me in her little circle of truth."

The bitterness in Vivian's voice gave Joan goose bumps. But Joan couldn't blame her for her resentment. She imagined she would have felt terribly betrayed too, if their situations had been reversed.

"That was around the time Howard started drinking in earnest," Vivian said. "Once I knew about my mother's deathbed confession, I understood why he had turned to the bottle so hard. Of course, you were too busy jet-setting all over the country to notice."

Joan squeezed her eyes shut, willing away the sting of Vivian's words. A part of her knew she shouldn't react, that Vivian was only lashing out at her because her true target—the parents who had kept her in the dark for so long—weren't here to absorb the brunt of her anger. But she also spoke the truth. That job Joan had accepted after college sixteen years ago had given her a gift she had never anticipated—distance from her father and his impossible expectations.

And apparently that distance had also made her blind to his struggles.

"Your busy schedule worked out to my advantage later," Vivian said, as Joan opened her eyes in time to see her wink. "Your boy Taylor was quite the stud in bed."

Joan ran her tongue around her dry mouth. "He's not my boy anymore."

"That's too bad. He really does love you, you know. He was always telling me how guilty he felt sleeping with me."

Then why keep doing it? Joan wondered. But that was a question for Taylor, not Vivian.

Vivian could answer one thing for her, though. "Did you pursue him on purpose?" Joan asked.

"Yes."

"Why? What did I ever do to you?"

"You never did anything for me. That's the point. You always had it all, and I had nothing."

"It was never a competition."

"You should have told that to my mother. She was always comparing us, holding me up to the bar you'd set. As kids I might not have known we shared a father, but she sure did. And she used that against me my whole life."

Despite all that Vivian had done, Joan felt a pinch of sympathy for her. "I'm sorry."

Vivian's dark eyes flashed. "I don't need your pity. In fact, you might want to save that for yourself. You know I have to get rid of you, right?"

Joan went rigid. "What do you mean?"

"Now that you know what I did, I can't let you live."

"You won't get away with killing me," Joan said, hating the way her voice wobbled. "Cô Tam is right upstairs. I can scream and have her down here in an instant."

"But you won't. Because then I'd have to kill her too."

Joan pressed a clammy palm against her chest. Her heart was beating so rapidly she thought it might crack her ribs. Vivian was right, of course. Joan would never do anything to endanger her aunt.

Vivian lunged then, outstretched hands reaching toward Joan's throat. A surge of adrenaline enabled Joan to spring off the couch and sidestep her. She sprinted to the far side of the room and ducked next to the grandfather clock.

But her efforts granted her only a moment's reprieve. Vivian was fast approaching, and Joan's unfortunate instincts had left her cornered.

Fueled by pure panic, Joan laid her palms against the clock's side and pushed with all her might, hoping beyond hope she might be able to move it far enough away from the wall to carve out a hiding place. She was startled when she actually felt it start to scoot across the floor.

Vivian was almost upon her now. Joan did the only thing she could think to do. She kept pushing. And pretty soon the clock did more than slide sideways.

Vivian let out a yelp of surprise as the massive timepiece tipped toward her. She crossed her arms in front of her face, but the defensive gesture couldn't prevent the grandfather clock from taking her down as it crashed to the floor.

Joan didn't move. The sight of Vivian lying motionless underneath her aunt's old clock had left her paralyzed. She knew she should call for help, that the longer she stood here doing nothing, the less chance Vivian had of surviving. But her body felt frozen, her muscles deaf to the silent commands her brain kept firing off.

Her feet were still rooted to the floor when the toppled grandfather clock marked the end of the hour. The single chime echoed throughout the room before everything fell dead silent.

* * *

"How do I look?" Tam spread her arms and twirled in the center of the living room.

Joan adjusted the black hat on her aunt's head. Tam was now one of the few living relatives Joan had left. Where would she be when her aunt finally succumbed to the ails of age?

Tam peered at Joan, her lips twitching with impatience. "Well?"

Joan blinked back the tears stinging her eyes. "You look beautiful, Cô Tam."

Tam tittered. "You weird child, you know that? But I take."

The grandfather clock, now standing upright again and none the worse for wear, chimed once, twice, twelve times as Joan followed her aunt out the front door and into the sunlight. She lifted her sunglasses up, catching a reflection of her own black hat in the lenses before she slid them onto her face. She wasn't used to wearing anything on her head, but somehow a full mourning ensemble seemed appropriate for her sister's funeral.

Joan still had trouble wrapping her head around the fact that she and Vivian shared a father. During the drive, she thought about the man who connected them, about the wife and son he had last seen dropping over the side of a boat, and how news of her own mother's fatal accident had felled him as quickly as an arrow to the heart. Had he collapsed again when he'd learned Vivian's mother had lost her battle with cancer? How had he felt when he'd discovered he had another daughter out there in the world, one he would never have the chance to truly know?

It was staggering, really, how much loss one person was expected to endure in a lifetime.

A sudden yearning for the brother she had never met slammed into Joan like a gale-force wind. She waited until Tam had parked the car and they were heading toward the grassy area where the outdoor service would be held before saying, "Cô Tam, do you ever wonder if my brother is still alive?"

"No. He go into ocean."

"But he could have survived. I mean, we don't really know what happened after that, right?"

"No, he dead."

She said it with such finality that Joan felt like weeping.

"How come you never told me about him before now?" Joan asked.

"Your Ba, he no want to tell. Too sad for him. But now he gone, I tell." Tam clucked her tongue. "Such shame. A life wasted."

Joan wasn't sure if Tam was referring to her brother or her father. For that matter, she could be talking about Vivian. They had reached the lawn where the ceremony would take place. Not many people were gathered, but Joan didn't know if that was a reflection of how Vivian had lived her life or because they had arrived early.

Joan looked at Tam, the urge to confess the events of that night burning inside her. She didn't want to have any secrets between them. She had seen how dangerous secrets could be.

She took a deep breath. "Cô Tam, I need to tell you something."

"What that?"

"My father had another child, a third child."

Tam gave her a curt nod. "Yes, yes. Vivian."

Joan rocked back on her heels. "You knew Vivian was my sister?"

"Yes, I know."

"For how long?"

"Eh, not long. I see your computer. That night. You leave top open, I look."

Joan had been so out of it after she knocked the grandfather clock over that she barely remembered how the crash had sent Tam running into the room. At some point Tam must have sneaked a peek at the ancestry account Joan hadn't bothered to log out of. Joan tried to work out when exactly that could have happened, but instead she found herself remembering how calm and self-assured her aunt had been when the police arrived at the house. Tam had told them how she was to blame for Vivian's death, because she had lacked the physical strength to move that old clock off the flat wooden dolly she'd bought years ago for the purpose of transporting it into the house. Joan had sat there, mute with shock, as Tam showed the officers the bed skirt she'd altered to mask the clock's unlikely podium and explained how Vivian must not have known about the dolly when she'd gone over to admire the unstable timepiece.

Joan's chest tightened. Tam had no idea that she was the person responsible for Vivian's death, not her.

"Cô Tam, about the night Vivian died. I—"

"Shh. It okay."

"But it's not okay. I—"

"Hush." Tam silenced Joan with a withering look. "You young, think everybody should know everything about everybody. Sometimes it okay to have secrets."

Joan's skin tingled. She had the eerie feeling that, in this case, her secret might not be as secret as she thought.

Tam patted Joan's hand. "You good child, you know that? Always want to do right. If I young, have baby, I would want girl like you. Much better than bad girl. Much better than boy."

Joan was glad the sunglasses masked the tears she could no longer hold back. She linked her arm with her aunt's and rested her head on her shoulder. Standing there side by side, both of them in their black hats, Joan could imagine how they looked.

Like witches. And this was their hour.

IN THE MATTER OF MABEL AND BOBBY JEFFERSON

By Christopher Chambers

Call center job. This is the Lake Cocytus of gigs, in that last circle of Hell where Hell has indeed frozen over. Reserved for the traitors, betrayers. Did I mention I was an English major and that's how I know this shit? Gets better: my supervisor's name is Virgil Dante. Made a literary joke about that to him during my online interview and just got deadpan silence. The Fates can't truly torture you unless they can amuse themselves in the process. It's going to get funny tonight, I can feel it.

Dante's watching me, up there in a nicer circle of Hell: a camera, hanging through the faux-stucco acoustic ceiling tile between two migraine-inducing fluorescent lights. Gives him a full sweep of the empty cubicles and the tchotchkes and cheesy vacation pics therein. Wonder what he's *really* doing— somewhere in Nevada, for a company headquartered in Oklahoma. Pizza, porn? I can't order out; my screen is locked. Barely a bar of cell reception . . .

. . . and before I can imagine a new way of killing myself . . . perhaps fentanyl dripped over a Good Humor strawberry shortcake ice cream bar . . . my screen kicks up a record, the phone line beeps. I'm going to be busy for the next four to seven minutes before I refer the matter to underwriting. Meaning a bonus of five bucks per call. Or I refer it to claims. Meaning I get a ding unless I roadblock, cockblock, chop-block before it gets to the adjuster. Dante may deign to listen in and render support. He's yet to deign in the month I've been here.

"Good evening, this is Shane at Eight Farmers Insurance. How may I help you?"

"Yeah . . . um . . . this funny, like the TV commercial where my nigga's on the phone late and his woman think he on a porno call, right?" The n-word? Really? "Yeah, an' she catches feelin's cause he say no, it's really the insurance man."

Bama alert. Still, I typically try hard to sound white when it's a policyholder rather than a perv caller or some doofus looking for the same info that's on the damn website. Sure enough, my screen's flashing that he's a policyholder.

"Yes, sir . . . to whom am I speaking . . . is this Mr. Jefferson?"

"What time y'all got there? I got twenny of twelve midnight . . ."

"Sir, right . . . it's eleven forty PM here in beautiful Syracuse, New York."

"It cold up there?"

"It is, sir. Seven inches of snow and counting." And I'm likely going to get stuck here if the damn plow doesn't come at sunrise. "How is it in"—I glance at the notes—"Bossier City, Louisiana? Balmy, I bet."

There's dead air, then laughter. "Ha! *Bwa-see-ay* City? My nigga, y'all, this ain't no Creole bu'shit like New Orlins. We say *Bo-zhur* City in these parts."

Training manual, page fourteen. Breathe. Redirect. "Well thank you, Mr. Jefferson, for correcting me. I love this job because it allows me to serve people all over this great country and such diverse—"

"Ain't got much time, my nigga." Yeah, he cuts me off. No laughter tacked on to his missives this time. "So let's get to it."

"I—I hear you, sir." I deflect from the n-word. "I'm presuming . . . let's see . . . yeah . . . that you wish to renew your term life policy . . . on your spouse, Mrs. Jefferson . . ."

"Yeah man, on Mabel. Expires at midnight. Lissen here, can y'all just hit whatever *renewal* button like before and it kicks in, youngsta?"

"Um, we can take care of that lickety-split . . ." Aw, man—I really said that? He's only seventy-three, not the Jim Crow, D-Day, and Hiroshima generation! "See, your first renewal was sort of automatic, as it was such a short initial term, even though you've taken out a policy on your spouse. This second renewal, however, of the term expiring tonight . . . if you read page twenty of the endorsements, it has new rules that kick in. Now, given Mrs. Jefferson's age and this being a second renewal term, your premiums are going to be *much* higher, so may I refer you to underwriting for our whole-life product? You may find that much better suited to your family's needs, and we can set up a tail policy tonight to bridge you the—"

"Don't sell me, silly youngsta, I need my damn coverage!"

If I get mad, I get fired. No gas-face expressions either. Dante's watching.

"Understood, sir. This will only take a few minutes, and you can have a good night's sleep knowing you've renewed in time. So, is Mrs. Jefferson available to speak? I'll also need a file or PDF of her most recent doctor's visit or health screening. You can email or text it to our secure network."

"Mabel asleep."

"Oh-kay . . ." I see a purple WHOLE LIFE notice suddenly flash on my screen, but hey, I gave him the opportunity. Whole-life might not make sense to these two, given their age, but shit, his premiums are going to geyser! The notice disappears, oddly, as I scroll to renewal entry, grit my teeth, then ask the required question: "Would you be able to wake Mrs. Jefferson—"

"Her name be Mabel!"

"Wake *Mabel* . . . so she can speak for no more than thirty seconds?"

"Aw . . . hold on," he snorts, all tinged with exasperation. I hear Mr. Jefferson, this time all flowery and sweet, whisper, "Mabel, honey, please talk this youngsta. Yeah, roll over an' take the phone . . . I'll fluff yo' pilla."

And then, "*I be so tired, Bobby Lee. Can't this wait till mornin'?*"

"*No, sweetie, my fault. I waited till the las' minute. All 'bout coverage.*"

And so I hear in my earpiece: "Young man . . . this be Mabel Jefferson. I certify I be in good health, God's care, and give Bobby Lee Jefferson permission to renew the insurance."

Nah. That's all I can say. I mean, this does not sound like an old woman. Definitely sounds like a sick person, but . . . she just sounds strange. At least she's not using the n-word.

And there's the damn whole-life prompt again, popping up! IT nerds need to fix that shit, but it's too late now. I dunno . . . let me try this . . .

"Sir . . . ma'am, I have a video chat option here from this end. If you are using phone or tablet of any kind, perhaps it's best if we can see each other."

"It ten till midnight, Godammit!" Mr. Jefferson snarls back at me. "Ain't gots no fancy iPhone, this be Ma Bell real 'murican dial phone shit, hea' me?" Oh my God. "Now, she say she okay . . . I needs this renewal, just this once!" Jesus, does some mutha have a pistol to his head? "We tryna get *coverage*. All about the coverage! *Coverage!* Can't y'all do me this?"

Okay, Dante's probably snacking and watching a hockey game, so I say fuck it and jump way badder than the manual allows.

"Mr. Jefferson . . . listen. I can't help you if you yell, if you use the n-word . . . and if you insist on circumventing . . . *okay* . . ." Color time! "If you keep *joanin'* me, right? *Gassin'*, right?" That shut him up. "Y'all've be paying premiums for a brick, but hey, that's between y'all and Eight Farmers. We don't wanna lose you as a customer, so can we start over from jump, pops? Hunned-percent on your side, *trust*."

"Well . . . uh . . .," he intones, like my secret identity's been revealed. He suddenly rescinds his wolf tickets and is all passive, pliant. "Y'all really need this health report and shit? Mabel's here, and just said she fit as a fiddle, right?"

"Come on, man, I need this job. So, no computer with internet access?"

"Nah-uh."

"Got an old fax machine?"

"Y'all young cats think er'ybody on the Tweets and shit. Ain't bu'shittin' you, youngblood . . . we need *coverage* . . ." There's that word again, yet he's not demanding. He's pleading.

He suddenly puts me on hold right as I hear something like pots and pans in the kitchen drop . . . weird, right, if he's in a bedroom with ole Mabel half snoozing!

He comes back and he's panting, dead-ass.

I think the old bastard's having a stroke when he entreats, "L-Look, youngblood . . . almos' midnight . . . h-help me out."

As if Cerberus has let the rest of the dogs out of Hell's maw, I hear my master's voice in my headset. He's chewing on something, loud . . .

"*Yeah, you copy?*" Dante prompts. "*I'm looking over his file. Just clear 'im for underwriting renewal, five-year term. Stupid old spooks like this are our bread an' butter.*"

I'm debating whether to get fired now. He's *seen* me. He knows I'm black, right? I mean, lots of "clear" people think I'm Puerto Rican or Arab sometimes, but Jesus Christ . . .

"How do you know he's African American, Mr. Dante?"

"*Hel-lo! He's a dark-ass moolie in his file pic, and credit report just screams nigger. 'Bout the only thing this asshole pays on time is our premiums! Choctaw Lodge Indian Red River Casino fuckin' owns him . . . on top of what . . . five finance companies? Shreveport Dog Track . . . fuggetaboutit!*"

What do I do? Yeah, it's not so simple. But . . . *shit* . . . I gotta summon back my sack. Been sitting on it too long.

"Dante!" Yep, I don't say *Mister* Dante to this racist guido. Yet does this jackass *not* hear me? Am I that forgettable?

"*Yeah, these niggers never plan, never build a thing— then blame it all on the white man. Count on hittin' the number or an insurance payout to be their angels. Yo, you listening . . . Hel-lo?*"

"Uh-huh . . . and I'm done with your—"

"*Just renew the fucker. It's almost midnight, you book a five-buck bonus . . . and hey, maybe the sumbitch'll pay off his debts when the wife goes. Like when the first Mrs. Jefferson croaked . . .*"

And he's out of my car. *Poof!* And all I can manage is a mouthed, hushed, "Hold up. Hold the hell up . . ."

Bye-bye, sack.

"Y-You still there, Mr. Jefferson?" I ask.

"Where're at, youngblood? Comin' to midnight. . . . Mabel be here, right as rain. She my blossom and I be her honey, hea' me?"

And then I hear something strange, and I mean stranger than this whole damn call's been tonight. It's not Mabel, in that bizarre voice of hers. Like, there's whispering. Men, whispering. He might be talking on an old rotary phone, but that ancient receiver's picking up this noise, and now I'm squirming in my damn chair.

A minute to midnight.

I swear I hear a whimper from this man who is dying to renew a predatory term life policy. On his second, elderly wife.

Almost serenely, he says to me, "I ain't got much time . . ."

I renew him.

I send the newly generated policy number to underwriting.

It's twelve AM. It's black as Styx outside, despite the snowfall.

"Mr. Jefferson, it's done."

I swear I hear him almost swoon in relief. And that whispering noise is gone.

"Look 'ere, youngblood," he gushes, "y'oughten've put my ass through all that, but we gotta do what we gotta do, eh?"

I'm not going to insult him and say it's my job. But I will insult him with *this*, since Dante was the one who did him the solid, not me, and I have time now to bring up the file. "Mr. Jefferson, what happened to your first wife?"

Maybe it didn't register, because I still hear him chuckling when he says, "Pardon?"

"You collected an eighty-seven-thousand-dollar death benefit . . ."

"Aw, that be Daisy. She fell an' hurt herself. Died in the hospital. Painful for me ta talk 'bout that."

"Death benefit on the renewal for Miz Mabel is one hundred large, Mr. Jefferson." Okay, I swallow hard and do it, because as bad as Dante and this corporation are, I'm not going to be party to some ole lady getting merked. "Mr. Jefferson, may I speak to Mizz Mabel . . . if, 'course, she's really there."

And he starts guffawing. I mean geeking, like he's over like a fat rat. "Ain't no thing now, eh? Gotta pick up the phone in the bedroom. *May-bell . . . May-bel, baby. Telephone, sweet thang!*"

So his ass wasn't even in the bedroom. Lying old mutha . . .

But here's fucking Dante again, in my ear.

"Hey, don't check your alerts?"

"Um . . . you mean the whole-life thing? I tried to up-sell him, but he said no . . . then you said renew him and get the higher term premiums. Was the next alert a network glitch?"

"Yo, moron . . . moron! We pay you to do IT? Fuck no! This is a cross-policy alert! Don't you read the manual? This Bobby Lee clown is listed as insured on another one of our products. A new whole life, effective midnight, today! Madrone . . . you

payin' attention? Check the screen, reconcile the policies, then get ready for the next call!"

He's gone. I check the screen.

Insured, Bobby Lee Jefferson. *The fuck?* Policyholder . . . Mabel . . .

. . . McCusker . . .

. . . Jones . . .

. . . Okafor . . .

. . . Silverstein . . .

Jefferson.

Oh,

Shit . . .

"Youngblood?" I hear as I fumble for words. "She truly tired . . . wansta know if her daughter . . . my stepdaughter Wanda . . . can do the email wid all that medical stuff tomorrow?"

"Ahhhh, Mr. Jefferson . . ."

"Bobby Lee, now that we frens . . ."

"Bobby Lee . . . um, I was researching your file, and . . ." Say it! Wimpy-ass English major!

"Know what—if it about my Daisy, past is past. Right now, I gots meet up wid some my fellas down the Do-Ray-Me Social Club, square some shit, y'all know . . . grown-folks bidness."

"At *midnight?*"

"Y'all think we old cats can't hang. Got m'self *coverage.* Good ta have in these perilous days, 'specially wid my Mabel being dead, dead tired all the damn time. Audi, youngblood."

Click. Beep. Gone.

And I'm sitting there, alone in the cubicle, alone in the damn building, snow piling up outside. I page Dante, and he isn't answering . . .

It's one.

Now it's two thirty. Two calls, and yeah, both are doofuses who can't understand the website's plain English . . .

Two fifty-eight AM, and after my "lunch break" of Trader Joe's lamb vindaloo from the hoary nasty microwave and a mug of bitter lukewarm coffee, I swear I'm seeing ghosts dancing across my corkboard.

And then my screen lights up, and the line beeps.

It's a mobile phone number, and I'm too looped and loopy to check the name.

"Good evening . . . I mean, good morning, this is Shane at Eight Farmers Insurance. How may I help you?"

"*Oh Father Gawd, oh Father Gawd, no!*" I hear a likely female voice shriek. "I—I dunno what to say . . . I have a police report they just handed me. I'm in the hospital."

The screen says she's a policyholder, but before I check the name, I try to calm her. Sometimes our cheap-ass anti-Obamacare med policyholders call up when they've been jacked up to find out what we won't cover, or how our deductible is the size of a mortgage payment. I can like a 911 operator.

"Slow down, I got you. Be calm. Where are you?"

"M-Magnolia Parish Regional Hospital . . . in the ER. Here with my mama . . . oh Jesus no . . ."

Her voice is breaking fast, so I check the name on the phone: *Simmons, W.* Nothing.

Now I read the policyholder's ID, and the name corkscrews into my eyeballs around the same second I hear it gouge my eardrums.

"Mabel Jefferson. My mama is Mabel Jefferson, and she has insurance with y'all."

"Are you . . . Wanda?"

"Uh-huh," she sniffles. "How'd you know?"

I can feel the acidic vomit biting its way up my gullet. "Is your mama . . . all right?"

Yeah, it's flooding past my Adam's apple when she says, "*Yes*, she's right here. Let me see if she's calm enough to speak . . ."

"Mrs. Jefferson?" I croak, upon battling the lamb vindaloo and coffee back down.

"Yes, hello . . . young man." Not a strain or wheeze or whispery weakness in her voice. And how'd she know . . . my age? "My husband, Bobby Lee, was shot in a robbery at his all-night social club in Bossier City. He . . . he frequented a lot of places with low-type scoundrels, I'm sad to say. Many a loan shark to tide him so he could pay our bills during my . . . infirmity."

Uh-huh. I'm monotone. I'm wheezy. Opposite of her brass-bell-gong voice. "Mrs. Jefferson . . ."

"Call me Mabel. I bet you have a lot to tell me."

"Mabel . . . *Miz* Mabel. This . . . this is a new policy. Midnight, in fact. I have to refer it to claims, and the adjuster's likely going to—"

"I know what the adjuster's going to need. Wanda, my daughter, will send it along."

"Yes, but . . . you're within the ten-day period. You can't get a payout. Burial expenses are covered, yes, but . . . the death benefit . . . assuming there're no . . . *questions* . . . is reduced to—"

"Two hundred eleven thousand dollars and fourteen cents . . . yes, young man, I know. I will also be canceling his term life policy on me, renewed before midnight. Now, do you have any more questions for me, or should I wait for the claim adjuster's call in the morning?"

"I'm done, ma'am."

"Thank you, Shane. Like the preacher says, this sour life is short, the sweet hereafter is long. It's unfair how one feeds the other."

Click. Beep. Gone.

Call center job. This is the Lake Cocytus of gigs, in that last circle of Hell where Hell has indeed frozen over. Reserved for the enablers, the abettors. And the chickenshit.

Did I mention I was an English major?

THE NIGHT
THE INTERNET DIED
By Rhonda Crowder

Samia sat at her home office desk, working, fighting to stay awake. She felt like she needed sticks in her eyes to keep them open. It'd been at least five hours since she'd stood up and nearly twenty-four since she'd started working on the report she needed to present to her team the following morning.

Her new job as CEO of the National Cybersecurity Center in Colorado Springs seemed taxing, considering she'd already deemed herself an "impostor," being the only African American woman in the organization's C-suite. Despite having military experience and a PhD in computer engineering from Stanford and having worked as assistant director for infrastructure security for the Department of Homeland Security's Cybersecurity and Infrastructure Security Agency (CISA), she still asked herself, "How did I get here?"

She could be so unsure of herself at times.

She ran her hands through her short, permed hair, then glanced at the clock on the wall. It read 11:59 PM. *It's still pretty early*, she thought.

"If I can manage just thirty more minutes. Thirty more minutes, I can wrap up this SWOT and get some rest before tomorrow morning's videoconference with my team," she said, clearly talking to herself, since no one occupied the room—let alone her swanky apartment—but her. "This has to be perfect. I'm sure they're just waiting on the poor black girl from the inner city of Cleveland to fail. Good thing they're a couple of hours behind."

Thoughts of inferiority stayed at the forefront of Samia's mind, probably because she'd always felt out of place. A math and science whiz kid in elementary school, she'd been made to feel like an outcast by the other children. As one of few blacks and even fewer women during her undergraduate studies at MIT, she hadn't fit in. Then, quickly rising through the ranks of the Air Force to become a brigadier general had made her stand out like a black sheep, to say the least. There had never been anyone who could relate to her, not even her mother or five siblings. She'd never known her dad. Her best friend since third grade, Tonya, sympathized but didn't fully understand. To make matters worse, her colleagues had referred to her as the AAC—affirmative action case—many times to her face. She'd found microaggressions in the workforce to be real.

Samia took a deep breath and a sip of Pepsi from a can before clicking on a secure browser she'd developed to search the internet. She typed *The Iranian government activated the internet kill switch* and awaited the results. She wanted to review some articles again, for the gazillionth time, that covered Iran's use of an internet kill switch to see how it worked in comparison to the one she'd developed for the United States. Since word of her kill switch had begun to circulate throughout the top levels of the government, it had become the biggest threat to U.S. cybersecurity and critical to how the Center planned to protect smart cities. In essence, despite her personal insecurities, Samia had become a master of the internet of things.

Being selected to attend that boarding school in ninth grade had paid all the way off.

She looked at her screen. Her computer continued to spool, and then finally an error message appeared. *Unable to connect to the internet.*

"The very last thing I need right now."

She immediately went into troubleshooting mode, trying everything she could think of. Nothing. She couldn't get on the internet. She picked up her personal smartphone, the newest Samsung Galaxy S20, and tried it. Neither her Wi-Fi nor 5G was available. Same thing with the iPhone she used for work.

"That's weird. Must be some kind of outage in the area," she said, still talking to herself. "Let me call Spectrum."

After calling and recalling from her landline for at least forty-five minutes because of the busy line signal, she finally got a representative.

"Yes. We are experiencing an outage. We're working as fast as we can to fix it," the woman said.

"Thank you," Samia responded, then hung up, thinking that still didn't explain her phones' internet outages. "What in the world is going on?"

Confused, Samia wandered over to the picture window in her top-floor apartment, located in University Circle. She could see Lake Erie just a short distance away and the duck pond behind the Cleveland Museum of Art—a spectacular sight even in the middle of the night. Oddly enough, she saw an unusual amount of traffic on Euclid Avenue. *Maybe they're still out celebrating the newly elected president?* she thought, and then her mind shifted to her fiancé, whom she'd met less than a year prior during a girls' trip with her best friend and sister.

* * *

"He sure is fine," said Tonya, Samia's best friend. "I think he's checking you out. I'm going to call him over here."

"Don't do that," Samia said, the more laid-back one of the three.

"Get that stick out of ya ass," said Sia, Samia's sister. Sia had enough spunk for the both of them, and Tonya had always been a firecracker. Tonya was the reason they were in Cabo San Lucas. She was always involved in something, and her latest moneymaking scheme was selling people five-star dream vacations at three- and two-star rates. She had convinced her two friends they needed to get away and let their hair down.

Samia knew that with her job, she could do nothing of the sort on United States soil, so she had looked forward to the opportunity to have some fun. Her work kept her in serious mode, on the edge twenty-four/seven.

Next thing she knew this young, handsome, Latino-looking man was standing before them and Tonya was starting to introduce her. He had skin smooth as shea butter and bright white teeth, and his smile made Samia melt. The tequila shots they had been taking all night probably didn't help either.

"Angel Sanchez," he said as he shyly introduced himself before kissing Samia's hand. "Would you ladies like to join me and some of my amigos over at Playa Del Amor?"

"Sure," Tonya and Sia said in unison.

"I . . . I . . . don't know," said Samia. "We don't . . ."

"We're here to have some fun," said Tonya as she jumped out and pulled Samia along. "Lead the way, Angel."

At Lover's Beach, the ladies danced, ate, and drank the night away with Angel and his friends. They had the time of their lives. They had so much fun that when the party concluded, Angel and Samia found it hard to part. Instead of the ladies catching an Uber back to their resort, Angel agreed to drive, and Samia invited him into her room.

He wasn't like most guys. He didn't try to have sex or take advantage of her. Instead, they sat under the early-morning sky, discussing hopes and dreams. He was single, with no children. He wanted to settle down and marry. He didn't seem intimidated when she mentioned her military experience and role. She didn't, however, tell him about her job with CISA. She typically kept that to herself.

But he told her he had studied engineering and worked for the CIA. They talked all morning. And, for the first time, she'd met a man who understood her. They were on the same team. Samia ended up spending the remainder of her vacation with Angel, and he promised to visit her in Cleveland upon her departure from Cabo.

At first they spent a lot of time video chatting via Duo— since he lived in LA—which led to their developing a virtual love affair. Then, about three months after their encounter in Cabo, he arrived in Cleveland for a two-week stay with a jaw-dropping engagement ring. Confident that Angel was "the one," Samia said yes without hesitation.

* * *

In the middle of Samia trying her best to finish pulling her SWOT together—without all the research she needed to back up her claims—her landline rang. "Who could be calling me this time of night?" She smiled. "It's probably Angel."

"General Browning." A frantic young male voice spoke.

"Yes, Pablo. What is it? Why are you calling me at one thirty in the morning?" she asked her senior technology analyst from CISA. She hadn't completely left that job yet.

"General. We need you at Burke Lakefront Airport in thirty minutes. A charter will be there to bring you to DC," Pablo continued with great anxiety. "The FBI is here."

"Why? What's going on? I'll need to pack."

"No time for that. We'll explain once you arrive." Pablo hung up.

Samia had been around long enough to know that when the government told you to be somewhere, you went. She hurriedly grabbed an overnight bag and a few essentials before jetting out the door to the parking garage. She didn't have the time or internet to order an Uber. Luckily, she didn't live too far from the airport and could be there in about seven good minutes—especially driving a brand-new Maserati.

* * *

As she pulled out of the garage, the number of cars out in the streets sent shock waves through her mind. All up and down Euclid Avenue were Ubers and Lyfts, seemingly suspended in time. She hadn't seen activity like this on the streets of Cleveland since the night the Cavs won the championship. People were riding bikes, walking, and just hanging out around the duck pond. A murmur buzzed through the air. She didn't have time to make sense of the activity. She needed to get to the airport.

By the time Samia had reached Burke, parked, and checked in, a pilot was standing on the tarmac to greet her. They saluted each other, and then she boarded the small aircraft. Once she was seated, an attendant appeared to inform her that they would begin taxiing the runway in less than five minutes.

Up in the air, Samia tried her best to relax, but being summoned to the Homeland Security office caused a great deal of jitters. She started to wring her hands and spin her five-carat princess-cut diamond ring. She thought about Angel, whom she hadn't spoken to in a few days, since he was on a secret mission. She respected that because, with her own levels of security clearance, she had secrets to maintain too.

She just loved the fact that she'd finally found someone who could relate to her.

Her family felt a bit skeptical of Angel, due to his nationality and their age difference—he was about ten years younger than her—but Samia had let them know black men seemed intimidated by her and so she'd never clicked with them. If she ever wanted to find happiness and have children, she had to date outside her race, and they needed to accept it as well as him.

After the attendant brought Samia a snack and a hot drink, she calmed just enough to doze off. She dreamed about her big day and life with Angel. And, by the time she woke up, they were preparing to land at Signature Flight Support DCA, Washington National Airport.

When Samia deplaned, a car awaited her. The driver helped her inside, put her overnight bag in the trunk, and took off within a couple blinks of an eye. During the drive to the CISA office in Arlington, she glared out the window and thought about how much she would miss working in the DMV area. But she looked forward to home being in Colorado Springs near her new job, where she planned to live with Angel. Even a new house being built for the start of their new life together. They anticipated moving in right after the wedding, set for June 2021, although they would probably have to reschedule it or scale it back due to the pandemic. She hadn't discussed canceling or postponing wedding plans with him, hoping and praying the ordeal would subside by then.

"I'll have you there in no time, General," the driver said.

"Thank you, Javiar," Samia responded.

As they got closer to Arlington, Samia noticed an unusual amount of people in the streets out here as well. "Javiar, you know why the streets are so crowded?'

"I'm suspecting it's because the internet is out. It's been down all night."

"Here too?" She hadn't bothered to check her phone since landing. She'd just assumed it to be an event isolated to Cleveland. *That's not irony*, she thought. *This is serious.*

"Plus, people have been celebrating the election results," Javiar added.

About twenty minutes later, Javiar arrived at CISA headquarters. He got out first, retrieved her bag from the trunk, and then opened the door for her. Over time she had developed enough etiquette to sit and wait for the driver instead of hopping out on her own. Just as she placed both feet on the ground, she heard gunshots from a distance. "Oh my," she said.

Javiar hurried her inside to Pablo, who ushered her to the main conference room, where the director and assistant directors from CISA, the secretary of homeland security, and two unknown gentlemen awaited her. Everyone looked like Nino

Brown's team in the movie *New Jack City* after the police had raided the Carter apartments.

"General Browning, please. Have a seat," said the Secretary, pulling out her designated chair at the table.

"Thank you," Samia said as she took her seat. Everyone else took theirs as well.

"We don't have much time, so I'm going to get right to it," her assistant director of emergency communications from CISA said. "We are under attack. Someone has activated the internet kill switch. It happened approximately at midnight, Eastern Standard time."

"But who, Director? Who could've possibly activated it? There's only a few people with the codes to do so, and I am one," Samia said. "I've guarded them with my life."

Oh Lord! Maybe this is a politically motivated attack in reaction to the election results, she thought, but kept it to herself. Many of the president's allies were present in the room. Although she disagreed with his policies, she had become pretty cozy with him too, having worked on the country's National Cyber Strategy a few years back.

"We think we've pinpointed the source in general. But first, we need you to get all systems back up and running before trading starts at nine thirty AM," said CISA's assistant director of cybersecurity. "Once that happens, the FBI and the secretary of homeland security will talk to you about who's responsible for this breach."

Samia looked over to the two unfamiliar gentlemen in the room. Both remained stoic.

"I've started to prepare some of the work we need to get done," said CISA's assistant director of cybersecurity. "Let's go to your office."

Samia led the way, trying her damnedest to masquerade her nervousness. She knew her job hung in the balance if she failed to restore the mechanism the country's economy depended on so heavily.

The assistant director of cybersecurity and Samia went straight to work, reviewing, evaluating, and rewriting code to deactivate the internet kill switch. They were so focused on the task at hand that neither uttered a word unless they needed verification or validation. Samia, because she was responsible for the development of the kill switch in the first place, was really the only one who could fix the problem. The other person in the room was there only to help her. She worked diligently until about eight forty-five AM.

"I've deactivated the switch. It's brought all but one mainframe back up. The one controlling the northeastern seaboard."

* * *

"Keep trying. That's the most important one," the director of cybersecurity said.

"There appears to be multiple attacks on it," said Samia. "Someone is trying to hijack data as well."

"Let me take a look," said the director. "See here—that's ransomware. There's a request for a hundred million in Bitcoin to unlock it."

Samia reached for her office phone to summon the secretary of homeland security and the FBI. Moments later they entered her office. She and the director explained what they'd encountered.

"We are aware of this, General. We're hoping you can hack the decryption key so we don't have to pay it," said the secretary of homeland security.

Samia looked at the men in disbelief. She knew she could, but completing it in less than an hour presented a challenge.

"We wanted to wait until you got all the grids back operating to tell you this," said the FBI agent. "But your fiancé, Angel Sanchez, is behind this breach."

Samia's heart crashed into bits and pieces. For the first time in her adult life, she'd decided to take a chance. Angel had felt so right for her. "No. Can't be," she said. "I did every kind of search on him possible. He checked out."

"He had a great cover," said the FBI agent. "His real name is Amin Ghorbani. His mother is Turkish and his father is Iranian. He grew up in Mexico but has been working for Russian intelligence agencies for the last decade or so, since his early twenties. His father was a spy too."

"We know this is devastating news, General; that's why we wanted to wait," said the secretary of homeland security. "But we are counting on you to save the economy. And we are highly confident you can do it."

Samia had to quickly gather her emotions and get to work. Although she loved Angel or Amin or whatever his name was, she refused to allow some spy to ruin her career and her reputation. She dug deep into her mental library of encryptions until she found the right one to crack the code, and at approximately 9:21 AM, all systems across the country were back up and running. The internet worked once more.

Back in the main conference room, her team and the others congratulated her for saving the economy. She even got a video call from the president thanking her as well.

"Don't feel like a failure about this breach," the FBI agent said. "You're not the only one this has happened to. We're just glad we were able to protect you and grateful for your skills and ability to quickly bring us back online. What would the cyber world do without you?"

"Thank you, Agent," Samia said. Even though she felt terrible for allowing herself to be compromised, she was ecstatic about her singular ability to save the U.S. economy.

I guess I am one bad sista, she thought.

MATA HAMBRE
By Raquel V. Reyes

"Meet me at la cafetería."
  "I'm not hungry."
"We're not going there to eat."

Pugi was the most chonga of the chongas and still chongaing at the old age of twenty-five. With black marker eyebrows, hair pulled back so tight it looked like guitar strings about to pop, big gold hoops, and a push-up bra on display from the low scooped neck of a tight tank top, my cousin was sex and intimidation stuffed into a pair of butt-lift skinny jeans. Her exaggeration of gender was one-eighty to my uniform of chinos and guayaberas.

"What time?"

"Eleven thirty."

"It's too late. I need my sleep."

"Too late? When did you turn viejo? Dee, it's not about food or sleep. Okay?"

"What is it about, then?"

"Thirst."

Pugi, always on the prowl, liked to drag me on her hunts. I wasn't competition. She took the men and I took the women, much to Mami y Tia's embarrassment and shame. And on the rare occasion she got into something she couldn't handle, my right hook was there to get her out of it.

"Fine. What's it this time?"

"The Medianoche at Medianoche contest."

The parking lot of Tres Palmas Latin American Café de Hialeah was alive and vibrating like it was the Calle Ocho Festival. The streets around it were blocked off. Ritmo 95.7, the Cubaton radio station, had a flatbed stage with ten-foot-high speakers blasting Cuban-accented reggaeton. A large white event tent twice as big as the actual restaurant stood monolithically in the center of it all. Despite all the chaos, I found Pugi easily. I followed the direction all the phones were pointed. She was doing her thing, gyrating and twerking like a Cardi B doppelganger. By the time the song ended, she'd be WhatsApp famous in Miami-Dade.

"You made it."

"You didn't give me much choice, mi querida ball and chain."

"Shut up. You love me."

"It's not like I could divorce you even if I wanted to. We're family."

"Hablando de familia, Mami saved us seats."

"Tia is here?"

"Your mom and my mom y Tio y Lenita y Ruben, y—"

"Coño. For real? The whole family is here?"

"Not the whole family. Just like eight of us."

"I thought this was a thirst mission."

"It is."

"Then where is he?"

"He's number five."

She took a folded, sweat-damp paper from her back pocket and waved it for me to grab. I read it as we walked to the tent. The program listed the sponsors. In addition to the restaurant and the radio station, there was Cruz Toyota, Donor of the grand prize, a red RAV4; Bembe Botánica; and Sedano's Supermarket. Twelve contestants were listed, most of them local celebrities. Number five was former Hialeah High quarterback and current UnMundo weatherman Alex Perez.

"Super."

"I know, right?"

Pugi hadn't gleaned the sarcasm of my superlative. Nothing good was going to come from Pugi lusting for her ex-boyfriend. Alex and Pugi had dated their junior and senior years of high school. Tia had heard wedding bells. But when Alex came home from UF that first Christmas, the sweethearts broke up in grand Pugi fashion.

"You keyed his car."

"That was forever ago."

"You spray-painted a pinga on his front door."

"Oh my God, that was so funny."

"His mother did not think it was funny. A huge dick in dripping black paint was on her house."

Every plastic-wedding-rental-chair seat in the tent held a body, except for the two in the front row right that were occupied by my mother's and aunt's purses. Pugi squeezed past drowsy abuelitos and kids jacked up on Jupiña to claim our saved seat. She waved for me to follow. I did against my better judgment. Mami gave me a kiss and a reprimand for dressing like a man. Tia did the same, except instead of chastising me for my appearance, she asked me why I couldn't do something about the way Pugi dressed. I'm not saying Tia used the word *puta* to describe her own daughter, but the way she said *fulana* was vicious.

"Why are we here?"

"Duh. Alex."

"The guy you were never going to forgive?"

"Ancient history, bro."

Pugi adjusted her boobs, crossed her legs, and puckered her lips. An air kiss flew in the direction of weatherman Perez as he and the other contestants pulled on aprons embroidered with the Tres Palmas logo. Alex flashed his above-market-salary smile. The UnMundo camera trained on him followed his gaze into the audience. It found a blond in a Cruz Toyota T-shirt. The woman grinned, flipped her hair off her shoulder, then clapped her hands together like she was sending a prayer to La Caridad del Cobre. Alex gave the woman a thumbs-up. His focus shifted from her to his workstation. The camera panned the audience and missed what I saw—Alex winked at Pugi. I lip-read the single-word message that accompanied it. *Later.*

"Who is that?"

"Who?"

"The blond across the aisle. The one primo Ruben is drooling over."

"Oh, that bitch? That's Cristina. Alex's girlfriend."

"Excuse me?"

"She's fake. I'm real."

The music died. Standing viewers pushed in from the open sides of the tent. The contest's MC tapped the mic. Feedback squealed. Once the levels were balanced, he welcomed everyone and explained the rules. There would be three rounds with a different sandwich in each. If a contestant touched the food with his fingers or any meats fell out of the sandwich, they'd be eliminated. At the end of each ten-minute round, there should be five finished sandwiches on the serving tray. Otherwise you didn't pass to the next round. Tres Palmas' lonchero, a lanky clean-shaven senior, was introduced to demonstrate the perfect sandwich-making technique. A butcher cart on wheels was pushed in front of him. With a long-tined fork in one hand and a sharp knife in the other, the lonchero deftly sliced a baton of Cuban bread into three equal parts, cut each lengthwise, and began the assembly of meats and cheese. His movements were swift, with no wasted effort. A smear of mustard and two pickle chips followed by slices of Swiss cheese, roast pork, and sweet ham piled tight and neat. It was a ballet of fork and knife. The audience applauded. When the lonchero bowed, his red-and-black eleke rolled from his collar. The Santeria bead necklace was for the orisha Eleggua. Not a good sign for the night. Pugi was mischievous and troublesome enough without any supernatural trickster help.

"What does that mean?"

"Mira. It's like . . . It's like part of his job."

"What?"

"She's like some rich bitch socialite that wants to have the handsome news guy as a boyfriend. So, papi and papi's money put the pressure on the station. It's not for real."

"Hold up. You're telling me Canal Veintitrés told him to date her?"

"Shhh. It's starting."

I looked at the fiancé, Cristina, who was looking at Alex, who was looking at Pugi. Alex turned his attention quickly to

Cristina. In that split second, it felt like a laser bounced from her to him to Pugi and made a neon-bright triangle. The two women whipped their heads toward each other following the path of the dangerous beam. I sat forward and disrupted their metal-melting stares before a real fire started.

"What the fuck is going on?"

"Nothing. She's nothing to worry about."

A bell rang and the contest started. Twelve pairs of knives and forks clinked and clanked. Each row of four had a judge watching for violations. Someone in the back row let their pyramid of bread roll off the cutting board and onto the floor. She was out. Next out was a big guy wearing a thick Cuban link bracelet. The meats in his sandwich had sloppy layers that fell apart during transfer from board to plate. The audience reacted with a collective "Ay." Before the end bell rang, two others were out. One for lack of mustard. The other for touching the bread with his finger when his fork got stuck in it.

"How long have you been back with Alex?"

"I'm not back with Alex. I'm fucking Alex. Big difference."

"You didn't answer my question. And I think the girl-friend won't see a difference."

"A couple-three weeks, más o menos."

"Does she know?"

"No."

"Are you sure?"

"She knows we dated in high school, that's all."

"The look she gave you said she knew something was up."

"She's the jealous type."

"Watch yourself. I don't want to have to break up a fight."

While the set was condensed, a spokesperson from Sedano's was thanked for supplying the bread and food. The woman was very Latina corporate. Her heels were high and her makeup perfect. She told the audience not to miss getting their five-dollars-off coupon from the Sedano's clerks walking around the tent. Bembe Botánica's support was acknowledged. The store owner reminded everyone that all despojos y limpiezas were on special until the end of the month. The MC asked the crowd if they were hungry. They replied with a loud "Si." Tres Palmas servers appeared with trays of mini sandwiches fresh from the press. Cuban link bracelet dude, dejected and deflated, took a fistful. He stepped over the low barrier separating the audience from the participants. He stood in front of Cristina like a kid who had lost at kickball. The man next to Cristina rose, patted him on the back, and gave the Cuban link his seat.

"Who's that guy?"

"A loser."

"Not him, the older guy?"

A plea was made for everyone to settle down. Round two was about to start. The remaining eight filed in from offstage. When Alex Perez passed in front of us, Pugi sprang from her seat and wrapped her arms around him like she was a giant squid and he was a sperm whale. Mami and Tia covered their mouths in shock. The UnMundo camera caught it, as did a few phones. I checked for a reaction from Cristina and saw what I'd expected. The hatred radiating from her was atomic level. What I hadn't expected was the shock wave of anger from Mr. Cuban Link. He was looking at Cristina the way she was looking at Pugi. Was this a love quadrangle?

"Who is the guy that got eliminated?"

"I don't know. I don't care."

I fingered my shirt pocket and found Pugi's folded program. Contestant number eight. DJ Peli, as in Peligroso. He and his homeboy Puñeta had a YouTube channel that was getting noticed.

The crowd was shushed again. Round two was the Elena Ruz challenge. The piles of pork and Swiss had been swapped for turkey. Made with medianoche sweet egg bread, the Elena Ruz had cream cheese, jam, and turkey. The trick to winning this round was not to rip the bread when spreading the cream cheese. The bell sounded. Ten minutes began to tick. Contestant number nine, the owner of several quince-dress stores, staked a bun to his cutting board and plopped a mess of cream cheese onto it. He tore two buns before frustration overcame him. He pinned the yellow bread in his thumb and index finger to spread the cream smoothly. Skin contact with the food meant instant elimination. Alex, in contrast, was calm and cool. Three sandwiches lined his tray, with plenty of time to finish numbers four and five. Alex set down his utensils, pumped his hands to relieve the tension, then rolled up his shirt sleeves. Pugi licked her lips.

"I thought you were thirsty, not hungry."

"Ja, ja, ja."

Four more contestants were dismissed. One minute remained in the round. Tia's phone beeped, as did several other phones in the immediate area. I looked left. She stared at the phone in her lap. The WhatsApp chisme grapevine was alive. The text read *Chanel 23 weatherman Alex Perez tiene una enamorada.* The video was more like a GIF of Pugi hugging Alex on endless repeat. A big red heart had been drawn over her ass. It was kind of funny. And others around us thought the same, if their giggles were any gauge. Tia looked to my mom for support, and they both sighed. The bell chimed. Applause boomed. The contest was down to three.

"You've made the gossip pages again."

"What are you talking about?"

"There's a video of you hugging Alex."

"Let me see."

"Ask your mom."

"I don't think so. Did they get my good side?"

"If you mean your ass, then yes."

Pugi laughed. Whoever had filmed and sent it had to be on our side of the room. And they were close to the front, judging by the angle. Curious, I scanned the rows behind me.

Who cared who'd done it? Obviously not Pugi. I noticed a few people pointing in Pugi's direction, then returning to their phones for a second viewing. The man who'd given his seat to DJ Peli stood behind the announcer. He tapped the screen of his phone, grimaced, then narrowed his eyes at Alex as he walked offstage. The MC cranked the crowd up with promises of cafecitos. The Tres Palmas servers passed through the audience with trays of thimble-sized cups of espresso. Once most of the seated patrons had been served, he introduced the owner of Cruz Toyota and donor of the grand prize. It was that man, the-seat-giver man. He twisted the cord off the mic stand and began speaking. His voice was practiced and performative. I realized he did the voice-overs for the dealership's ads.

"Alex better win that car like he's supposed to."

"I'm sure he can afford a new car with his new job."

a.g

"Duh. The RAV4's for me. He promised. Plus, he's been practicing for a month."

"Practicing?"

"With the lonchero. Alex has some deal with Cruz."

"That Cruz? The Toyota guy?"

"Sí."

"Isn't that cheating?"

"It's advertising. Like Alex is gonna talk about Cruz Toyota on the weather. Whatever."

Mr. Cruz finished his soft-sell sales pitch and invited the audience to stop by the showroom soon. I thought that was the end of it, but he kept talking. He waved into the front row, and both DJ Peli and Cristina stood. They bookended him onstage and were introduced as his daughter and the star of his soon-to-be-released new theme song. There was a burst of applause. Mr. Cruz and his daughter returned to their seats. DJ Peli took the mic to debut "Cruzin' in a Cruz Toyota." He unzipped his black hoodie to reveal a Cuban link necklace fatter than his bracelet on which hung a diamond-encrusted Toyota emblem. When he hunched and postured to swagger with the Cubaton beat of the song, the pendant swung from pec to pec.

"Tengo sed."

"You can't be serious. You called him a loser like two minutes ago."

"No, I didn't. He's kinda sexy."

"Chill your thirst, cousin."

The lyrics to the song were the standard get a big car, be a big man, party on the beach, and get a pretty girl. When DJ Peli rapped the lines about the pretty girl, he pointed to Cristina. Cristina made a fake smile and cut her eyes to her father. He ignored her. He watched DJ Peli like Gollum looking at the gold ring. The song ended. Mr. Cruz stood and clapped with vigor, which got twenty or so others on their feet. Pugi and I kept our butts in our chairs. The MC asked the three remaining contestants to return for the final stage of the contest. All the vacant work areas had been removed during the rap performance. The three stations left were placed center stage. The sandwich to be prepared was the famous Medianoche, similar to the Cubano sandwich but made on tender egg bread. The lights in the tent dimmed as the spotlights on the stage came up brighter. First to walk to their station was the ex–superintendent of Miami schools. Second was a distant member of the Julio Iglesias family.

"Stay in your seat. No more hugs."

"I'm not taking you out with me anymore if you're going to be pesada and no fun."

"Promise."

Our jesting halted—a streak of red and blond vaulted over the partition and onto the stage. Cristina kissed Alex on the mouth. All cameras, UnMundo and cell phone, recorded the action. My arm instinctively went out to bar Pugi from starting a fight, but I was too slow. Pugi pried Cristina off Alex and pushed her away. Cristina recovered and lunged at Pugi. Alex told the women to calm down. Pugi never liked to be told to calm down. Soon she was throwing roasted pork and jamón dulce at Alex. Cristina came to Alex's aid and blocked the flying meats from hitting him. Words were exchanged. *Whore. Cheap. Basic. Daddy's girl.*

Alex told the women there was enough of him to go around. The women weren't listening to him. Pugi's pointed acrylic nails dug into Cristina's scalp. Cristina yelped like an injured dog. Pugi held tight to a fist of blond hair. The women fell to the floor, with Pugi on top and with the advantage.

DJ Peli entered the ring. He cussed at Alex. Called him a pedazo de mierda who dated Cristina only for the money. Alex faded into the shadows and away from the heat. DJ Peli encircled Pugi's waist with his husky arms and wrenched her off Cristina. Tia asked if I was going to help Pugi. I replied that Pugi appeared to be fine. She waved a ball of blond strands, validating my assessment. As Pugi kicked and screamed to free herself from DJ Peli's shackle, Peli professed his true love to Cristina. When Cristina rebuked his love, he set Pugi on a butcher block and fell to his knees. He wailed and begged. Why? Why Alex Perez? Why not him? He loved her, not Alex. All eyes and cameras were on the melodrama. It was like a live telenovela.

Cristina ignored the man groveling at her feet and insulted Pugi instead. She called her a chonga bitch. Pugi stood on the rolling table as she balanced herself, bread and pickles tumbling this way and that. She prepared to jump like a lucha libre wrestler from the top rope. A guttural scream silenced the entire tent, followed by an equally primal, "You ruined everything!"

Alex Perez staggered from the dark part of the stage and fell onto the center workbench. Blood gurgled from a wound in his back. I watched the UnMundo camera zoom into the shadowy background beyond him. Someone brought up the tent lights, and the audience gasped. Mr. Cruz had a bloody fork in one hand and a knife dripping blood in the other. He repeated the same two lines over and over. "You ruined everything. You ruined my business."

A chorus of sirens closed in on the tent. I yanked Pugi off the stage and into the seat next to me. Her black eyebrows and eyeliner were still crisp, but her face had gone from the color of a coconut shell to the color of coconut milk.

"Are you still thirsting and hungry?"

"I think I've lost my appetite."

ACKNOWLEDGMENTS

As a group, the anthology authors would like to thank Crooked Lane Books for taking a chance on our collection of short stories. To our editor, Terri Bischoff, and the entire Crooked Lane team, we appreciate your support and hard work and all your effort to turn our manuscripts into this anthology. As editor, I want to extend a heartfelt thanks to all the contributors to *Midnight Hour* for creating and sharing their stories. A special shout-out to the Crime Writers of Color, a community of more than three hundred people of diverse backgrounds who identify as crime/mystery writers, where we are all members. And to the awesome Stephen Mack Jones, what an honor to have your foreword as part of our book. Thank you!